DA ...hor

Born in 1970, Paul Dixon grew up in County Durham in the north-east of England. He graduated from Sunderland University with a master's degree in Film and Cultural Studies in 1999. He lives just outside Durham City with his wife and two children. *Two Rubber Souls* is his debut novel.

Dedicated to Mick and Pauline

CHAPTER 1

Too Late For Goodbyes

There were a million and one better places to be on a scorching hot Saturday afternoon than spending it trapped inside the claustrophobic confines of an overpopulated train carriage. Given that the journey had suffered an unscheduled twenty-minute stop at Seaburn station due to signal failure, it was accurate to surmise that the patience and good humour of the travellers on the 12:40 p.m. Sunderland to Newcastle train was stretched to the limit.

As the train rumbled wearily over the High Level Bridge into Newcastle, the deflated spirits of those onboard rose at the sight of sunlight glinting on the murky waters of the River Tyne, its legendary fog long since burnt away for the day by a golden yolk of a sun. Realising their journey was entering its final stages, passengers began to gather their belongings and gently stretch their limbs in the limited space available. The broadcasting of a barely audible apology by an employee of the train company – clusters of broken words lost within a series of hisses and crackles – received a muted response from the intended audience, apart from a solitary curse that spilled from the mouth of one disaffected individual.

Taking his cue from everyone else around him, Pete Davies turned to his sleeping cousin. "Wake up, Liam. We're nearly there," he said.

"Leave me alone," mumbled Liam, keeping his eyes firmly closed.

Within minutes of their departure, Liam had complained of feeling ill. Informing Pete that he needed to close his eyes for five minutes or so, Liam had immediately fallen into a state of slumber. This annoyed Pete deeply, leaving him with little choice but to spend the majority of the ride in subdued contemplation.

As the train began to slow down, it entered the cool interior of a dark tunnel, causing the temperature inside the carriage to plummet. Although this offered a welcome respite from the stifling conditions, Pete shuddered with the sudden change, feeling the hairs on his arms stand to attention. He responded by vigorously rubbing at his exposed limbs to apply a burst of instant warmth.

With the windowpane suddenly inverted into a temporary object of reflection, Pete winced upon finding himself face to face with his own image. All summer long, he had been praying for his much despised, secret affliction – his physical immaturity – to recede. The anguish it caused him was a heavy burden to bear, and something that to date had been endured in silence. He could only imagine how crushing the embarrassment would be should his fears become public knowledge at school. As far as Pete was concerned, a problem shared would not be a problem halved. On the contrary, he believed if so much as one word was breathed to anyone else, the news would multiply and spread as quickly as a highly contagious virus, making him a laughing stock in no time at all. Pete knew he would be cured. One day. However, that day, frustratingly, did not appear to be on the horizon anytime soon.

What he craved in the interim was a tangible sign to display to the world that the transition from boyhood to maturity was in progress: a distinctive deepening of the voice; the acquisition of muscle to his stick-thin physique; or the replacement of the wispy bum fluff on his chin with a few flecks of thick, dark stubble. On all counts, there had been no notable improvement since the final day of school in the summer term. An unchanged boy still stared back, so youthful in appearance that Pete believed he could easily be mistaken for a child of eleven or twelve years of age. With such harsh truths came the realisation that he would continue to find it difficult to gain entry to a world that, in his opinion, newfound maturity made eligible: peer acceptance and romance.

Pete was also acutely aware that, with the return to school just around the corner, he was destined to remain vulnerable to the taunts and bullying that were accepted practices within the confines of the PE changing rooms, and the dreaded communal showers. In no other area of school life was Pete's self-consciousness and sensitivity more exposed than in this harsh environment. To his relief, he had not, in his preceding three years of secondary schooling, been singled out for cruel treatment from his classmates, apart from a couple of stinging wet towel flicks to his back. However, Pete had witnessed shocking levels of maltreatment firsthand, with the principal victims tending to be John Thames and James Appleby.

They were universally accepted as being easy targets, primarily because it was not in their armoury to retaliate. The chief perpetrators, Giles Morgan and Bryan Fawcett, enjoyed carte blanche to dish out a wide range of harsh treatments. The towels of Thames and Appleby would be pulled away from their waists while they were getting changed and thrown into the steaming shower room, followed by any other items of their clothing hanging on the pegs that Morgan and Fawcett saw fit to soak. The tormentors, squealing and howling derogatory remarks like a pair of over-excited, demented monkeys, would then point at the exposed, overweight torsos of their victims in mock horror, encouraging everyone else to join in.

Back in the classroom the teasing would resume, with the additional humiliation of the boys being forced to sit in their damp, clinging clothes. Thames would blush bright crimson, while on one occasion a visibly distressed Appleby had snapped, bursting into tears and running from the classroom.

Now that Pete was entering the penultimate year of school, he had eagerly exploited an option in the school curriculum that allowed O-level pupils to drop one of the twice-weekly sports lessons in order to study a second foreign language. This offered Pete a small crumb of consolation, despite the prospect of additional homework that this entailed.

Emerging from the train tunnel back out into bright sunlight, Pete's mirror image evaporated, jolting him back into the present. His thoughts returned to his imminent concern, and the reason for today's excursion.

It was Saturday, 1 September 1984, and was a date Pete had been dreading. It had been looming in the background all summer; a cloud of melancholy, constantly loitering in his thoughts to rain on his mood.

Finally, it was time to say goodbye.

The seed of Pete's all-encompassing pathos had been planted on the first day of the summer holidays, six short weeks ago. For Pete, this period usually ranked alongside Christmas and his birthday as the most eagerly anticipated date in the yearly calendar.

The Saturday in late July had begun with Pete in an upbeat mood. With his weekly visit to his father's house nearly over, he was planning to spend the afternoon browsing the shops of Newcastle city centre with Liam.

Pete was sitting at his father's kitchen table eating a prompt lunch of scalding hot tomato soup. Dipping a slightly stale slice of white bread into the contents of the bowl, he made a mental note to remember to wash his face before leaving the house. The liquid always left red marks on the side of his mouth that resembled unsightly scabs if allowed to go unnoticed.

On the black and white portable television set, attached to the kitchen wall by a metal bracket, the monotone weather presenter was urging the nation to make the most of the Mediterranean warm front sweeping the British Isles. "So," he said, bringing the forecast to its conclusion, "with heavy downpours due by the middle of the week, bringing with them a spell of cooler temperatures, it is indeed a matter of making hay while the sun…ahem…shines."

The attempt at humour was delivered in a slightly forced, unnatural manner. An uneasy smile crossed the presenter's face, making it difficult for the viewer to decide whether he was pleased or slightly embarrassed by his own joke. It reminded Pete of Mr Glanville, a strict disciplinarian maths teacher who ruled with an iron rod. No pupil dared to intentionally cross him. Sporadically, though, Mr Glanville did attempt to convince others that there was a thin sliver of humanity in his blood by displaying a humorous side to his personality. Pete was present on one such occasion to witness a quip made to a room of petrified adolescents, so used to his no-nonsense, authoritarian manner that it predictably elicited a stunningly quiet response. Pupils were scared to laugh just in case he was actually being serious. After several seconds, Mr Glanville broke the silence with his sledgehammer voice. "That was a joke, class. You are allowed to laugh…" he said, pausing ominously for maximum impact, "…sometimes. I'm not a monster, you know," he continued, flashing a thin-lipped, twisted smile reminiscent of Vincent Price in a Dracula film, his eyes twinkling with sadistic malevolence.

Pete never joined in with the choruses of sycophantic, false laughter in Mr Glanville's lessons. He had not forgiven the teacher for the occasion when he was humiliated in front of the whole class for getting an algebra question wrong. Pete hated algebra. When Mr Glanville spoke about algebra, he made it sound as if it was a country with its own language. For all Pete cared, and for all the sense it made to him, it may as well have been a planet a million miles away. He imagined Algebrans to be weird-coloured aliens, a bit like the Clangers, only not as cool, with names like Pythagoras and Equation.

"Stick to the day job, Michael, and get *Grandstand* on," muttered Pete's father, entering the kitchen from the backyard. His gardening chores completed, he rinsed his dirty hands quickly under the tap before drying them on a tea towel. Grabbing a can of lager from the fridge, he wandered into the front room to put his feet up and prepare for an afternoon of televised cricket.

Ian Davies liked his sport. Regardless of the type, if it was on the television, then he was more than happy to watch it. His main love was football. Even though he was forty-one and carrying a little more weight than when he was in his prime, he still played once a week in the local over-forties league. Come rain, hail, or shine, every Saturday morning between August and May, he would consistently turn out for his team, Hendon United. Unfortunately, from Pete's perspective, he was expected to accompany his father. Assigned the arduous role of ball-boy, he would spend a large proportion of the morning retrieving wayward shots that had failed to threaten the opposing team's goal.

With the new football season not due to begin for a further month, Pete was currently enjoying a temporary reprieve. However, he did not get off completely scot-free during the summer months. Each Saturday morning, it was expected he would accompany his father on his early morning walk to the local park with Knuckles, his brown and white patched Staffordshire Bull Terrier.

This particular Saturday morning had been a rarity for Pete. His time had been primarily his own once his dog-walking duties were completed, with his father content to potter about alone in the backyard. Pete's father had built a multi-tiered rockery bed several years ago, populating it with a wide variety of plants and flowers, and had spent the morning weeding, watering and having a general tidy up of the area. Pete seized the opportunity to watch *The Saturday Morning Picture Show* on television in peace, keeping his fingers crossed that he wouldn't be found any chores to do, which was usually the case when his father was doing some DIY, or attempting to rectify one of the seemingly never-ending faults with his car.

Lacking the funds to take his Cortina to a car mechanic and have it professionally repaired, his father would frequently park his car in the back lane, lift the bonnet, scratch his unshaven chin, slurp on a mug of tea, and attempt to diagnose the root of the problem. At some point while tinkering away, with his head stuck under the bonnet or laid flat out on his back under the vehicle, he would call out to Pete for assistance, his voice carrying all the way from outdoors, through the open backdoor into the front room.

"Pete... Pete."

"Yes, Dad."

"Fetch me the set of ratchets from the garage, son. They're in the orange box under the bench."

"Yes, Dad."

The ratchet set located and passed to his father, Pete would return to the comfort of the sofa. Five minutes later, a second shout would emanate from outdoors.

"Pete...Pete. Hand me my torch. Not sure where it was last."

"Okay, Dad," Pete would reply, silently fuming.

This would be the pattern for the remainder of the morning. Whenever a task was assigned to him, Pete would rummage furiously among the contents of numerous toolboxes and workbenches, full to bursting point with hand tools, loose screws, boxes of rusty nails, and other miscellaneous items.

"Have you not found it yet?" his father would bellow impatiently.

In desperation, Pete would grab the first tool to hand and proffer it.

"Not that one, son. The one I want is the same shape, but smaller."

After four or five attempts, Pete would eventually find the correct implement, but it was painfully obvious to both of them that Pete was never going to follow in his father's handyman footsteps. He sensed a general air of disappointment in his father over his lack of enthusiasm to become familiar with the workings of a car engine, to learn how to tile a bathroom, or become skilled in the erection of fences. A 'chip off the old block' Pete most certainly was not.

A loud knock at the front door just as *Grandstand* was starting snapped Pete out of his thoughts. He had lost track of time, and set about wolfing down a custard slice, safe in the knowledge it would be another week before his father required his gofer services, and an eternity before Mr Glanville and ball-boy duties crossed his path once more.

"Take a seat, Liam," Pete heard his father genially say upon answering the door. "Pete's just finishing off his dinner."

It irked Pete that his father always seemed to adopt a more favourable manner and tone of voice when talking to Liam. His father was never like that with Pete, always appearing to be on the verge of losing his temper, and lacking patience if Pete needed to be asked to do something twice. Pete often thought that his father secretly liked Liam more.

Pete wondered what the pair were talking about, as their chat was unusually hushed. Whatever it was, it seemed to be taking Liam an eternity to finish his story. Normally their opening exchanges of verbal sparring were jokey and vociferous. He switched off the portable television and silently entered the corridor between the two rooms, so that he could strain to hear what Liam was saying.

"Excellent news, son," boomed his father. "I'm really pleased for you. There's nothing around here for lads your age. You're better off joining up and seeing the world."

Pete froze. His head began to spin furiously. Had he just heard correctly? Liam was joining up.

Pete cast his mind back to just before the previous Christmas. Liam had been giving him earache about how cool it would be to join the army, and how he was seriously thinking about applying. Liam had even obtained a brochure from the careers office, detailing what life in the armed forces involved for new recruits. The prospect of Liam leaving home did not fill Pete with comfort. But ever since January, Liam had neglected to mention it, leaving Pete to conclude it had just been another of his cousin's passing fancies and that nothing solid would come of it.

Pete continued to hover at the doorway to the front room, remaining out of sight.

"When do you leave then, son?"

"First week in September, Uncle Ian."

"Blimey, that's not too far away."

"I'm at Aldershot to begin with, until my initial training is completed. After that, the regiment will be deployed abroad. Germany, probably."

Pete was crushed. Out of the blue, a new major upheaval to his life had been set in motion. Summer felt ruined before the holidays were even a day old.

He tiptoed back into the kitchen, rinsed out his soup bowl, and then placed it in the dish rack to dry. Pete then hurried upstairs to the bathroom. Locking the door, he stood in the middle of the room, battling the tidal wave of emotion that threatened to explode from within him.

It had been a difficult six years for Pete – first having to navigate himself through the choppy waters of family disharmony and his parents' eventual marital breakdown, before adapting to a new set of circumstances as both his father and mother slowly reconstructed their lives, eventually meeting and setting up homes with new partners. His mother, Sheila, as well as gaining permanent custody of her son, had formed a relationship with a travel agent called Trevor Braithwaite, which was cemented by the birth of a daughter, Carla, in 1981. With a successful business located in Durham City, thirteen miles away from Pete's hometown of Sunderland, the decision was made to relocate to Newton Moor, a modern private housing estate in the suburbs of Durham City. With a predominantly middle-class population, it was so different to anything Pete had previously experienced, and he had found it difficult initially to settle in at his new school and acquire friends, due to his crippling shyness and low self-confidence.

Pete's father chose to remain in Sunderland, moving to the staunch working-class district of Hendon with his new partner, Val.

With all the upheavals that had taken place in his life, Pete felt like the figure in the old snow shaker he had bought as a six-year-old on a day trip to Blackpool, which now stood on his bedroom windowsill. When he shook it, the flakes swirled around like snow in a blizzard, while the miniaturised child at the centre was the only thing to remain static and unchanged.

Throughout this period of confusion and loneliness, his cousin had been the one positive; a buoy to cling onto. At the weekend, they would spend hours together engaged in something that had been sorely missing from Pete's seminal years to date: fun. Whether browsing music and clothes shops, playing pool, or hanging out at amusement arcades, the pair were always doing something exciting. Liam encapsulated the spirit that existed between the two boys by christening them the two musketeers, a label that Pete believed in wholeheartedly. Away from the chaos, discipline, and finger-wagging of parents, teachers, and authority, Pete could relax, be himself, and enjoy his first experience of independence.

As soon as a weekend was over, Pete would be sad, but consoled himself with the thought that the slow countdown to the next one had already commenced.

Struggling to accept what he had just heard spoken between his father and Liam, Pete felt as if he was crumbling both physically and emotionally, and was worried about how he was going to be able to disguise his tearful reaction. He twisted the cold tap on the sink until the water began to spurt out, before repeatedly scooping icy cold water onto his face until his skin was numb to the touch. Inspecting himself in the mirror, Pete saw that his features were sickly pale, apart from the blotchy patches around his eyes. Taking several deep breaths, and composing himself as best as he could manage under the circumstances, Pete weakly made his way back downstairs before his lengthy absence drew unwanted attention.

Like a finger pressed unremittingly down on the fast forward button of a video machine, the remainder of the summer holidays had flashed by at a rapid pace, with Pete expending hours lamenting the way life in general always seemed to spring nasty surprises upon him when least expected. He pondered the question of why the important people, who he loved most in life, felt a necessity to seek new lives for themselves with different people, to his personal detriment. Pete also struggled to accept the immediacy with which a seemingly unbridgeable gap between Liam and himself had opened up, as if Liam couldn't wait to shed the skin of his old life and move on to new friends and fresh experiences. All of a sudden, his cousin was barely recognisable as the person he had been before his acceptance into the army.

Sadness was not the only emotion Liam's impending departure had stirred in Pete. He also experienced intense feelings of jealousy at the manner in which Liam was poised to make an effortless leap from teenager to standing on the brink of adulthood. It frustrated Pete that he was going to remain ensnared within a seemingly eternal chasm of torment, being neither a child nor an adult, tethered by heavy, binding chains that refused to break.

The train crawled into the station before stuttering to a halt at platform nine. Pete gave his cousin a scathing look of contempt. He had no sympathy for Liam's suffering, as it was all self-inflicted. Like a loose lid on a full pan of boiling water, Pete was struggling to contain his raw anger, mortally offended by his cousin's open apathy to the monumental importance he had attached to this day. He was so frustrated that he wanted to hit Liam, but knew Liam would only laugh at his feeble attempt to inflict physical harm on him, just as he used to do during the numerous fun fights they had when they were younger, when Liam would toy with him the way an expert matador would treat a naive, junior bull. He never took anything seriously. Everything was a joke to Liam.

Pete gave him a sharp nudge in the ribs with his elbow. This time, his actions were more successful.

"Jesus, are we here already?" asked Liam, gingerly opening his bloodshot eyes. "Did I drop off?"

"As soon as we left Sunderland."

Pete could smell on Liam's breath an unappealing mix of stale beer, vomit and cigarettes. The repugnant aroma told its own story of the reason for Liam's dishevelled state. It was the smell of the day after the night before, the occasion being Liam's farewell night out on the town. Currently denied to the fourteen-year-old Pete, the world of pubs, music, alcohol, nightclubs and women had become second nature to Liam that summer. Although he was only sixteen and a half years of age, Liam easily passed for an adult in appearance.

"Come on, then," said Liam, springing to his feet with urgency when the carriage was nearly empty. "I'm gonna piss myself if I don't get to the bog soon."

Freshly relieved, Liam returned from the station toilets a great deal perkier than he had been all day. He had seized the opportunity to revive himself with a quick splash of water to his face, and a hint of colour had returned to his cheeks.

From the moment Liam discovered his destiny lay beyond his hometown, he had been determined to enjoy every remaining drop of freedom. His final weekend was his opportunity to complete the round of farewells, not just to family and friends, but also to his old self. Liam was no longer the adolescent who had spent most of his life verbally and physically battling anyone who chose to stand in his path, particularly his teachers at school. To be constantly told you would never amount to anything in life, and that you were a total waste of space, would have crushed a lesser-willed person. He, however, had been born with unshakeable inner confidence, and believed fate would deal him a good hand if he hustled long enough.

Although proud of his working-class roots, Liam knew his prospects on Wearside were non-existent. He was a rare breed among the group of friends who had all left school together, successfully managing to find an escape route from unemployment, crime, and the slave labour of youth training schemes, directly into a career that would allow him to earn a wage while travelling the world for free. A few months of life spent on the dole queue had been enough to convince Liam he was doing the right thing, and he was not about to allow sentiment to sway that conviction.

Exiting the station through its austere stone arches, Liam flinched under the harsh scrutiny of the all-pervading bright sunlight, like a vampire exposed to its greatest nemesis. He shakily slipped on a pair of sunglasses as they walked over the zebra crossing, and headed in the direction of Pink Lane. His thumping hangover was beginning to ease, but he was severely dehydrated.

"This heat hasn't let up all day," he complained. "I'm dying for a can of pop. My throat's as dry as sandpaper. Must have had nine or ten pints last night, at least."

As Liam began to set a swift pace in pursuit of refreshments, he was not the only one to be physically suffering. Every step taken by Pete that morning had caused a sharp stabbing pain to shoot through the heel of his right foot. The blame for this increasingly debilitating condition Pete unanimously attributed to his mother. At her insistence earlier in the week, Pete had worn a new pair of school shoes at home in an effort to break them in. He was usually banned from wearing footwear indoors by his house-proud mother, and it was ironic that on the one occasion the strict house rules were relaxed, it should prove so painful. After only a couple of minutes with them on his feet, Pete admitted defeat and gratefully removed them. Attempts in subsequent days to break them in had proven equally agonising, like a rodeo rider being repeatedly thrown to the ground by a wild stallion determined to resist all attempts at subjugation. In a last ditch attempt to make them tolerable, his mother had stuffed the troublesome shoes with scrunched-up newspaper to stretch them. For Pete, though, the damage was already done. A circular area of his skin had been scythed away, leaving a large, tender area of exposed flesh that required a constant application of germolene and plasters.

A quick inspection undertaken on the train had revealed his current plaster to be caked in blood and dislodged. Pete had been unable to adequately reapply it, and the resumption of the journey on foot had begun to inflict upon him a new course of tooth-grinding, eye-popping agony.

"Slow down a bit, will you, Liam? My bloody foot's still killing me."

Liam laughed. "Aah, did Mummy's plaster come off her little son's foot again," he teased.

"Shut your face," snapped Pete, real venom in his retort.

Liam was slightly taken back by his tone of voice. "Calm down, couz. I was only kidding. We'll stop off at that department store by Grey's Monument. I'll buy you a pack of plasters when I get some pop."

Hoping that his offer had placated him, Liam began to regale Pete with the tale of his exploits from the previous night. "Pete, I had the best night ever," he began, barely able to contain his euphoria. "Me and Stevey went on a pub crawl around Sunderland town centre, and then we ended up going to Finos. It had gone midnight by the time we got in. Nearly half an hour we had to wait outside in the queue. Missed happy hour by minutes," said Liam. "I've never seen the place as packed. You could barely move on the dance floor. Full of totty, it was. And the tunes were amazing. All the latest chart hits. Fantastic."

Pete was struggling to match Liam's level of enthusiasm. Whenever Liam mentioned Stevey, Pete became moody and sulky. It was bad enough for Pete that the age barrier denied him the opportunity to attend Liam's leaving night out, but for Stevey to be there in his place was sickening.

Knowing the lack of love between Pete and Stevey, Liam was keen to get to the key point. "Come on, Pete," Liam persisted. "If you listen a bit more you'll enjoy it when I get to the best part."

Satisfied Pete was still listening, Liam resumed.

"It was Stevey's round at the bar," continued Liam. "You should've seen his face when he saw the price of the vodka and orange. His chin nearly hit the floor. Moaning on he was, saying how he would have no dole money left until his next giro. But I put him right. I told him I always have to go onto shorts, as I can't stand the fizzy, yellow piss they sell in there. It always gives me heartburn."

Liam glanced at Pete to check he still had his attention.

"We knocked two trebles straight back. My bloody head was spinning, as if I'd been chinned by Barry McGuigan. Well, as much as I wanted to, if I'd sat down

I wouldn't have got back up again. So, we hit the dance floor, and within a couple of minutes we'd both scored."

This revelation halted Pete in his tracks. The unexpected news of Stevey's success made his heart sink. "Stevey managed to pull a girl?" he asked, eyes widening in disbelief.

"Aye. How he managed it dressed in those horrible clothes he buys from the catalogue is a mystery. But, Pete, you should have seen her. She was a right dog. Really ugly."

The direction the conversation was taking immediately lifted Pete's spirits. "How ugly?" he asked.

Liam smiled as Pete's inquisitiveness began to get the better of him. "Definitely a ten pinter, couz. I wouldn't have touched her with a bargepole. She had a brace over these horsey buckteeth, an absolutely massive nose, and was a bit on the large side, to say the least. Apart from that, she was a stunner," he joked. "And Stevey was able to use his one and only chat up line, the one about having more to them than fat. Like the line from *Grease*."

Pete reckoned that *Grease* was more popular in Sunderland than Jesus. Everyone he knew who lived there seemed to own the record and film.

"Normally he gets a slap in the face," continued Liam, "but even he was shocked it worked this time. Honestly though, she was the type of bird you go with once, knock up, and spend the rest of your life regretting. Stevey will be well under the thumb if he sees her again. She'll have his dole giro in her purse before the envelope hits the carpet."

The animosity that existed between Pete and Stevey had originated years ago. The instigator had been Stevey, who for some reason had taken an instant dislike to Pete when they first met. This baffled Pete, as he had never knowingly said or done anything to cause offence to him. More recently, Stevey had been upset when Pete received a batch of Liam's clothing cast-offs. These items included coveted designer labels such as Lacoste, Taccini, and Boy. To purchase them brand new was not an option for Pete, with his meagre income of pocket and paper round money, so the occasional item was gratefully received, even if they had seen better days and were slightly too large for his slender frame.

Stevey's taste in fashion did not extend further than a Leo Gemmelli lemon and grey striped cardigan. Champagne and water in comparison, was Liam's favourite saying to describe the difference in quality between Stevey's and his own clothing preferences. Liam's putdown name for Stevey was Leo, particularly if he had been unnecessarily taunting Pete by calling him virgin, or mischievously asking when he was going to enter puberty. This type of teasing always hit the mark, making Pete blush furiously with embarrassment. He was incapable of firing back any kind of verbal punch against something so damning, so it would be left to Liam to stick up for him.

"Stevey's mood went right downhill," continued Liam, "when I told him I was going home to my bird's place, leaving him to fork out for a taxi alone. Her Mam and Dad are on holiday so she had the house to herself," he explained, obviously still unable to believe his good fortune. "She was worth it, though, a right stunner. Debbie, I think her name was. Slim, long tanned legs, and a lovely figure on her. She was like one of Wham's backing singers," he gloated. "She had a cracking personality, too. Must have been at least eighteen, maybe nineteen. We started off with a coffee, and the rest, as they say, son, is history. Well, what I can remember of it. It's all a bit hazy at the minute."

Liam's triumphant grin was of the smug cat that had got the cream.

"She gave me her phone number as well. When I told her I was joining up, you should have seen her reaction. Guess she loves a bloke in a uniform."

Pete wished he could be as successful with girls. It seemed that all Liam had to do was click his fingers, and he would effortlessly acquire a girlfriend. Pete had a vision of Liam from the night before, drink in hand, surrounded by a crowd of adoring females. Pete found it unbearably difficult just to pluck up the courage to talk to a girl he liked, as all thoughts would become immediately erased from his mind, and his mouth would lose the ability to form the most basic of coherent sentences.

"Anyway, I rang Stevey this morning, and boy is he in a huff with me for leaving him last night. So, I thought, 'stuff you mate.' We don't need that loser with us today, do we, Pete?"

Pete was heartened a little by Liam's words. Some of his original anger from the train journey began to thaw a little as he realised that the day may not be quite as bad as he had originally feared.

As they approached Grey's Monument, they passed a large group of tough-looking football fans, men in their thirties and forties.

"Look, Pete. It's the enemy. Where's your Keegan gone, where's your Keegan gone?" sang Liam, loud enough to turn numerous heads.

When promotion to the top flight of English football was secured the previous May, the figure proclaimed as the messiah by Newcastle United supporters had immediately retired from football, dramatically whisked away into the sky above St James' Park stadium in a helicopter at the end of his final game. The tears of thousands of hardened Geordie males reputedly spilled into the Tyne for weeks afterwards.

"Shut up, man," hissed Pete, warily looking around for any potential repercussions. "Those blokes were on the train coming here, which you would have known had you not been out for the count. They look rock hard, especially the big bald one."

Pete was in no mood to put to the test the joke that sometimes did the rounds at school – that you could insult a Geordie's girlfriend as much as you liked, but be equally offensive about his beloved football team and the gloves were off. Pete preferred to avoid the threat of physical conflict at all costs. His father was fond of bluntly berating his son over his inability to physically defend himself, saying he couldn't fight his way out of a wet paper bag. Such psychology may have been designed to rouse Pete strongly enough to prove him wrong when the occasion arose, but instead had the opposite effect of making Pete shrink further into his shell.

"Calm down, son," replied Liam, unflustered. "We could outrun those fatties any day of the week. Besides, they haven't got time to bother with us. They need to drink at least ten pints before they can go and watch that rubbish, and they're running out of time before the kick-off."

To Pete's immense relief, Liam's taunt failed to elicit any response. Whether they were ignored or unheard, he did not care. "You'll get us killed one of these days," said Pete, keen to register his displeasure.

"Oh, stop being so bloody soft," retorted Liam, undaunted and clearly relishing the agony his actions were inflicting upon Pete. "There's nothing like a bit of risqué humour."

As the football supporters slowly shuffled towards the nearest public house, Pete noticed a crumpled piece of paper fall to the ground, carelessly dropped by one of the group. Without a word to Liam, he dashed across to pick it up. Unravelling it, he was surprised by what he held in his hand. A twenty-pound note.

"What's that you're holding, Pete?" asked Liam, before a knowing smile crossed his face. "Bloody hell, Pete. Twenty quid. It's your lucky day, mate."

Liam's last remark fell on deaf ears. Pete was already running towards the men.

"What is that idiot doing?" whispered Liam to himself, shaking his head in disbelief.

Pete caught the group up, darting in front of them to block their entrance to the pub. As one, they came to a halt. Even though they realised the thin youth confronting them offered no physical threat, they were confused as to why he was so bold as to bar their path.

"What?" barked the bald-headed leader, stooping down to look at Pete, his face so close that Pete could see the vein pulsing frantically on the side of his head.

"It's just...th...that. You dropped this back there."

CHAPTER 2

Two Tribes

While Liam headed off in search of band-aids and cans of pop, shaking his head in disbelief at what he had just witnessed, Pete hobbled over to the plinth of Grey's Monument. Carefully avoiding the plethora of fresh pigeon droppings, he sat down and removed his training shoe. Tentatively rolling down his blood sodden sock to inspect the troubled area and allow soothing air to circulate around his bare foot, Pete flinched as he extricated a small piece of cotton fabric that had embedded itself in his heel. A couple of tentative probes with his fingertips elicited a secondary wave of discomfort. Resting his foot upon the warm pavement, Pete awaited his cousin's return.

The hub of the city centre was a hive of lively activity. Blackett Street was filled with the constant drone of traffic, emanating from a slow-moving procession of grime-coated yellow double-decker buses snaking through the epicentre of Newcastle, spewing thick jets of fumes from chugging, cylindrical exhausts, like a heavy smoker taking a draw on his first cigarette of the day. Hordes of lobster red, energy sapped shoppers ambled sluggishly through the pedestrianised area around the Monument, physically wilting in the sticky, mid-afternoon hairdryer heat. Most of the people congregated in and around the statue were there simply to have a leisurely afternoon, lapping up as much of the sun as they could, aware it was too good to last. Some had a specific purpose for being there, such as the owners of the two long, portable tables, displaying black and white information leaflets and other paraphernalia, manned by supporters of Amnesty International and the Campaign for Nuclear Disarmament. In amongst all of this chaos, streetwise town pigeons strutted confidently on the congested pavements, pecking gleefully at the remnants of discarded pasties and sandwiches thoughtlessly dropped on the ground.

One individual stood out to Pete in the midst of so much commotion. Talking into a handheld microphone that was plugged into a small amplifier, a man in his late forties paced the pavement as far as the lead on his device would allow in pursuit of an audience, furiously reciting passages from the Bible. Beneath a thick, unruly thatch of black hair, bulbous eyes fizzed with frenzied mania. His choice of clothing was at odds with the weather. He wore a thick, woollen tank top over a navy gingham-checked shirt, combined with a pair of tight black trousers that were slightly too short for his matchstick thin legs. He was a figure of fun to the youngsters lazing around the plinth, who pointed and laughed at him. The reaction from the adults was merely apathetic, as they simply ignored him. In the heat of the day, they were more interested in the instant salvation of a vanilla ice cream. Unfazed by their amused and impassive reactions, the man tirelessly soldiered on.

Pete felt a tinge of sympathy for him. Although he had no way of knowing for sure, Pete guessed that he was a loner, with no family or real friends. Pete wondered what twists and turns a life has to take to end up like this man

– a figure of ridicule talking nonsense in the middle of the street.

Regular visitors to this area of the city were used to peculiar individuals promoting their religious beliefs in public, jostling to be heard beside the extreme political parties and end of the world proclaimers. In that respect, Grey's Monument was to Newcastle what Speaker's Corner was to London.

Liam finally returned, clutching two cans of Coke. Pete gratefully took his. It was ice cold and tasted heavenly. Almost as an afterthought, Liam threw Pete a pack of plasters and sat down next to him to smoke a cigarette, while Pete tended to his wound, wishing that a miraculous band-aid could be as easily applied to the mental discomfort he was feeling.

"Look at those old fogeys," said Liam, indicating with a nod of his head in the direction of a host of pensioners occupying a handful of weather-beaten wooden seats. "They'll do themselves a bloody mischief dressed up like that in this heat," he remarked, shaking his head. The majority of them were wearing garments more appropriate to a bleak winter's day, such as heavy knit cardigans and overcoats. "I'm buggered if I'm gonna give them the kiss of life if they keel over with heat exhaustion. I'd rather take on Stevey's lass from last night. Imagine that, Pete, getting a lungful of Fisherman's Friend, and all those false teeth banging against your lips," he joked, doing an exaggerated comedy shudder of the shoulders.

Despite his determination to maintain a cold exterior, Pete laughed. For a split second, it felt to him just like the old times again.

"Bless them, though," continued Liam, adopting a serious tone. "It must be horrible when you're getting on a bit. Your best years behind you, nothing to look forward to but bingo and crap television. A country that you went to war for to protect not giving a holy shit about you. The joys of getting old, eh?"

Pete nodded in agreement. It was difficult for him to appreciate at such a tender age that one day he, too, would grow to be a similar age, even though he knew it was a fact. He couldn't imagine himself being eighteen, never mind retirement age.

After a few minutes of silence had elapsed while they recharged their batteries, Liam hit Pete with an unexpected, daunting proposition.

"Hey, Pete. How do you feel about helping me out with a little job I have to do today?"

Pete's frown was one of initial confusion, not understanding what type of work Liam could possibly be undertaking on the last day before his departure.

Liam pressed on. "Do you fancy helping me nick some records?" he asked, his voice dropping to a whisper. Liam glanced around to check nobody was paying attention to the illegal tone of their conversation.

"What?" A bolt of unadulterated fear shook Pete. His heart rate felt as if it had instantly trebled.

"Stevey always backs me up normally, but obviously he isn't here, the puff. But you are," said Liam, launching into his act of persuasion. "You won't have to do anything, I promise you. It'll be me doing all the risky stuff. All you have to do is follow me out the door when I give the signal, and stay close to me from behind. What could be easier than that?"

"But I thought we were going to look around the shops and do all the usual stuff," said Pete feebly, knowing his voice already betrayed in it a slight tone of surrender. All of a sudden, Pete wished he was anywhere else but where he found himself, being put on the spot by the one person he found most difficult to refuse.

"I promise you, Pete," continued Liam, holding up his hands to acknowledge the integrity of what he was about to say, "we'll do whatever you want for the rest of the day if you just help me out on this one little job. I've got a list as long as my arm of people who have ordered stuff. I can't let them down now, can I? Plus, I need the readies. I won't be picking up my first pay packet for ages, so I need the income from this to tide me over for the first few weeks down in Aldershot. And, you have to admit, you do owe me. Look at all the records I've given you in the last year or so."

It was true. Pete had been more than happy to reap the fruits of Liam's generosity in the past, including most recently The Kane Gang's "Closest Thing To Heaven," numerous remixed twelve-inch versions of Frankie Goes To Hollywood's number one hits, George Michael's current record "Careless Whisper," and the debut Style Council LP.

"They were stolen? You told me you had bought them for me."

"I was a little economical with the truth, couz. You're that naïve; I knew what the mind didn't know, the heart wouldn't grieve over."

It was true that Pete was slightly wet behind the ears, particularly in his relationship with Liam. He always believed everything Liam told him, no matter how far-fetched it sounded. Trust was engrained in his nature. Theft, however, was an act he had never participated in, and he had no desire to do so.

In opposition to Pete's honest nature was the fact that this was Liam asking for a favour. Liam had always been the pied piper to Pete's unquestioning innocent child, the Jesus to his disciple. What Liam said went. No argument and no discussion. Pete had always acquiesced unconditionally in the past, accepting Liam as the natural leader. Just this once, though, Pete really felt he had no option but to stand his ground and decline Liam's proposition.

Feeling the pressure of the moment bearing down on him, Pete closed his eyes and rubbed the chilled can over his forehead.

"Why can't you just leave it alone?" remonstrated Pete a moment later, unable to look Liam in the eye. "On today of all days," he pleaded earnestly. "Just stop for one minute to think about it. How much you stand to lose if things go pear-shaped."

"Come on, Pete. Don't be a bottler," replied Liam. "Not on my last day."

Pete grimaced uncomfortably as he considered the repercussions of getting caught. "I just don't think I'm cut out for it, you know. I'd go to pieces. And if Mum and Dad find out, I'm dead meat."

"That's exactly how I felt before I did it the first time," replied Liam, cigarette hanging loosely from his lips. He was warming to the challenge of coaxing Pete, in much the same way a football manager sweet-talks a nervous rookie player before a big game into believing he can rise to the occasion. "But that's how it is, Kidda. You have to feel the fear before you can conquer it. And to tell you the truth, even now, I still get a little flutter of butterflies in my stomach beforehand. It's only natural. But once you've got away with it, the buzz you get is unbeatable. It's like an addiction you have to feed over and over."

Pete was unresponsive, stubbornly gazing out into the near distance. Feeling he was getting nowhere, Liam felt an inner surge of anger and impatience. He took his last shot.

"Listen, Pete. From tomorrow, you're on your own. Now I know you're not happy about that, and I don't expect you to be. And to tell you the truth, I'm going to miss you, too. You're a top lad, and we've had a few laughs over the years, haven't we?"

A wistful smile crossed Pete's face.

"I know we're family," Liam continued, "and they always come first in my book. I know you have a heart of gold, but living on that posh estate has made you soft. You need to toughen up a bit, be willing to take a few more risks in life. I promised myself I'd make you more street-savvy, and pass on some of the tricks of the trade. I suppose you could call it the handing over of the baton."

Liam put his hand onto Pete's shoulder, squeezing it to cement the feeling of brotherhood he was attempting to articulate.

Pete turned to face Liam, whose rhetoric was beginning to kindle a flame of loyalty inside him. His scales of decision-making were beginning to slowly tilt back in favour of blood ties over common sense, regardless of how uncomfortable in reality that proposition made him feel.

"Okay, I'll do it," said Pete softly.

Liam smiled as he realised his act of persuasion had been successful. "You'll do for me, Pete," he gushed, rubbing Pete's head affectionately. "You'll do for me."

They stood up and set off on the short walk to Northumberland Street, leaving Liam with the dual task of quickly briefing Pete on his role while attempting to boost his shaky confidence. Within five minutes, they had arrived at their destination.

"This is it," said Liam, pausing across the street from Hit World Records, the largest megastore chain in the north of England. He turned to his cousin to deliver a final pep talk. "Just remember, Pete, it's Saturday afternoon, so the shop is packed to the rafters because there's a sale on. The staff working behind the counter will be too busy serving customers to notice us, as the queue will be a mile long. That just leaves the security guard on the door. Put yourself in his shoes. It's nearly the end of a long day, of a long week. You're underpaid. Your legs are aching from all that standing, and you're tired and dying of thirst. You hate your boss and the company. You're not concentrating properly, are you? All that bloke's thinking about, Pete, is going out on the piss and getting his leg over with a slapper in the Big Market tonight. We can't fail. Now let's get in there and clean up."

A quarter of an hour had elapsed since Pete and Liam first entered the store. For Pete, performing his role in the clandestine operation exactly as Liam had instructed, each minute was slow and tortuous as he browsed through the racks containing rock and pop albums.

With Pete in place, Liam eventually swooped in beside him so that they were shoulder to shoulder, and began to flick through the records. Whenever Liam's arm nudged Pete's, that was the signal for the pair of them to shuffle along one place to the right. Using the width of their combined bodies as a shield against prying eyes from behind, and with a wall straight ahead of them, a great deal of camouflage was created for Liam to work in. His plan was simple: assemble together in one rack the items he proposed to thieve, sandwich them between the two plastic carrier bags he had fetched from home that each contained a record, lift the haul out of the rack, and walk out of the store with them held down by the side of his body. Pete's primary role, then, was to as casually as possible follow a few paces behind Liam, just to his side, in order to further assist in concealing the ill-gotten gains from any prying eyes.

A further five minutes passed, and still Liam offered no indication that he was ready to undertake the most problematic part of the whole mission: exiting the store undetected. A nauseous cocktail of apprehension, fear, and adrenalin was swirling around inside Pete like a washing machine on maximum spin. Glancing down to his left, he could see Liam had placed his two bags onto the bottom shelf of the rack he was browsing. Pete's heart missed a beat as Liam, at last, lifted them out of the rack, and began to head towards the exit.

The dramatic opening bars of the summer's ubiquitous hit "Two Tribes" rang out around the store, adding to an atmosphere already crackling with tension.

One of Liam's tips to Pete had been at all costs not to panic. Should he feel an attack of the jitters coming on, Liam advised him, he should focus on nothing else but his breathing. Inhale slowly, hold, count to five, and then exhale as slowly as possible. This technique, he promised, would allow Pete to remain calm, and feel in control of the situation. Liam told him the SAS adopted similar methods, deriving their mental strength from being able to disengage from their usual thought patterns in order to function to their highest capability behind enemy lines.

Liam's advice sounded good to Pete in theory, but he was experiencing considerable difficulty in putting it into practice. He felt like the main character at the beginning of *Midnight Express* as he attempts to smuggle drugs through a Turkish airport. Anxiety had eroded the calm, cool exterior Pete wished to display. Sweat glistened on his forehead. His breathing was rapid and shallow, and his heart thumped like a child furiously banging on a door to be released from a dark room. Blind panic was setting in.

Standing by the doorway was the security guard Liam had mentioned. Dressed in black trousers and khaki short-sleeved shirt, the blonde haired man reminded Pete of an older, overweight version of the police officer from the cop show *Chips*. Arms crossed, and intensely chewing on a piece of gum, he stared impassively ahead.

The two boys emerged from the long, congested aisle into the vast ocean of space that stood between them and the exit. Pete felt as if he was radiating an aura of guilt more visible than the glow surrounding the Ready Brek kid. It was a struggle placing one foot in front of the other, but each step he took was one step closer to freedom.

Ten paces to go.

Chips subjected Pete to the most quizzical, probing stare he had ever experienced.

Nine paces to go.

Under such close personal scrutiny, Pete gulped as he felt his jaw begin to quiver.

Seven paces.

A refreshing blast from the air-conditioning vent above the exit broke the spell of the moment. With his hair blowing in all directions, Pete ran a hand through it to try and pat it back down into place. Chips relinquished his gaze as the pair walked past him.

Pete emerged out into the sun soaked street with all the joy and relief of a marathon runner crossing the finishing line. His smile, however, faded just as quickly when he noticed Liam pulling slightly ahead of him at a brisk pace. Jogging to catch him up, Pete was surprised to see Liam's face had gone a ghostly shade of white, no mean feat considering how suntanned he was.

"They're onto us," hissed Liam, not attempting to disguise the rising panic in his voice, casting nervous glances over his shoulder every couple of seconds.

Pete twisted his head around. It was true. The security guard was standing out on the street, hands on hips, surveying the sea of heads. Next to him was a younger member of staff, wearing National Health glasses and a Smiths T-shirt.

"Bloody hell, Pete. Don't look back."

The rapid change in Liam's demeanour was far from reassuring, leaving Pete with a general feeling of foreboding.

Liam took a deep breath and gathered his thoughts. Telling himself this was not the time for panic, he quickly weighed up the best course of action to take. Within a few seconds, the initial shock at how fast events had turned on their head, with the hunters suddenly finding themselves the prey, was replaced by a plan of action.

"This could be a false alarm, Pete, or it could get hairy. Either way it's best not to take any chances, so just follow me and try to keep up. Okay?"

"Yes."

"Right. Move it."

Like greyhounds out of the traps, they took a sharp right turning and accelerated with impressive velocity towards a four-storey department store. Bursting though the set of double doors, Liam led the way. With Pete hot on his heels, they blazed through the ground floor departments at what felt to Pete like the speed of sound. Entering the female clothing section, the pair twisted and weaved around all obstacles in their path, until they arrived at a fire exit at the rear of the store. Pushing it open, Liam ushered Pete through, quickly taking the opportunity to catch his breath and see if anyone was on their trail.

"Shit," cursed Liam.

The unmistakable sight of Chips and his colleague, standing at the double doors where the boys had been seconds previously, eradicated any notion of the situation being a false alarm. As if smelling Liam's fear, the guard looked up and the pair momentarily locked gazes, before the chase resumed.

Finding themselves in a deserted back lane, full of precariously stacked, empty cardboard boxes and a coating of litter, Liam turned to Pete.

"Right, Pete. Time to split up. You go that way," he said, pointing right. "That leads back to the city centre. You'll be fine once you mingle back in with the crowd. I'll go left."

Pete could only gawp helplessly.

"Get going," Liam urged, taking off in the opposite direction.

Resisting the temptation to follow Liam, and with no other option open to him, Pete began to run as fast as his legs allowed. Within seconds, the excruciating pain in his foot had returned. Pete guessed that the recently applied plaster had already gone the way of its predecessor. Previously a hindrance, the fresh wave of discomfort now acted as a spur, like the crack of a whip from a horse jockey.

Alone and scared witless, Pete felt the poisonous shame of his guilt course through his veins, cursing the fact he had allowed Liam to persuade him to become embroiled in such a stupid act. Only now in the aftermath of the failed theft, the desperate act of damage limitation, did the penny drop as to just how far out of his depth Pete actually was. This self-truth suddenly merged itself to an awareness that had been slowly dawning on him these past few weeks, like someone who struggles for hours with a jigsaw puzzle before painstakingly matching the elusive pieces to finally complete the picture. Pete realised that, however much he dressed and acted like Liam, deep down inside they were chalk and cheese and always would be. He could now see how ridiculous the rebellious, tough persona he adopted whenever he hung out with Liam was. It was something, Pete promised himself, he would rectify should he manage to escape his present predicament.

Pete knew that the potential ramifications of being apprehended were too horrendous for words, with borstal the most daunting outcome imaginable, a self-contained world where only the fittest survived, and the weak were trampled upon. Pete was under no illusion which category he came under. He envisaged cold, sleepless nights broken by the sound of cell doors slamming shut, the abrupt rhythm of patrolling wardens' footsteps on bare concrete floors, and lone, pitiful cries piercing the night.

After thirty metres, Pete passed two concrete bollards, and the lane narrowed into a gloomy alleyway. Struggling for breath amid the thick stench of stale urine, he was heartened by the steadily increasing sound of traffic in the near distance. A sliver of daylight up ahead gradually widened. He was nearly home and dry, and felt a tingle of optimism at the knowledge that within seconds he would be an anonymous face in the crowd, a needle in a very large haystack. Any pursuer would have a near impossible task seeking him out.

With only twenty metres to go, Pete found himself nearing the side entrance to The Blaydon Vaults, a small backstreet pub. The potent smell of beer and cigarettes was wafting out through a small open window, accompanied by the loud din of a rip-roaring heavy metal song from a jukebox. With small groups of men chatting outside while drinking their pints, Pete slowed to a jog in order to thread himself through them.

The sound of an angry voice from way behind him shook Pete out of any complacency he was beginning to feel. "You, boy. Stop right there," it demanded.

For some inexplicable reason, Pete did just that. He turned around to discover Chips had doggedly remained on his scent. Doubled over by the concrete bollards, he was red-faced and gasping for breath. With a mad as hell, determined expression on his face, Chips eyeballed him. Pete gulped as it hit home that his anticipated freedom was no longer a guaranteed certainty.

The drinkers congregated outside all stopped talking to take in the drama unfolding in front of them. With no other choice but to continue onwards, Pete held his breath as he approached them, expecting at least one of them to intervene and block his path until Chips caught up.

By some miracle, Pete found himself through and beyond the men in the blink of an eye. A quick glance behind showed Pete had put yet more distance between himself and Chips.

I don't believe it, he thought, yards away from safety. I've done it.

As Pete turned to face forwards, he crashed into a man making his way into the alley. Swept backwards off his feet, Pete hit the ground with a heavy thud. With the wind knocked out of his sails, he was helpless to do anything other than stare up at the concerned faces circling above him. A voice in his head was desperately urging him to get back onto his feet and continue with his escape.

As Pete struggled to raise himself up, a hand grabbed hold of the top of his shirt and roughly yanked him up. Leaning against the wall initially to steady himself, Pete attempted to continue running, only to discover the vice-like hand clamped onto his shoulder was refusing to yield its grip. Pete looked helplessly at his captor, a heavyset man in his early thirties, with tightly curled black hair, a thin moustache, and silver granny glasses. Having pinned Pete to the wall with his right arm, he was using his free hand to gesture to someone further up the street. Pete knew it had to be Chips. Finally, it appeared the two foes were about to come face to face.

Unable to believe the misfortune that had just befallen him, Pete made one final titanic effort to wriggle free, tears of frustration falling from him as the gravity of the situation began to sink in. However, his frantic efforts were to no avail, with the adult being simply too strong.

Reduced to a walking pace by this stage, Chips was nearing The Blaydon Vaults when a bunch of tattooed, denim-clad football fans spilled outdoors, immediately creating a human wall between Pete and his subjugator on one side, and the security guard on the other.

"What's going on here?" a gruff voice demanded, instantly recognising the youth being held against his will, as well as taking note of the security guard attempting to brusquely force his way through his comrades. "Benny. Chalky. Keep that guard away from us for a minute," he ordered.

Pete looked towards the group of men. It was the large, shaven headed man he had returned the twenty-pound note to, barely an hour ago.

"What the hell do you think you are doing to that kid?" he barked menacingly at the man stubbornly holding onto Pete. "He's my mate. Let go of him. Now," he ordered.

A deathly silence fell upon the alley. Pete felt the man's grip loosen a little, but not enough to break free.

"I said now," reiterated the bald man, moving forwards with a look of no-nonsense intimidation.

Immediately realising he was seriously out of his depth, the Good Samaritan relinquished his hold and, in a curious twist, found himself backed up against the wall and rounded upon by Pete's saviours. No longer the dominating force of the situation, and with the fear of God in his eyes, he made a panicked appeal.

"Now then, lads, let me explain. This isn't what it appears."

"Come on then, pervert, pick on someone your own size," yelled the leader, his face centimetres away from the Good Samaritan's. Predictably, the man failed to react violently, closing his eyes in fear and shrinking down into a crouched position, holding his arms protectively around his head.

"Go on, son," shouted Pete's liberator. "Get yourself away. Whatever you've done, I guess it can't be all that bad," he said, winking at Pete. "He'll not give you anymore grief."

"Hey, you there. Don't let that boy get away," shouted Chips, from behind the human wall that was preventing him from intervening.

"Go," urged the bald man.

Pete didn't need telling again. Within seconds, he was back in Grey Street, feeling a great deal safer among the crowds of human traffic. The only problem remaining was to decide, in a split-second, the best plan of escape from the several options available to him.

The quickest choice was staring him in the face, with the entrance to the Monument underground metro station situated yards away from where he stood. Pete was tempted to run down the stairs into the station and jump onto the first train that arrived, just to put some distance between himself and the city. However, he knew that should anyone come looking for him while he remained on the platform, he would effectively be trapped with nowhere to go.

Pete contemplated heading back to the main train station and using his return ticket back to Sunderland. A plus point was that the vast size of the station's interior would allow him to remain relatively anonymous once inside, but the one major disadvantage was it only had one narrow entrance, and should it be under surveillance, then he would be an easy target and vulnerable to being apprehended.

Pete's third and final choice was the one he opted for. He turned right and walked quickly up the road in the direction of the Haymarket area of town. After a few hundred yards, he took a prompt right-hand turn into the fume-filled, dimly lit bus station, located in the bowels of Eldon Square shopping centre. The shadowy, night-like atmosphere was most welcome, and Pete felt safer and less conspicuous rubbing shoulders with the hundreds of people waiting to board the buses that left from an array of bays every few minutes.

Wanting to escape the clutches of the city as soon as possible, Pete had planned to jump onto the first bus he came to that was due to depart. For the second time in the space of a few minutes, lady luck smiled on him. A bus to Durham was parked in bay seven at the bottom end of the terminal, and was only two minutes away from departure. Boarding swiftly, Pete found a seat at the rear of the downstairs tier. Chewing his bottom lip, Pete nervously kept his gaze on the entrance to the bus, half expecting a deluge of police officers to enter at any moment.

Nobody came.

The doors hissed shut, and the bus juddered out of the station into daylight, the grime-smeared windows providing a degree of cover from any probing eyes on the street. Pete felt like a pursued undercover spy who, having overcome numerous obstacles by hook and crook, was now one last hurdle away from the sweet taste of freedom.

Five minutes later, the bus finally left behind the clogged up city centre roads, and the tentacles of the constantly changing traffic lights, crossing the Tyne Bridge into Gateshead. Leaving behind the most chaotic hour he had ever experienced in his life, Pete swore to himself he would never be so stupid again.

CHAPTER 3

Life In A Northern Town

The sound of Barry Manilow's music woke Pete up from a frequently disturbed sleep. Opening his eyes, he was relieved to discover the darkness of night banished from his bedroom. The demons that had descended upon his consciousness in the dead of night did not appear half as daunting or fearful in the cold light of day.

In the early hours, it had been a different matter. Restless and perspiring, his feverish paranoia had spiralled into overdrive. The slam of a car door from outside at 2 a.m., closely followed by muffled voices and footsteps, had Pete trembling under the sheets.

An hour later, the blanket of silence was punctuated by the sound of a car engine running. Pete feared it was the police, deployed to swoop when least expected to arrest Durham's newest public enemy number one. He braced himself for armed officers to abseil down from the roof and crash in through the bedroom window. Blindfolded and handcuffed, he would be whisked away to an isolated, deserted building in the middle of nowhere. A murky room lit by a low wattage bare bulb, unfurnished apart from a splintered, rickety table and several bare wooden chairs, would be the scene of his interrogation. A pair of detectives, comprising good, friendly cop and sadistic, horrible cop, would inflict upon him the full range of brutal torture techniques at their disposal, until he was pleading for mercy and ready to come clean.

The act of confession for Pete, however, would be a case of jumping out of the frying pan, only to find himself in the middle of an all-consuming fire. He would be a grass, a snitch, and a traitor. Such badges of dishonour and shame, once bestowed, were not so easily shaken off.

Over and over, Pete relived his close escape, his mind a malfunctioning video machine.

Play, stop, rewind.

Play, stop, rewind.

Play, stop … until he fell into an uneasy slumber just as the first birds of dawn began to sing.

In Pete's experience, life never seemed to remain carefree for long. The drama of the previous day had been a closely fought battle settled in his favour, no matter how tenuous the victory. Nevertheless, the main war that was his life continued unabated. Today marked the return of an age-old adversary, a familiar hated feeling that had been temporarily banished over the summer, but which now returned with a vengeance: Sunday sadness.

It was a ghost that haunted him; so tangible he could almost touch it. It manifested itself in numerous guises: the smell of fried breakfasts intermingling with Sunday roasts in the late morning outdoors air, seeping out from slightly ajar, steamed up kitchen windows; the nostalgic radio shows that played sad ballads from previous decades; television channels dominated by programmes related to religion and farming; and the monotonous, never-ending transmission of ceefax pages.

Exposure to any of these symptoms immediately filled Pete with dread, but were mere bit-part players in comparison to the primary factor that contributed to his negative emotions, as the weekend dragged right on to its bitter end: the return to school on a Monday morning.

Having not been to school for so long, Pete was feeling the pain of this particular reality more intensely than normal. The dreaded thought that this time tomorrow he would be back in an educational institution was firing at him like a hail of bullets from all angles. With the clock ticking on the final countdown, he felt like a condemned man ready to face the hangman.

Pete hated the way time always seemed to accelerate just when you wanted it to do the opposite. It only felt like yesterday that he had walked excitedly out of the school gates on the last day of term, removing his hated school tie for the last time. Six weeks of heaven had beckoned, an oasis of spare time to spend as he wished: long, lazy lie-ins; Radio One road shows to listen to; dozens of frames of snooker to play; hours free to entertain himself on his ZX Spectrum computer; piles of frequently refreshed library books to plough through; and, when all else failed, he could rely on his film collection, consisting of nearly one hundred video cassettes that were packed with movies such as *Gregory's Girl*, *Escape to Victory*, *Star Wars*, and numerous others starring the likes of Clint Eastwood and Bruce Lee. With so many hobbies to be engrossed in, for a short time life for Pete was almost bearable.

With more time than usual to spend around the house, there were other benefits available to Pete. His culinary diet was freed from the choice of mundane slops served up as school dinners, or the greasy chips and battered sausages from the lunchtime visit to the local chippy. Endless quantities of banana sandwiches with liberal coatings of sugar, and packs of custard creams and bourbons biscuits, were devoured, washed down by an almost constant flow of the tea that he had been addicted to ever since he was out of nappies.

The soundtrack to these days came from his record collection. Beatles and John Lennon music were his favourites, followed closely by current acts such as The Style Council, Aztec Camera, Thompson Twins, and Howard Jones.

Through the paper-thin floorboards that separated the floor of his bedroom from the kitchen, the sound of contented Sunday morning domesticity could be heard: the boiling of the kettle; cups, plates and cutlery being placed on the table for breakfast; the relaxed voices of Pete's mother and Trevor, his stepfather, chatting.

Pete didn't need to be wearing a pair of x-ray specs, the type that are frequently advertised in the back of Sunday newspapers next to the all in one slippers and adult film adverts, to be able to picture the scene. Trevor was sitting at the oblong-shaped pine kitchen table, dressed in his Sunday clothes of cords and old denim shirt, reading the financial supplement from the *Daily Mail*, while occasionally stabbing at a segment of lightly sugared grapefruit. Opposite him, Pete's mother was still in her lemon-coloured terry towel dressing gown, munching on her toast, with a cup of tea, while humming along to her records. Their adored three-year-old daughter Carla, Pete's half-sister, was playing on the rug in the centre of the room with her My Little Pony figures, chattering away to her toys as if they were real-life creatures.

Pete hated the image they portrayed of a cosy, happy family when he was not present in the room, only for the atmosphere to change when he walked into the room, making him feel as if he was an unwelcome intruder.

At dead on 9:30 a.m., Trevor Braithwaite finished his breakfast and folded up the newspaper. "Okay, love. Time to get cracking outside," said Trevor to his wife, while pulling a funny face at Carla. "The car won't wash itself."

Carla looked up. "Is Daddy going to wash his car?"

"Yes, darling. Daddy is."

"Can I come and help Daddy?"

Trevor laughed, while his amused wife looked on. "It's very nice of you to offer, Carla, but I have a job for you to do for Daddy."

"Carla do what?"

"I would like you to stay and look after your ponies, and I promise I'll come and play with you as soon as I'm finished."

"You go and do your jobs, darling," said Sheila. "I'll keep an eye on Carla while I get on with the cleaning."

Trevor leaned over and kissed his wife, a big grin on his face.

"What's that for?" she asked.

"For making me the happiest man alive," he replied, before leaving the room.

Full of the type of inner satisfaction that tells you life cannot possibly get any better, Sheila stood up and began to clear the dirty dishes off the table, stacking them on the kitchen bench while the sink filled with hot water.

Once the kitchen was cleaned to her impeccable standards, Sheila removed the old plastic ice cream container that held the cans of polish, disinfectant, sponges and cloths, from the cupboard under the sink and moved into the lounge. With Carla still happily playing, Sheila flipped her record of *Barry Live in Britain* over onto side two, placing the stylus at the beginning of the first track. Armed with polish and duster, Sheila methodically sprayed and wiped clean the room's few ornaments and photo frames, half-dancing along to the song "Bermuda Triangle."

With the more delicate items completed, she set about cleaning the larger items, such as the television set, mantelpiece, and coffee table. Sheila was extremely house proud, and believed the home was a reflection of the people who lived within its four walls. She took the view that if a friend or neighbour was to call around unexpectedly, she should not feel embarrassed enough not to invite them inside just because the lounge was in need of a good clean.

To ensure such dilemmas never presented themselves, Sheila had certain rules chiselled in stone in order to guarantee the house was always kept to an acceptable standard. Firstly, it was a definite no-no to enter the house wearing shoes. They were to be removed in the front porch, or at the back door, before entering. Furthermore, no main meals were to be eaten in the lounge, especially off laps while sitting on the sofa watching television, and it was unthinkable to even comprehend placing a coffee mug onto the carpet, lest a drop of liquid stain the surface. Newspapers and magazines were not to be left on the sofa or floor, but placed in the newspaper rack when not being read.

Having polished the wooden, ceramic and metallic items to within an inch of their lives, Sheila removed the Hoover from the cupboard under the stairs, fired it into life, and set about methodically sucking the carpet free from dirt.

With the downstairs and stairway carpets freshly vacuumed, Sheila temporarily switched off the machine on the upstairs landing. She paused outside her son's bedroom door, and gave three sharp knocks before entering.

"Rise and shine, Pete," she said, walking over to the window. She pulled back the curtains and opened the top window. "Just letting in some fresh air," she said.

Pete shivered as a sharp blast of cold air infiltrated his room.

"Oh Mum, it's freezing," protested Pete. Regardless of whether it was a bright summer's day in June, or a dank November Sunday morning, his mother always saw to it that a blast of fresh air was just what Pete's bedroom required. The fact that he could be in the middle of a deep sleep, or feeling under the weather with a heavy cold, was unimportant.

Pete hated the weekly tidy up of the house on a Sunday morning, when his mother always made it her personal mission to be as generally disruptive as possible. Pete felt it was a deliberate ploy to make him so fed up with the noise, and her nagging, that he would decide to venture out of the house. His mother was always complaining about the amount of time he spent lazing in his bedroom, or lounging around the house in front of the television watching films. Pete would remonstrate as to what exactly he should be doing.

"Go for a walk, or go and play with your sister," was always her two-pronged response.

Apart from the fact he objected to being forced out of his bedroom against his will, albeit temporarily, Pete hated the way his mother treated herself to a good nose around at what he was currently up to: what books he was reading, the computer games he was playing, and the records he was listening to. If he was reading a book that she objected to, such as one of James Herbert's horror stories, she would ask him if such material was suitable reading for a fourteen-year-old boy.

"*The Fog* and *The Dark*," she would say to him, tutting disapprovingly. "That stuff will give you nightmares, you know. What happened to reading comics like *Roy of The Rovers*?"

A despairing shake of the head from Pete was the only response she got from such questions. Pete would wonder when she was going to realise that comics were only for kids.

A further pet hate of Pete's, in relation to his mother taking command of his personal habitat, was the tendency she had for putting records and computer games away in the wrong cover or box, making it a pain when it came to laying his hands on them. If she did happen to miraculously pair the correct record to its matching cover, it also irked him how she would put it back inside his storage box without any thought for its correct alphabetical placing. The previous week Pete had flicked through his records to find John Lennon's *Imagine* album not with the rest of his other Lennon records, but placed in between Madness and *Now That's What I Call Music One*. When Pete complained, she retorted that if he couldn't be bothered to put it back himself, then why should she waste time and effort returning it to its correct place?

"Up, Pete," she persisted, standing over him with her hands placed ominously on her hips. "I want you washed, teeth brushed, dressed, and up and about, so I can clean the lavatory, bathroom, and in here."

Pete groaned, covering his eyes with his arm. He hated the way his mother called the toilet a lavatory. It was just one of many new words she had added to her vocabulary in recent years. Another phrase she used that was a pet hate of Pete's was "that chap." In the old days, Pete would hear her refer to a male in conversations as a "bloke" or a "gadgy." Since the move to Durham, they were now referred to as "that chap." Pete cringed whenever he heard her say it.

Knowing there could only be one winner when confronted by the wrath of his mother, Pete sulkily slid out of bed and made his way into the bathroom, her muttered complaint that "it isn't normal to shut yourself away in your room all day" ringing in his ears.

There was a terrible smell lingering in the clammy air of the bathroom: Trevor's sickly deodorant spray. Pete didn't know what brand it was; only that it wasn't Tidal. Pete had received a gift pack of Tidal as a present from his Gran the previous Christmas. Initially overjoyed by this unexpected gift, he had applied it religiously for several days as advised by the sports stars endorsing it in the television adverts, in the hope that it would act as some kind of magic manly potion and encourage his body to develop physically. But magic potion or not, Pete quickly dispensed with its services, as he could no longer bear the peppery aroma it left on him, causing him to develop sneezing fits of epic proportions. Pete was planning to slyly donate it to a school jumble sale or the local church fete when the opportunity arose, careful to ensure knowledge of his actions did not get back to his Gran, and she put him in her bad books. He didn't want to hurt her feelings by making her think she had wasted her money on him. She was a pensioner and didn't have a great deal to live on.

Pete loved going to visit her. Her kitchen cupboards were always full of amazing food, and she never seemed to tire of making sure Pete always left on a full stomach. It was not unusual to be treated to salty slices of thick corned beef, together with large portions of deep-fried chips, not the tasteless frozen oven chips his mother bought by the ton. His Gran stocked many varieties of Heinz soup, which he devoured with slices of fluffy white bread for dunking, not the brown stuff with chewy bits in that his mother had converted to. If his Gran had been baking, Pete could expect savoury and sweet pies of all types, with firm shortcrust or flaky puff pastries. Pete loved the way she would place all of her freshly cooked food onto racks to cool, and allow Pete to help himself. She would sit opposite him at the table and quiz him on what he had been up to since his previous visit, as well as asking his opinion on the food and what he would like to sample on his next visit.

"You're a growing lad," she would say, disbelievingly, when Pete told her about some of the food his mother prepared these days. "You need proper, old-fashioned home cooking inside you. Not all of the fancy stuff that has sprung up these days. Cabbage pancakes. Huh. What will they think of next?"

Pete would feel slightly treacherous for siding against his mother, particularly as he knew somewhere along the family grapevine his complaints would wind up back to her. Gran would mention it to his father, who at some point in the near future would use it as ammo during one of his protracted and heated arguments on the telephone with his ex-wife. All fingers would then be pointed at Pete, with the blame for any resultant disharmony between the estranged parents and their collective armies laid squarely at his door. But Pete felt such abandoning of loyalties was worth his while if it ensured his Gran, in a wave of pity, gave him second helpings, as well as a cold food parcel to take home for a supper or lunch the next day.

Pete was quick to get washed and changed. Now that he was actually out of bed, he had decided to get out of the house for the morning. Although the intensity of the previous day's episode had died down a little, with no telephone call from Liam to confirm his successful escape, Pete could not be one hundred percent certain he was out of the woods yet. The prospect of several hours moping around the house on tenterhooks, waiting for the phone to ring and bad news to be delivered, was much too tortuous to contemplate. Pete knew Liam's coach departed at 12:10 p.m., so he reckoned that if nothing to the contrary had been heard by then, it could be safely assumed that everything was hunky dory and Liam had set off on the long journey to Aldershot.

Grabbing his four pounds paper round money from under his pillow, a spare plaster, his personal Walkman, and a couple of C90 audio cassettes, Pete dashed down the stairs into the front porch and slipped on his coat and trainers. Walking down the driveway, Pete saw Trevor standing on the front lawn talking to Mr Evans, their next-door neighbour. Noticing Pete on his way out, Mr Evans shouted a greeting.

"Good morning, young Peter," he said, his voice always sounding as if he was struggling to contain the funniest joke in the world that he had been sworn to keep secret. Mr Evans always attempted matey camaraderie with Pete, usually something along the lines of "Ah, what a beautiful morning, young Peter. Makes you glad to be alive," or "Off to school, are we? What I'd give to be your age again." Today was no exception. "Not giving your Dad a hand with the garden, then?"

Pete flinched. He hated it when Mr Evans, or Geoff, as he insisted on being called, referred to Trevor as being his father. Too shy to say anything, Pete would smile feebly while inside he was a cauldron of rage. Pete wanted to grab hold of Mr Evans and scream at him, "He's not my real bloody Dad."

Mr Evans's reference to gardening made Pete recall the time when, not long after moving into the brand new house, his mother had coerced Pete into helping Trevor out in the garden, in an attempt to get the two of them to bond. It was a disaster. Having been brought up all of his life in a terraced street that had no gardens, Pete was puzzled as to why she thought he would be interested in getting his hands dirty with the man who had stepped into his father's shoes.

Continuing to edge closer to the pavement, and getting further away from the two men, Pete shook his head in response to Mr Evans's question. Past experience told him that he would be trapped in a conversation of pointless idle chatter if he stood still.

"No, Mr Evans. I'm going into town. I'm running late, actually," lied Pete, keen to avoid any further dialogue.

"Oh, I am sorry," replied an apologetic Mr Evans. "You get going, lad," he said, a sad smile on his face, before resuming his chat with Trevor.

Pete knew Mr Evans was basically harmless, but wished he would just mind his own business. He knew, however, that his mother and Trevor were just as much to blame for Mr Evans's constant erroneous references.

Keen to keep up appearances, his mother had made it plain that she did not wish to shatter any image of perfection that was presented to the neighbours, lest they be the subject of gossip and were cast in an unfavourable light. Certain aspects of the past were forbidden to be discussed, such as her divorce, and were swept under the carpet as she gradually befriended and integrated herself into the local neighbourhood. When she was asked to host a wine and Tupperware party, she knew her neighbours had finally accepted her.

On the night in question, Pete was banished to his bedroom, fobbed off with a hastily assembled plate of buffet food: chicken supreme filled vol-au-vents, sausage rolls, and half a dozen sticks of skewered cheese, pickled onion and pineapple pieces. Liquid refreshment was in the form of a small glass of rose wine, taken from one of the three-litre cartons stockpiled for the occasion, diluted with lemonade. Unable to concentrate on reading or watching television, due to the noise generated by the crowd packed into the lounge and kitchen downstairs, Pete ended up playing his records as loud as he dared in order to drown out the annoying racket.

Pete hurried along the sedate street of identical three bedroom semi-detached houses, where narrow stretches of grass verges separated the smooth asphalt road from flagged footpaths on both sides. Apart from Trevor and Mr Evans, there were a small number of local residents who had ventured outdoors, relishing the prospect of an hour or so of comparative solitude. There were gardens to be tended to, with borders containing late-blooming flowers of red, yellow and blue to be weeded, and lawns to be cut. Likewise, nothing satisfied them more than giving the motor cars that stood on their driveways, consisting of the latest models of Escorts, Rovers, and Granadas, a wash and a polish until their bodywork shone as impressively as the day they had stood in the showrooms without a mile on their clocks.

The Newton Moor housing estate had its origins in the early 1970s. A fast-growing local workforce, recruited to the likes of the local prison service, police constabulary, and local government authorities, as well as multiple private industries that were located in and around the city centre, were employed in an area of the north-east where the demand for property far outstripped the supply. Various housing development firms set in motion plans to counter this unequal equation, drawing up plans for construction on several square miles of land a five minute drive away from the city centre.

Owned in the previous century by a solitary upper-class family, by the start of 1984 the same area of land was reputed to be home to the largest private housing estate in Europe; the modern dwellings were highly desired by families who aspired to climb up the social ladder, and who were not put off by the expensive price tag.

Pete cut through the narrow footpath that ran between house numbers nine and eleven, bringing him to the large communal field at the rear of his street. Taking a short cut across the grass brought Pete to the summit of a short steep hill, leading him down to the silver metal footbridge that spanned the main east coast railway line. This structure was the doorway between the eastern periphery of the housing estate, and the rural landscape that lay just beyond.

Pete paused to take in the impressive panorama that lay before him. It was a magical world, a two-mile journey of yellow brick road proportions that culminated with the centuries-old Norman cathedral, an omnipresent Oz in the background of the postcard landscape.

The first stage of the route carried him along a gently winding, narrow dirt track that led through wide fields of open grassland, full of sheep and cows grazing leisurely. Gradually widening out into an unmade road, the route ran past a farmhouse and its adjacent barn and stables. Here, Pete paused briefly to peer over the boundary wall of the farm's inner yard. Small clusters of hens were strutting around the yard, pecking at the ground. Penned in at the far corner were a group of boisterous, mud-splattered pigs, eagerly awaiting their next batch of swill. The potent, earthy aroma of the animals permeated the air, forcing Pete to hold his nose.

Leaving behind the sound and scent of the animals, he continued among the shadows of a stretch of highway, lined on both sides with legions of tall trees. Snatches of birdsong emanated from lush, overhanging branches that conspired to blot out a significant proportion of the natural daylight.

Reaching the lowest point of the valley, the trees fell away to leave Pete on a flat, exposed section of terrain, between fields containing crops of green and gold. Pete imagined whole families of rats scurrying through tunnels situated below the ground's surface, just like in the story of Nimh.

By the time Pete arrived at the newsagent's shop in the Market Place, a light drizzle had begun to dampen the quiet city streets. Grateful to have reached shelter just as the heavens opened, Pete busied himself with browsing through the weekly music magazines, before agonising over what to purchase from the confectionary and snacks aisle. In need of a serious amount of comfort food, Pete chose a can of Coke, Mars bar, packet of Polos, and bag of Tudor pickled onion crisps, as well as a Sunday newspaper.

With well over an hour to kill before he deemed it safe to return home, Pete crossed the street and wandered up the medieval-like, narrow lane of Saddler Street. Bearing right for the short but steep ascent of cobbled Owengate, Pete reached Palace Green. With the rain pelting down in fury, Pete quickened his pace towards the cathedral, located at the far end of the peninsula.

It was gloomy and draughty inside the nave, the first section of the cathedral Pete found himself in upon entering by the main knocker entrance. The only source of natural light came courtesy of the large stained glass windows, built high into the stone walls. In the near distance, the faint glow of a shimmering cluster of candles, where the nave met the crossing tower in the middle of the building, added some much needed illumination.

Pete had visited the cathedral once before, as an eight-year-old on a school trip, but he remembered little of that particular occasion, apart from the exhausting climb to the peak of the sixty-six-metre tower that made him feel as if he was standing on top of the world.

Feeling exposed and conspicuous standing in the middle of the open floor, Pete began to slowly stroll around the hushed interior, occasionally pausing in the numerous chapels and walkways to read the inscribed tombs, or to gaze incredulously at the feats of grand architecture on display, such as the prominent stone columns that rose all the way up to the elevated ceiling.

Arriving back at where he had started, Pete noticed that more and more people, dressed smartly in their Sunday best, had begun to occupy the rows of seats in the main hall. Standing on a podium in front of the expanding congregation, a reverend was talking to an organist who was warming up his fingers by playing little snippets of hymns.

It was obvious to Pete that some kind of Sunday service was about to begin at any moment, so he took his leave. Finding an empty seat outside the university library building on Palace Green, conveniently sheltered from the rain by a nearby tree, Pete slipped on his Walkman headphones and unfolded his newspaper.

Concluding his tour of the cathedral at the information desk, Alistair 'Barney' Barnett turned to address the tour party.

"And here, I'm afraid, is where our journey ends," he began, pausing to smile at the round of gentle groans. "Thank you very much for travelling all this way today to see the delights of our wonderful church. I hope that it has not disappointed, and I have very much enjoyed meeting you all. I have a spare five minutes for those of you who have any questions, and for the rest of you, thank you once again, and please feel free to wander around to your heart's content for the remainder of your visit."

Barney accepted the compliments and handshakes of the dispersing group with humility and grace. In his role as a volunteer church steward at Durham Cathedral, it truly lifted his spirits when his efforts were genuinely appreciated.

Once the final few queries were politely but efficiently dealt with, a glance at his watch told him he had a little surplus time on his hands before his services were required once more. Unusually for so early in the day, a heavy fatigue had threatened to overcome him in the last stages of the tour, so he hoped that an invigorating burst of fresh air would be the ideal tonic. Before anyone else could approach him, Barney made his way outdoors to grab a few moments to himself, and take the weight off his legs. He always found it ironic that in a building dedicated to prayer and peace, the only real solitude was to be found outside its walls. He would, however, have it no other way, thoroughly relishing his role as ambassador to the thousands of visitors that flocked to the city each year.

"Morning, Mac," shouted Barney, walking past the car park attendant perched inside the doorway of his wooden hut, impassively surveying the damp morning.

"Good morning, Barney."

As Barney approached his favourite seat, he noticed one-half of it was occupied by a young boy, hunched over a newspaper laid out on his knees. Barney sat down in the space next to him, adjusting his purple gown as he made himself comfortable.

Whenever he had a few moments to spare, or needed time to himself to gather his thoughts, Barney liked to come to the wooden seat outside the university library building. He had always found Palace Green to be a place of great tranquility, particularly on days like today where, apart from a few parked cars, the scene he contemplated was almost a carbon copy of the view that previous generations would have experienced.

Situated upon the city's natural peninsula, the inner heart of Palace Green is dominated by its oblong-shaped, immaculately maintained green, with the buildings that line its perimeter all harking back to bygone eras. Across from where Barney was sat were the original city almshouses, now reinvented as university departmental buildings and a teahouse. Like the library behind him, they dated back to the Victorian period. To his left stood the antiquated Durham Castle. Originally owned by the Durham prince bishops, it had been handed over to the university in the 1830s, but still managed to retain its air of majestic grandeur. To his right was the city's most pivotal feature, the world-famous Durham Cathedral. Home to the remains of two of the key figures of early Christianity, the Venerable Bede and Saint Cuthbert, the iconic symbol of Norman architecture had dominated the landscape for nearly a millennium.

"Good morning," said Barney to the youngster.

He smiled to himself when no reply was forthcoming, the headphones covering the boy's ears obviously drowning out his greeting. Barney patted the youth on the arm, gesturing to him to remove them from his head.

Pete pressed stop on his cassette player and allowed the headphones to rest around the base of his neck. He warily turned to face the man, anticipating a ticking off for some kind of rule he must have inadvertently broken. The white-haired stranger had a round face, with a tough, weather-beaten complexion, and a distinguishing large bulbous nose that was lined with broken veins. Pete couldn't assign an accurate age to him, guessing only that he was definitely older than his father, but looked younger than his sixty-four year old grandfather.

"I take it you are a Sunderland supporter?" enquired Barney.

Feeling uncomfortable at being spoken to by an unfamiliar person, Pete nodded, wondering how he could possibly have known that.

Barney's shoulders shook as he laughed, enjoying the look of sheer puzzlement on the boy's face. "Don't worry, young man. I'm not a mind reader, although sometimes I wish I had that particular trick up my sleeve. I saw that you were engrossed in the football match reports from yesterday, and you had an all too familiar look on your face as I approached just now. It is one that I know only too well, as I'm a Sunderland fan too, for my sins. All of these defeats are difficult to take, are they not? If you were a follower of our rivals, then you would have looked a great deal more jovial, I think."

When the man paused, as if expecting a response, Pete felt slightly awkward. Unable to think of a reply, he wanted to return to his newspaper, without appearing rude. In social situations such as these, Pete always struggled with self-confidence.

"Alistair Barnett," said the older man, extending his right hand to Pete. Briefly hesitating, Pete quickly shook it. The man's hand was icy cold. "Barney to my friends – I so despise formalities. And you are?"

"Oh, sorry. Pete," he mumbled.

"It's a pleasure to meet you, Pete, especially a fellow fan of the red and whites," he said. Removing a small apple from a concealed pocket in his gown, Barney took a crunching bite, gazing thoughtfully around the street as he slowly chewed.

Pete's initial discomfort was alleviated by the man's proclamation that he liked football. Pete had never entertained the thought that religious people, such as the person next to him, would have such normal interests.

"Did I notice you in the cathedral a little while ago?" asked Barney.

Pete nodded.

"Ah, I thought that was you. Are you not with anyone else? Your parents? A friend?"

"No," muttered Pete, shaking his head.

Barney was curious. It was unusual for one so young to turn up alone in the cathedral. In his experience, children were reluctantly dragged along at the behest of parents, or teachers on school visits. Accordingly, rather than attempt to appreciate their surroundings, they tended to be more intent on making a nuisance of themselves. The youngster's presence Barney found fresh and heartening.

"Never fails to take your breath away," said Barney, gazing admiringly in the direction of the cathedral. "I've seen it a million times over the years and it still inspires awe and humility. Do you know, Pete, that I've been sitting in this very spot for the past forty-odd years, ever since I was about your age. Can you believe that? I have memories of sitting in this very spot during the last war, as a young choirboy, when all of a sudden the skies were filled with the sound of the approaching Luftwaffe."

Pete looked up at the grey sky. He couldn't imagine the Germans being so close, bringing the threat of imminent danger to Durham.

"Weren't you scared?" asked Pete, the thought slipping out of his mouth before he had time to think.

"Terrified," replied Barney, pleased to detect an element of curiosity in the youngster. "My mother wouldn't hear of sending me away to the countryside, out of harm's way. She believed that the Nazis were the devil incarnate, and that any God in existence would surely protect us from any bombs in the shadow of God's sanctuary here on earth. Whether by luck or divine intervention she was, thankfully, proved correct. That didn't stop me from running as fast as my legs would take me to the air shelter, though."

Barney looked across the green as if watching his younger self running off in the direction of Dun Cow Lane. "Yes," he sighed, taking hold of the silver cross hanging around his neck, briefly rubbing its smooth surface with a fingertip, "so much of life has passed me by as I've sat here, and still I never tire of this spot. Between you and me," whispered Barney, as if about to reveal a startling conspiracy, "I think it is the most beautiful place on earth, with an unspoilt magic all its very own. But let that be our little secret," he said, tapping the side of his nose with his index finger, "otherwise, the whole world and their cat will be queuing up to steal our little piece of paradise."

Barney glanced at his watch. "Ah ha. Nearly time for my next tour. How time flies. I'm afraid I must be going in a few moments."

"You mean you actually work there?" asked Pete.

"Yes, I do, young Pete. In a voluntary capacity, as a church steward. I'm afraid I retired from active service last year, for reasons that I do not wish to bore you with, although one never retires from his beliefs and devotion. I like to keep busy, and I cannot think of a better way to stay occupied than to introduce the public to the many charms and delights we have here. I'm afraid I'm not one for sitting around doing the crossword, or pottering about in the garden. While I can, I would like to remain active and do something useful. Have you been inside before today?"

"Only once."

Barney smiled again, as if confirming to himself that his initial impression of Pete had been correct. "Oh, you really should keep returning. After all of these years, I still get surprised by things I've never noticed before."

The cathedral bells, housed in the central tower, chimed for the hour. Barney looked incredulously at his watch. "Goodness gracious, it's midday. My watch must be slow. I really do have to be going," he said, rising quickly from the bench. "I have a party of Americans from Chicago, and a magical mystery tour from Cleethorpes to attend to. Two parts of the world you would normally struggle to bring together, but that is the lure of our little place. Amazing when you think about it," he said, shaking his head in wonder. "At least it gets me out of peeling the potatoes and carrots at home for Mrs Barney. If there's one thing I've learnt after all of these years of marriage, it's to be busy whenever my wife is at home, otherwise she has a nasty habit of finding a chore or two for me to do."

Barney brushed off a few specks of dirt from the rear of his gown. "Maybe I'll see you around the place again in the near future, young Pete," he said, preparing to depart, "and maybe it will be when the fortunes of our team are on the up. But don't hold your breath," he joked. "Enjoy the rest of your day, and try smiling a little bit more. It will make you feel better, I promise. God bless," he shouted over his shoulder, as he hurried back to work.

As Pete rounded the corner into his street, he was presented with a scene of suburban normality. He had half expected to discover half a dozen police officers milling around the street, walkie-talkies at the ready, awaiting a sighting of the criminal at large, but nothing out of the ordinary was occurring in the damp, sleepy surroundings.

Pleased to find Trevor's car was absent from the driveway, Pete stepped tentatively into the hallway of the house. Apart from the gentle hum of the refrigerator, the house was deadly silent. The usual telltale signs of activity for a Sunday were absent: no radio on in the kitchen, no noise from Carla, and no sound of a Barry Manilow video playing from the lounge.

Pete ascended the first four stairs and cocked his ear for clues of occupancy upstairs.

Silence.

The answer phone machine, on the small table by the front door, indicated there were no unread messages. Pete took that as a good sign.

On the kitchen table, a short note written by his mother awaited him:

"Out for lunch. Back late afternoon. Grab something out of the freezer."

Everything normal there, too, thought Pete. If he was in trouble then he knew it would have read something along the lines of "wait till you get home." Piecing together the fragments of evidence available to him, Pete deduced that nothing untoward was now going to rebound back upon him from the previous day. Conclusive testimony to this fact was displayed on the kitchen clock. It was 12:30 p.m. Liam was now twenty minutes into his journey to Aldershot. If events had taken an unexpected turn the previous day and Liam had been arrested, then Pete was sure that the ripples of tumult would have washed up onto his shores by now.

With this realisation came a mixed set of emotions. The pang of real loneliness Pete felt at Liam's fresh departure was sweetened slightly by the way events had panned out since his own misguided foray into the world of criminality.

On a less serious note, Pete felt it was an added bonus to be granted a reprieve from the ordeal that was the family Sunday lunch. The roast meat, usually chicken or beef, Pete had no qualms with. Copious mounds of buttery, fluffy mash potato with hot gravy drizzled over was complete heaven, and his mother's extra large Yorkshire puddings were to die for. Where Pete struggled badly was in his attempts to eat the assortment of vegetables that she unfailingly presented on his plate. Like two rival gladiators going head to head with swords and shields, sparks would fly around the kitchen table at Pete's stubborn refusal to allow one forkful of despised root or green vegetables to insult his taste buds. The previous Sunday had been a typical example. The untouched remains of Pete's dinner plate left to go cold included sickeningly sweet parsnips, cunningly cut by his mother to resemble roast potatoes, putrid tasting strands of cabbage, and rubbery stalks of cauliflower.

"There's no pudding if you don't even attempt to eat them," threatened his mother, while Trevor busied himself with assisting Carla to eat her lunch, obeying the unwritten rule that nutritional well-being was a domestic drama to be participated in by mother and son only.

"I don't care," replied Pete, sensing a get-out clause, knowing an early evening walk to the off-licence would supply more than enough confectionary consolation.

"It's apple crumble and custard," she stated, knowing her verbal punch was well below the belt as it was her son's favourite dessert.

"Oh Mum, I'm allergic to this type of veg, though," he pleaded desperately.

"It's good for you, Pete," she declared, with added emphasis in her voice. "You'll never be strong and healthy if you don't eat what's good for you."

Pete spent an agonising minute pushing the offending pieces around his plate, dreading what was about to follow. Attempting three small mouthfuls in quick succession, washed down with several large mouthfuls of water, he glanced at her to see how much, on a scale of one to ten, his attempt had appeased her. She gave him the nod that confirmed he could progress onto dessert, although her expression conveyed the impression it was with extreme reluctance.

Lately his mother had begun to cook meals based on exotic sounding recipes, not the type of cuisine that was readily available on the shelves of their local Fine Fair food store. Pete sometimes glanced at the shopping list compiled in readiness for yet another session of experimental cookery, and would be left none the wiser as to what the finished article was going to be, such was his ignorance of many of the ingredients.

With many of the meals taking two or three hours to prepare and cook, Pete wondered why she wasn't content to simply place a ready meal into the microwave for several minutes, wait for it to ping, and instantly serve up a delicious, satisfying meal. For this very reason, Pete loved their new kitchen gadget, as it freed him from being reliant upon anyone else for his meals. Pete also loved the fact that he could leave the kitchen to watch television or play some music while the food was cooking, without fear of burning the house down.

A quick survey conducted of the freezer shelves revealed an unopened packet of McCain pizzas. Pete knew that would be sufficient for his tea in a few hours time. The only tricky aspect to preparing pizza – one that Pete frequently encountered – was knowing how long to allow it to cool before eating. He had made the mistake on numerous occasions of taking a bite and beginning to chew, only to spit it out a few seconds later as the mildly warm tomato covering on top revealed it to be deceptively scalding hot underneath.

Content to make a beef pot noodle for his lunch, Pete filled and switched on the kettle. While he waited for it to boil, he switched on the Betamax video recorder in the front room and rewound the cassette in preparation for watching the Clint Eastwood cop movie he had recorded the previous evening.

Chapter 4

Nobody Told Me

The inaugural school week of the autumn term at Framlington Hall Comprehensive School had passed by at a snail's pace for Pete. By the time Year Four congregated in the main hall on Thursday morning for their weekly assembly, he was already wishing the weekend was upon him. A suffocating air of seriousness had pervaded the atmosphere in classes all week, as a steady procession of teachers reiterated how imperative it was for pupils to knuckle down with their school work in the coming months, and how it would only seem like five minutes before the all important O-level exams were upon them in less than two years time.

Already the barely completed summer break felt to Pete like a distant dream.

A contagious feeling of apprehension spread throughout the gathered throng as Mr Glanville, Head of Year Four, entered the hall with ominous purpose, dressed in twilled, dark brown trousers and his ubiquitous weed green tweed sports jacket, complete with leather patches on the elbows. The noisy chatter was brought to an abrupt halt with three steady whacks of his wooden ruler against the podium he stood behind.

Two hundred pairs of eyes stared intently at Mr Glanville, ensnared by his fearful reputation like rabbits in the beam of car headlights.

"Welcome, Year Four, to the most important stage yet in your education," he solemnly announced, milking his undisputed authority for all it was worth. An orator who believed in seeing the whites of an audience's eyes up close, Mr Glanville immediately stepped away from the platform. Continuing his speech while pacing the floor space in front of the seated pupils, he subjected the first few rows of extremely attentive pupils to the infamous Glanville pong, an unmistakable scent of stale nicotine that was a symptom of his two packets of cigarettes a day habit.

Gripping his trusted ruler, Mr Glanville accentuated with zealous gravitas what he expected from his pupils in the coming year, raising his arm and repeatedly bringing the object down with a purposeful whack in the palm of his hand at the key points he wished to accentuate:

"...hard work..."

Swish. Whack.

"...good behaviour..."

Swish. Whack.

"...abide at all times by the school's code of conduct..."

Swish. Whack.

"Otherwise," he said, pausing to cast a sweeping gaze around the room, successfully conveying the impression that he was individually addressing everyone present, "it will be punishment."

Swish. Whack.

Having managed to effectively inject an element of terror into the majority of those present, including several of the teachers in attendance on the sidelines, Mr Glanville proceeded to run through his agenda in a matter-of-fact, less intimidating manner.

Ensconced in the middle of a row towards the rear of the hall, Pete felt sufficiently camouflaged amongst his peers, and insulated by the distance between himself and the front of the hall, to allow his concentration to drift away from the speech. He returned to thoughts of the forthcoming Saturday. Pete was, much to his annoyance, resigned to spending the morning deployed as ball-boy for his father's football team on some windswept playing field. For the first time ever, there was no Liam to turn to as a get-out clause on the afternoon, leaving Pete to guess his father would be expecting him to spend it sitting in the pub with his teammates. Pete would much rather hop onto a bus back home to Durham when the game ended, leaving him free to hang out by himself at home for a few precious hours.

Pete felt as if he was fast approaching a crossroads in his relationship with his father. He no longer felt like the little child he once was, happy to follow in the shadow cast by him. Pete's time spent in Liam's company had given him a taste for independence, and the desire to pursue his own interests. The way Pete saw it, if his father wasn't prepared to participate in activities they both enjoyed, then he would begin to dig his heels into the ground and refuse to go and stay over at weekends. Pete knew this course of action would severely rock the boat, placing him on a collision course with his father and risking the full raw wrath of his explosive temper.

Although it was looming on the horizon, the potential problem of Saturday was well and truly on the backburner for Pete until he had negotiated a more immediate hurdle: the fast approaching first PE lesson of the year. Scheduled for the following morning, it signalled a return to the trauma of the dreaded showers.

Before Pete could ruminate further on the quandary that lay ahead the following day, he received a sudden rude awakening.

"Davies," shouted Mr Glanville, pointing an accusatory, nicotine-stained finger in his direction. "Are you paying attention, boy?" he roared.

Stirred without warning from his thoughts, it took Pete a moment to realise that everyone in the hall was staring in his direction. His cheeks reddened, and he felt a perplexed sense of injustice at the severity of Mr Glanville's tone of voice. All Pete could guess was that he was being wrongly blamed for an indiscretion committed by someone else around him: the flicking of an ear, a stifled giggle, or a barely concealed yawn.

For a split-second time froze as the shell-shocked youngster and stern teacher exchanged glances, the latter's creased, walnut-like features poised to explode in thunderous rage. Pete shifted uncomfortably in his seat as the uneasy silence continued, every passing second increasing the agony, a psychological Chinese burn.

After what felt like minutes, but was no longer than a dozen fluttering heartbeats, Mr Glanville averted his withering gaze from Pete and picked up where he had left off.

He was off the hook. Every set of eyes in the hall removed themselves from the visibly shaken Pete and turned to face the front. Pete burned with the indignation that only the unfairly wronged can feel, but was inwardly relieved by the realisation that he had escaped lightly. Mr Glanville had a reputation for toying with his victims, slowly grinding them down and publicly humiliating them until they were reduced to feeling small and inconsequential.

Whatever his reasons for singling out Pete, Mr Glanville had succeeded in sending out a stark warning to everyone present: easy days were over, and he was back doing what he did best, resuming his universally acknowledged dual role of chief sadist, and public enemy number one.

Relieved when the bell finally sounded to signal the end of assembly, Pete gathered his belongings and made a quick dash through a heavy morning shower to the Languages block for his introductory French lesson. Mightily relieved to have avoided one of the two allotted PE classes on the timetable, Pete had still managed to approach today's lesson with characteristic misgivings, and by the time he set foot into the classroom did so with a degree of trepidation. He had heard that French was a million times more difficult than German to learn, and what he had seen of the language on late night, subtitled movies merely confirmed that impression.

A cheery Mrs Watson breezed into the classroom to discover her new intake of students sitting sensibly at their desks, quietly taking in their new surroundings.

"Oops," she said, making light of her own clumsiness, as she dropped the pile of books she had been precariously carrying onto her desk. "I'd make a hopeless waitress," she said, more to herself than to anyone else, before facing the class. "My, this makes a pleasant change," she smiled. "No chaos. No shouting. If first impressions are to be believed, then I can see I'm going to get along with you all just fine."

Mrs Watson always felt it paid off to begin on a positive, good-natured level with a new group, believing that it would be reciprocated, and reduced the potential of getting off on a bad footing.

"Hello class," she continued, "or should I say 'bonjour!' Welcome to French with me, Madame Watson. For the next two years, I am going to be your guide for what I very much hope will be an exciting, fun-packed journey."

She selected a pile of the textbooks she had unceremoniously dumped a moment ago and began to distribute them, continuing with her introduction as she did so.

"Now, I know that many of you have chosen to study for a second language, because between French and PE, it is the lesser of the two evils."

She paused to raise a hand to cover her mouth, as if having unwittingly let slip a thought meant to remain unspoken. "Oops. What I should have said is that you have chosen my class as you have a magnificent passion for France, its fine language and amazing culture. This being the case, it is my job to ensure that, come your final year exams, you will be sufficiently conversant with this beautiful language to be able to add it to your list of skills. Now then, before we jump straight into learning one or two basic phrases, let me tell you a little about how we will work as a group. It will be very informal. You can call me by my name, Christine, and I will call you by yours. You are now young adults, not babies, and I will accord you the respect this deserves until anyone acts otherwise, and then it will be back to the old boring routine of calling me Mrs Watson, which is very dull, don't you agree, and will make our teaching sessions together a good deal less enjoyable than they could be."

She paused to take an exaggerated deep breath before continuing.

"As you can see by looking all around you, I have attempted to create a mini-France in our humble room of learning; putting up a few symbols of French life, hopefully adding a little colour to our surroundings. I find plain, boring walls such a depressing sight."

The class surveyed the photographs and posters pinned to the walls in tribute to everything that was quintessentially French: landmarks such as the Eiffel Tower and Arc de Triomphe; examples of art and culture such as the impressionist artist Monet's water lilies painting; historical figures such as Napoleon; and national emblems such as the red, white and blue of the French flag.

Mrs Watson had one final trick up her sleeve, a logistical tactic that over the years she had successfully deployed to produce a stimulating, well-disciplined learning environment.

"One more thing, class. I have compiled a seating plan that I would like you to adhere to for each lesson. As many of the learning modules will involve acting out everyday scenarios from French life, between a brother and sister, I would like each desk to consist of one male student and one female."

She smiled at the resulting chorus of groans. Striking while the iron was hot, Mrs Watson produced her list and began to organise the group accordingly.

"Okay, class. I adopted the highly scientific system earlier this morning of putting your names into a hat and pulling them out at random, so please, if you do not like the person you are next to, do not blame me. Once your names are read out, if that pair can please find a desk as quickly as possible, that will be very helpful."

Mrs Watson perched her spectacles onto the tip of her nose, and began to read out the names of the allocated pairs.

Two names included on the list, unsurprisingly in the light of recent history, were Appleby and Thames. For once, they appeared relaxed and happy within their chosen academic environment, knowing that for an hour a week they would be part of a gentler fraternity.

As Mrs Watson neared the end of her list there were still three pupils sitting without partners: Pete, Samuel Bainbridge, and Helen Davenport.

Known more commonly as Sam, Bainbridge was someone who until now had rarely crossed Pete's path during his time at the comprehensive school. With Year Four students now grouped together in terms of academic, as opposed to mixed, ability, the two boys had found themselves in the same class for most subjects that week. Pete got the distinct impression that Sam did not like him. This puzzled him, because in all of their time at the school, the two boys had not even held a single conversation.

Pete would soon learn that, in this respect, he was far from alone. Sam was adept at remaining aloof from those he did not wish to have as a friend. Gangly and physically weedy, he maintained an attitude of snobbish superiority with those he felt were beneath him, sneeringly looking through narrow, sly eyes down his hawk-like nose at those he despised.

"Helen Davenport. Your partner will be Sam Bainbridge."

Sam grinned with relief at this news. He would have been upset to be the odd one out, particularly at the expense of Pete, whom he treated to a stare of victorious contempt.

"And finally, you must be Pete Davies, then," said Mrs Watson, ignoring the element of uncharitable behaviour that had already crept into one of her class members.

Pete nodded.

"Please stay seated where you are, Pete, your partner must be running a little late. It will be Frances Bailey-Jones. So, moving on…"

Pete was flabbergasted by this unexpected development, as were several other boys in the room, judging by their disappointed expressions. While doing his best to publicly disguise how overjoyed he was by this news, internally Pete's heart was leaping for joy. It was universally acknowledged among his male peers that Frances was one of the most desirable, enigmatic girls in their year group, and possibly the entire school. With her long, straight blonde hair, ice blue clear eyes and pale skin, she resembled a Scandinavian goddess to her legion of private admirers.

During the past year, only a couple of people had summoned up the courage to ask her out on a date, most memorably Giles Morgan. Loud, self-confident, and not used to taking no for an answer, Morgan had approached her at the school disco the previous summer term. So confident was he of success that he made his move on the dance floor, the most public of romantic domains, in full view of everyone. To the strains of Lionel Richie's "Hello," it was an emphatic goodbye for Morgan as his overtures were firmly rejected. Morgan's reaction to being rebuffed was predictably explosive. Storming out of the main hall in a blind fury, he momentarily paused to punch an innocent bystander in the corridor, bloodying his nose. Earning Morgan a suspension from school for two weeks, the incident triggered major debate and gossip in the corridors and classrooms for the remainder of the term.

In hindsight, it was not too difficult to work out why Frances had given Morgan a categorical thumbs down. Although he was arguably the greatest sportsman and toughest boy of his age group at the school, in terms of academic ability and personal interests they were poles apart. Morgan was less than average in the classroom, with his hobbies not moving beyond the boundaries of sport. In contrast, Frances was academically strong, always achieving top grades. In terms of personal interests, she was more concerned with issues such as the welfare of animals, human rights, and the threat of a nuclear war. She couldn't see how the world could get worked up about trivial matters, such as football and fighting, when there were bigger matters going on in the real world. To these ends, Frances was a vocal voice on the school council, more interested in grabbing hold of the reins of power and steering them towards topics close to her own heart.

Two minutes later, the door opened and Frances made her entrance.

"I'm sorry for being late, Mrs Watson."

"Ah, Frances, there you are. I will let you off just this once, but please do not make a habit of it. And that applies to you all, class. Our time here is short and precious. We really do need to make the most of every available minute. Please," said Mrs Watson, gesturing to the vacant seat next to Pete. "I will fill you in on what you have missed at the end."

As Frances sat down, Pete apprehensively chewed his lip, pretending to be more interested in the content of his textbook than the arrival of his new partner. He did not glance across at her for fear his inner excitement would betray the calm and composed demeanour he was attempting to portray. Pete also wanted to avoid her gaze in case he detected in her expression abject disappointment at being forced to suffer his company for a whole year. The blow to his confidence would be so crushing that Pete feared he would never recover from such weighty damnation. As much as he wished to make a good first impression, Pete's instinct told him time was on his side. For today, he was merely content just to muddle through without coming across as a bumbling idiot.

At the mid-morning break, Pete had a great deal to reflect upon. Following the personal embarrassment inflicted upon him by the Glanville incident, Pete marvelled at how quickly life could turn around. It really looked like the gamble of an additional academic subject was going to pay off, in more ways than one. The hourly lesson would undoubtedly be the highlight of his week, bringing a ray of sunshine into his otherwise monotonous existence. Pete felt a little smug at the knowledge that he would be the envy of so many, most of whom would give their right arm to be in his position.

Four days into his new job as Head of English at Framlington Hall, Derek Brookes finally felt as if he was beginning to acclimatise to his new surroundings. With it being a more prestigious post than his previous teaching position, the opportunity to take a major step up the ladder of his career had been too much of a temptation to refuse. A born worrier, he had then spent the best part of the summer break pondering whether his decision had been such a wise one, particularly as he had been professionally settled and happy. Thankfully, his feelings of insecurity and sleepless nights in the run up to his first week had been a false alarm. With a few days teaching under his belt, and the initial nervousness that comes with any new job beginning to settle, Brookes felt a great sense of well-being with himself and life in general. He had met all of his departmental colleagues, who consisted of a couple of stalwart veterans, a novice fresh out of teacher training, and a maverick eccentric counting down the final remaining years to retirement. The layout of the school and the names of its buildings were now gradually beginning to stick in his head, with experience telling him that a couple more weeks down the line would find him wondering what all the fuss had been about. In the meantime, Mr Brookes was navigating himself around the school on a need to know basis.

Arriving for the last class of the morning, Mr Brookes was met by a mass of pupils congregated around the classroom doorway. With this being his inaugural session with this set of pupils, he felt thirty sets of eyes simultaneously weigh him up and cast instant judgement.

"Good morning," he said, forcing his way through them. "If you can just let me get to the door and unlock it, you will actually be able to sit down a lot quicker."

On his first ever day of teaching ten years ago, a colleague had imparted one piece of advice that had been worth its weight in gold to Mr Brookes ever since: do not show a new group of students that you are human whatsoever, or at least not until the following Easter. This meant never smiling or laughing in the presence of pupils, never showing any degree of favouritism, or allowing individuals who attempted to take liberties and undermine his authority to go unpunished. The colleague of Mr Brookes maintained that pupils would latch onto any signs of weakness, and make your life hell.

At first, he had found such a stance difficult to adopt, flying as it did in the face of his own easygoing nature. Nevertheless, Mr Brookes persevered, and miraculously it worked. He cultivated a reputation, and that, he discovered, was the key to everything. Children reacted to the perceived image of you, and not to the real person underneath. If they entered a classroom believing you were tough and uncompromising, they would react accordingly. Likewise, if you were perceived as an easy touch, then your life was not worth living.

Mr Brookes stood at the front of the classroom while his students found a desk and removed their coats.

"Okay, everybody. Please settle down as quickly as possible," he began, keen to impose his own personality and rules upon them from the off. "Put your bags and other possessions on the floor. All I want to see on your desks for now are your pens and rulers."

As if by magic, everyone complied with his instructions. Mr Brookes wanted to smile, but contented himself with the warm inner glow he experienced at the automatic acceptance of his authority.

"Now, I'm sure you are up to here with speeches about how you are expected to get real and serious this year. I'm sure I will bore you all with similar themes in the coming weeks, but for today, I want to give you a break from all of that. Today, we are going to allow a little freedom of expression to reign. For the first half of the lesson, I would like you to get creative and write about something that is a big passion in your life."

Mr Brookes noticed one boy at the back of the classroom mouth the word "sex" to his companion.

"Keep it clean, please," he said.

Helen Davenport stuck up a hand.

"Can it be a story, Sir?"

"Yes. It can be a story, maybe a poem, or a news story, even. Anything you like. For one day only, it is entirely up to you. In the second half of the lesson, I will randomly choose several of you to discuss what it is you have written about, and from there conduct a class discussion on the main points arising. And just to ensure that you all participate, you can take it away as your first set of homework of the year."

A predictable round of groans echoed around the room. It was water off a duck's back to him, as expected as cries of "he's behind you" at a pantomime.

"And for your second set of homework for the week, let's have your new exercise books backed, please. I'm sure you all know the drill by now as to what is suitable, and what is not."

Having safely secured a prized window seat at the back of the classroom, overlooking the yard and sports track, Pete had already opened the blank exercise book that had been waiting for them on the desks, and was thinking about what to commit to the page. English was by far his favourite subject, and he was eager to hit the floor running, excited at the prospect of finally getting to grips with some serious literature and poetry.

Looking up to face the front as he sought inspiration for his opening line, Pete chewed thoughtfully on the top of his biro. Mr Brookes was stood with his back to the class, writing a few pointers and ideas on the blackboard to assist the less inspired class members.

Looking at him more closely for the first time, even from behind there was something unsettlingly familiar to

Pete about Mr Brookes, but he couldn't quite place where he had seen him before. He was sure that if they had previously been introduced, Pete would have been able to recall where. Maybe, thought Pete, he was confusing him with a football player. In his early thirties, tall and solidly built, with a short crop of tightly curled black hair and neatly trimmed moustache, Pete reckoned Mr Brookes would not have looked out of place lining up for Everton, Liverpool, or any other Division One football team. However, it was not so much his appearance, more the smell of his aftershave that had first struck Pete – a heavy, woody fragrance. Pete was quickly flicking through the millions of thoughts stored within the recesses of his brain, gradually homing in on where he had recently encountered it, until...

"Oh, shit," exclaimed Pete, loud enough for the people sitting at the desk in front to turn around.

In an instant, Pete's world sank to the depths of despair. He felt physically sick, and his head began to spin. It was the reaction of one who knew his luck had well and truly ran out.

Mr Brookes finished writing on the blackboard, and began to make his way up and down the aisles, distributing stickers for the class to write their names onto and attach to their clothing. When the teacher eventually arrived at Pete's desk, and began to explain to Pete what he was to do with the sticker, he paused in mid-sentence, rendered speechless at his unexpected reunion.

Pete had been rooted to the bare wooden seat outside the Head of Year's office for nearly an hour. Apart from the first few minutes, when Mr Brookes spoke briefly to Mr Glanville in private in his office, and the school secretary arrived carrying a personal file, Pete had been left alone to ponder his fate. All he had been told was that Mr Glanville must make some phone calls.

The only sound for what seemed an age was that of Pete's own chattering teeth, as he shook fearfully with all the force of emerging hypothermia, dreading what fate had in store for him.

The corridor's hushed air of upper authority was eventually shattered by the noise of a thousand teenagers, temporarily reprieved from their studies, going about their lunchtime business outside. Pete sensed that many of the voices would be centred on him, with rumours and gossip regarding his mysterious eviction from the English lesson spreading like wildfire around the school.

When classes recommenced for the afternoon, and a forced calm descended once more upon the school, Pete was beginning to wonder if he had been forgotten about. His stomach was rumbling with hunger, and he desperately needed to go to the toilet.

Five minutes later the uneasy calm was broken when Pete's father unexpectedly burst through the double door entrance at the end of the corridor. Pete had assumed his mother would be the parent to be contacted by the school. As he walked towards his son, with the school secretary struggling to keep up, Pete could see the expression of anger on his face.

"What's this all about, Pete?" he demanded. "Your teacher says you've been involved with nicking stuff. Is that right?"

Pete's power of speech was paralysed. He looked down at his feet, his bowed head telling his father all he needed to know.

"Jesus Christ, Pete. I never expected this of you. What have I told you about not getting into trouble?"

Hearing the fresh commotion in the corridor, Mr Glanville's door creaked open, sounding to Pete like Dracula emerging from his coffin.

"Mr Davies, I presume? Ronald Glanville. I am sorry you have had to travel all this way, but we were unable to contact Pete's mother."

Both men briefly shook hands.

"Please," he said, gesturing to Mr Davies to enter his office. "And you too, young Mr Davies," he said wearily to Pete. "It wouldn't be a party without the guest of honour," he added drily.

Stiff all over from being sat in the same position for more than two hours, Pete followed his father into Mr Glanville's office, wondering if he would ever emerge into the outside world again.

"Now then, Mr Davies. Mr Brookes, who is Pete's English teacher, has told me about a rather disturbing incident that occurred in Newcastle city centre last Saturday afternoon. He states categorically that he witnessed your son being pursued by a store detective from a music store, because he was suspected of stealing a number of records."

Pete's father sat pokerfaced, listening intently to what Mr Glanville had to say.

"Mr Brookes intervened and apprehended your son, only to be manhandled by a bunch of drunken thugs who intimidated Mr Brookes into allowing your son to make good his escape. Or so he must have thought at the time," he added, raising an eyebrow at Pete.

"Mr Glanville, before we go any further, can I please have a couple of minutes alone with Pete? This has come as a big shock. I really think I need to have a chat with him first, in private, to get the facts clear in my own head before we can go forward with this."

Mr Glanville stood up. "Yes, Mr Davies. That sounds reasonable, under the circumstances. You're as much in the dark about this as the rest of us, I expect. I'll go and have a cigarette for five minutes. It's been such a long morning."

With Mr Glanville temporarily out of the room, Ian Davies turned to his son.

"Okay, son. I promise not to shout at you, or get angry with you, but if I am going to be able to help get you out of this mess, because that's what it is, then I need to know the truth, and nothing but. Otherwise, this teacher is going to throw you to the lions, and I have to say I wouldn't blame him, based on the facts as he sees them. So, Pete, let's have it before he returns. Everything."

Unsure exactly how his father could possibly save the day, Pete took a deep breath and relayed everything that had happened: how Liam coerced him into acting as cover; how Pete had never personally handled any of the goods or benefited from the theft; and how this was a common occurrence for Liam, with a never-ending list of ready customers waiting with cash.

When he had finished, Pete was surprised to see his father looking at him with something akin to admiration. "You mean to say you haven't mentioned this to anyone else?"

"No, Dad."

His father playfully rubbed Pete's head with his hand.

"Good boy. Good boy, Pete. I'm so proud of you for not grassing up your cousin. If the police get involved, and Liam is dragged into this mess, then he can kiss his army career goodbye. I've no doubt about that."

From the corridor came the sound of footsteps approaching, accompanied by a loud, chesty cough.

"Right," whispered his father, "say nothing, son. Leave all the talking to me. I might just have found an answer to this." He gave Pete a knowing wink, slipping back into serious mode as Mr Glanville entered, reeking of cigarettes.

"Now then, where were we?" asked Mr Glanville, sitting back down and looking expectantly at Davies senior.

"Mr Glanville," he began. "Pete has told me the whole truth about what happened, and based on these facts, I have a proposition to put to your good self."

Mr Glanville leaned back, intrigued to hear what was about to be submitted to him. Pete's father took Mr Glanville's continued silence as his cue to continue.

"It was our Pete who was involved, he admits that, and for that reason alone, under normal circumstances, there could be no defending him. However, part of the blame lies solely with myself. I was with him on Saturday, and had arranged to meet him outside this store, but was running late. It was my wife, Pete's stepmother, getting carried away in the sales that made me forget the time. Anyway, while he was waiting he was gently persuaded, shall we say, to help some lads out who had been hanging around in the street. Being afraid and a bit timid, he reluctantly went along with it, hoping I would turn up in time. When he was pursued by the shop's staff, he panicked and ran, which is when he bumped into Mr Brookes, who I'm sure will confirm Pete was not carrying anything on him. Afterwards, he went straight home on the bus as he was worried what would happen, and that no one would believe him. I'm disappointed that he didn't come and tell me the truth straight away, and then this other boy could have been found at the time. That doesn't let our Pete off the hook, though. He's been foolish, and I intend to punish him severely. I'll be having words with his mother too, to see that his pocket money is stopped, and he is grounded. Also, he would like to offer Mr Brookes a full apology at an appropriate time."

Mr Glanville looked thoughtful as he digested everything he had just heard.

"Hmmm, I must admit, having glanced through Pete's file that it does sound like a case of Dr Jekyll and Mr Hyde. Never in trouble of any note, and no detentions in all of his time here. Pete's school reports are promising, and he's well behaved, quiet in class, and no evidence of homework not being handed in on time. In other words, a model pupil. This trouble may explain why he was looking so distracted in assembly this morning."

"If you will excuse him for the rest of the week, Mr Glanville, I intend to nip this in the bud and go to see the shop manager first thing in the morning, in order to put right the wrongs of this sorry state of affairs. I will explain what happened, offer my sincerest apologies, and reimburse the store for their losses."

Mr Glanville nodded, relieved that a satisfactory resolution for all parties was slowly emerging, assuming the store manager could be placated. He could see that the boy's father, although rough around the edges, talked a lot of common sense. "And you will telephone me personally to let me know the outcome of your visit to the store?" asked Mr Glanville.

Pete's father nodded. "From the first telephone box I come to."

Mr Glanville glanced at Pete. "And if no charges are brought, then I can see no reason for Pete not to report back for lessons first thing on Monday morning. For today, however, let us leave things as they stand. Tomorrow, as they say, is indeed another day."

Mr Glanville stood up and shook Mr Davies's hand. "Until we speak tomorrow," concluded the teacher.

"Thank you, Mr Glanville," said Pete's father. "Until tomorrow. Come on, son," he ordered Pete, heading for the door.

A goth band were playing their latest single live on Friday's early evening music show *The Tube*. It was rare for Pete to be watching the programme from the beginning at his father's house. Usually at this time on a Friday, when the weekend was in a blissful state of infancy, Pete would be on the last leg of his drawn-out journey from school to Sunderland, on his way to another weekly sleepover. Consisting of one short bus journey from school to Durham City's bus station, followed by a more arduous hour-long second journey through thirteen miles of rush hour traffic to Sunderland town centre, it was completed with a fifteen-minute walk to his father's home in the inner city area of Hendon.

Pete was mentally and physically worn out, the stressful activities of the past day and a half well and truly catching up with him. Following the meeting with Mr Glanville the previous Thursday afternoon, Pete's father had insisted his son spend the night at his house. Once there, Pete was sent out to buy the evening local paper from the newsagent while his father called his ex-wife and broke the news to her of the day's events.

With his father determined to smooth everything out as soon as possible, the pair had risen early that morning and caught the train to Newcastle city centre, and were standing outside the record store with ten minutes to spare before the doors opened for business.

Davies senior, dressed in suit, shirt, and tie, restlessly paced up and down the street, glancing at his watch every few seconds. Pete had never seen his father so smartly dressed. As soon as the shop opened, Pete waited nervously outside while his father darted inside, emerging a couple of minutes later to beckon him inside.

They were led by a dishevelled looking sales assistant, unshaven and dressed in a creased blue chambray shirt, through a door marked 'Staff Only' on the second floor. They climbed up a further flight of stairs, walked down a long corridor full of half-opened brown boxes containing recently delivered stock, until stopping outside a door marked 'Manager.'

The assistant returned to the shop floor. Pete's father straightened his tie, took a deep breath, and knocked.

"Enter."

Pete's father had been expecting somebody of his own generation, dressed in similar attire. He was surprised to be greeted by a much younger male, dressed informally in black jeans and Prefab Sprout T-shirt, with a thick mane of tinted hair cut sharply across his ears and flowing down to his shoulders. He thought the store manager resembled a Butlin's entertainer or a radio disc jockey far more than a figure of authority on the high street.

"Robin Waters," said the manager, formally rising to shake his hand.

"Ian Davies."

The manager beckoned to them to take a seat.

"Now then, Mr Davies," he enquired, after everyone had made themselves comfortable. "What is it exactly I can do for you?"

Pete's father quickly ran through a story similar to the version he had offered to Mr Glanville the day before, reiterating how out of character it was of Pete, and how he blamed himself for not meeting his son on time and allowing him to be preyed upon by the town's more unscrupulous characters.

All the time Mr Waters sat stony-faced, nodding attentively, until Pete's father came to the key part of his speech.

"So that's basically what happened, Mr Waters. I would like to make an offer to you to bring the matter to a satisfactory conclusion."

Mr Waters's eyes widened. "What exactly do you have in mind?"

Pete's father put his hand into the inner breast pocket of his jacket and produced a thick wad of notes, counting out a sum of money before slapping it down on the desk.

"One hundred pounds, Mr Waters. Does that cover the cost?"

Mr Waters picked it up and checked the sum himself. "Oh yes, I'm sure that's more than enough."

"Let's just call the extra payment for overheads, and the inconvenience we've caused you."

Pete was innocently oblivious to the knowing look that passed between the two men. He wanted to tell his father that Liam had only stolen fifty pounds worth of records at most, but held his tongue.

"Well, then, in light of what you have just told me," began Mr Waters, "and your willingness to bring the matter to a swift conclusion, I cannot see any reason why we should involve the police and the courts. I do hope, however, that your son has learnt his lesson from all of this. Stealing is a rocky road to stray down, particularly for one so young."

His father turned to Pete, his signal to personally apologise to the manager.

"I'm very sorry, Sir. I won't let it happen again."

Mr Waters smiled and clapped his hands together to signal the brief meeting was over. "Well, that appears to conclude matters, Mr Davies," he said, opening the door for his guests. "Let me show you the way out."

Pete wept tears of relief back out on the street. It felt as if the weight of the world had just been lifted from his shoulders. To Pete's immense surprise, his father did not deliver the expected "let that be a lesson" speech.

"It's all over now, son," he began, placing a consolatory arm around his shoulders. "I know what Liam did was wrong, and he shouldn't have involved you. But like I said yesterday, I'm proud of you for not grassing him up. Blood's thicker than water, and you've shown guts in front of your teachers and that bloke back there in the shop. Liam's done the best thing, getting away from this place, and to bollocks that all up over a few daft records isn't worth it. You know, son, that could be something for you to start thinking about too, in a year or so. You're bright enough. A spell in the navy or the army, see the world for free, and get paid for it. You've got youth on your side and the world is your oyster. There's bugger all around here for you. The bloody Tories have seen to that."

The coward in Pete shuddered at the very thought of joining the armed forces. However, he nodded his head, implying he would give his father's suggestion some thought. To give voice to his true feelings would only bring an unwanted argument, and Pete preferred not to bear the brunt of his temper. If that meant agreeing with everything his father said, whatever his own private opinion, then so be it.

Pete recalled the wad of money the shop manager had just received, and felt guilty. He knew for his father that was a small fortune, particularly as he was not in regular employment.

"I promise to pay you back, Dad. Every last penny."

His father laughed. "Don't be daft, son. That's what dads are for, to help their kids out of tight spots."

Pete decided not to protest further, parking the issue in his head for consideration at another time.

"Right then," said his father. "Let's give your Mr Glanville the good news, and hopefully by next week all of this will be forgotten."

Dead on 6 p.m., barely a third of the way through *The Tube*, Pete's father came dashing into the front room, made himself comfortable in his favourite chair, and switched over to BBC One for the evening news.

Pete sighed, preparing himself for a long boring hour until the light entertainment programmes began. As usual, the miners' strike dominated the news headlines. The main story focused on the hardships affected families were being forced to endure six months into the dispute, and with no end in sight. A camera crew had followed a typical family for the day. The father was interviewed as he pushed his young daughter on a set of swings at a playground. A look in their kitchen cupboards revealed little in the way of appetising food, as his wife spoke of the constant struggle they faced to pay the never-ending bills that dropped through their letterbox. The report concluded with the family speculating about the kind of Christmas they would have if the dispute continued, but with the father defiantly stating that, having come so far and sacrificed so much for the cause, he and thousands like him would not be tempted into crossing a picket line.

"See that," said Pete's father, pointing at the screen. "That's what it's all about, son. People prepared to stand up and be counted. Solidarity. That's what those Tory buggers don't understand. The way the working man will stand side by side with his workmates, and not be bought off by the offer of a few extra quid to return to work. That," he said, through clenched teeth, "is why the miners have to try and win. But that bitch, Thatcher, the woman's pure evil. She'll do her damn best to crush them."

Pete's father never minced his words when it came to voicing an opinion. His coarse, industrial language was that of the shipyards he had once worked in.

Pete perked up when the news finally ended, replaced with the opening credits and familiar theme tune of *Blankety Blank*.

"You can turn this bloody rubbish off, son. I cannot stand that Irish fella. If I had the chance, I'd shove that bloody microphone of his where the sun doesn't shine. What a waste of licence-payers' money."

"But we don't have a licence, Ian," interjected Val mischievously, always ready to rub her husband up the wrong way.

"Just as bloody well, isn't it?" he unashamedly replied. "I've better things to do with my dosh than line the pockets of the likes of him."

"Give it a rest, will you? The bairn just wants to have fun by watching a bit of telly, especially after the couple of days he's had."

The anger vanished from his father's face, replaced by a large grin when the new host of the show walked on. "I bloody love Les Dawson. Now he is someone who deserves to be on this. He's got more jokes in his little finger than that other bloke has in his whole body."

It made Pete happy when his father slipped back into one of his good moods, rare though they were, just like in the old days. Pete had vague, warm memories of being five years old, when he would sit next to his father on the sofa at weekends and watch television until he fell asleep.

"Come on, you daft sod," said Val to her husband, with one eye on the clock. "Go and get ready. It won't be worth going out at this rate."

Friday night was pub night.

"All right, woman," he said, rising up from his chair. "Don't nag."

"And get a shave," she shouted, as his feet clumped upstairs.

It had been a momentous day for Hendon United football club. Four nil winners over their closest rivals, Thorney Close Workingmen's Club, they had preserved their unbeaten start to the season, moving five points clear at the top of the Sunderland over-forties football league.

Pete usually dreaded the post-game celebrations back at the local pub, but even they, for once, had not been too much of a drag. His father was in high spirits, revelling in his unofficial role as chief joke teller and raconteur. The only uncomfortable moment arose when his father recounted the full story of Pete's run-in with the record store and his teacher, and subsequent events. His father, voice slurred from several hours of heavy drinking, wrapped a strong arm around Pete.

"I'm proud of you, son. Fucking proud for not grassing up Liam."

The remaining teammates sat around the table all acknowledged their approval of Pete, giving him a round of winks, thumbs ups and raised glasses.

"Aye, you've got a good one there, Ian," remarked Ernie, the bespectacled goalkeeper.

Flushed with pride by the unanimous chorus of approval for his offspring, his father dug his hand into his pocket and pulled out a note. "There you go, son. Sorry I've not been too regular of late, but you know how things are. That should tide you over for a bit."

Pete glanced at the gift. A twenty-pound note. Unlike the previous Saturday, Pete did not intend to return this sum, swiftly pushing it into his trouser pocket before his father changed his mind.

For the remainder of the afternoon, Pete cheered up considerably, as he pondered over which records he could treat himself to upon his next visit to the second-hand record shops.

Father and son returned home just after 3 p.m. With his father slumping straight into his chair in the front room and reaching for the remote control, Pete went through to the kitchen and fetched for him the plate of salad from the fridge that Val had prepared for her husband.

As the pair began to watch the pre-recorded *Football Focus* programme from earlier on that afternoon, his father slowly picked at the salad balanced on his lap.

"What a goal, Pete. Did you see that?" asked his father, smiling in admiration at the television. "I used to bang them in like that for fun at his age," he continued.

Pete raised his eyebrows as his father once again relayed the tale of how his knee injury as a teenager tragically robbed him of a stab at a career in professional football. He had heard the story so many times before.

"On Sunderland's books, I was, at fifteen. Training with the reserves, cleaning the first team's boots. What a life I could have had. We could have been living a life of luxury now, son, if things had turned out different."

Pete smiled weakly in muted acknowledgement, while munching on his corned beef and beetroot sandwich.

The phone ringing in the corridor cut short his father's familiar story.

"Go and answer that, son," ordered his father, vigorously shaking the near empty bottle of salad cream to extract the final few drops of sauce from the bottom. His pet hate was being disturbed when he was watching anything to do with sport on the television. "Tell whoever it is I'm not in, if it's for me," he added, as Pete retreated from the front room. "It'll be Val's bloody mother more than likely. She can talk under water, that one."

Pete lifted the receiver.

"Hello. Ian?" said a familiar voice.

"Hi, it's me, Mum," replied Pete.

"Oh…Peter. Can you put your father on the line, please?"

Pete immediately tensed up, detecting the hard tone in his mother's voice. Cold, businesslike, and devoid of maternal warmth. She sounded poised to engage in battle.

Pete sensed storm clouds brewing on the horizon. The warning signs were on full display, the clincher being her addressing Pete by his full Christian name. In the final throes of his parents' marriage, when a seemingly innocuous discussion could swiftly escalate into a barrage of verbal insults and abuse, he would be banished from the room with a terse, "Peter, up to your room. Now."

"Dad, it's Mum for you," said Pete meekly, dreading what was about to ensue.

"What the hell does she want now?" cursed his father, placing his tray on the carpet and rising from his chair.

Handing the phone receiver over, Pete returned into the front room, nervously running his hand through his hair as he waited for the sparks to begin to fly.

"Yes," spat Ian, his eyes hardening.

"Ian? I thought you were going to call me yesterday?" began Sheila Braithwaite, immediately on the offensive. She had been adamant with her ex-husband during their last conversation that he should telephone her straightaway with the outcome of Friday's meeting. For all of his vague assurances then that it was "all but sorted," she now wanted to know the full details of the incident, and why it was her son who had been labelled the instigator and chief suspect. If she knew one thing in life, it was that her son was not a thief.

Annoyed that he had been left with no option but to drive all the way through to Durham the previous Thursday to sort out his son's mess, when his ex-wife was unable to be contacted by the school, Ian Davies felt that it was not his job to be chasing her with news of the solution that he had negotiated.

This had led to a tense stand-off as each party waited for the other to pick up the telephone and call, finally broken by Sheila that morning. She had been attempting to make contact for hours.

"Oh, that," said Ian. "Yeah, it slipped my mind," he lied.

"Slipped your mind," squealed Pete's mother. "How can the future of our son simply slip your mind?"

"Don't worry, Sheila. We went through to the shop yesterday, and I managed to smooth everything out."

"By telling them the truth, I take it?"

"Well, yes and no. Pete admitted being involved, but I said that some other kid forced him to do it."

"You lied to the shop, and the police?"

"Just the shop. The police weren't involved."

"Oh, well that's okay, then," she said sarcastically. "So, it's our son who has shouldered the blame?"

"Sheila, it has to be this way," stated Ian, setting out his stall. "If Liam gets dragged into this, then that's his army career over and done with before it's started."

"Well, he should have thought about that before he dragged our Peter into one of his little schemes. You know how easily led he is around Liam."

"Listen, Sheila, let's just draw a line under the whole affair, shall we? Pete's got off with a warning from the shop, they're not going to press charges, and they were reimbursed for their losses."

"Oh, and have you thought about the stigma attached to our son?"

"Oh, I get it. What you're really worried about is how your little posh friends and neighbours will react when they think there's a thief in the family."

"This has nothing to do with what I think," she said, increasingly exasperated by his attitude. "This is about how Pete's school treats him in the future, and what his teachers and friends think of him. Ian, you've acted irresponsibly, and not for the first time in your life, it has to be said."

"Irresponsibly! I'm the one who has just saved our Pete's arse. If it was left up to you, the whole thing would have blown up in all of our faces by now. I did what had to be done to sort it out. It worked, and that's what rankles with you. End of story, Sheila. Okay?"

Sheila stood with the phone receiver to her ear, silently fuming, cursing Ian for always managing to have the final say. It infuriated her that she was trying to teach her son right from wrong in life, only for his father to undermine her by showing Pete how lies and deceit could prevail. She slammed the phone back down, terminating their heated discussion. Her ex-husband had backed her into a corner with nowhere to go, knowing that for her to go to the school and contradict his, and by proxy Pete's, version of events would simply make the whole family appear even more scheming and unlawful. Reluctantly, Sheila decided to let things lie for now.

Pete glanced at his father from the corner of his eye as he sat back down. It was apparent that the run-in with his mother had completely shattered his good mood.

"Bitch," he spat, his face contorted in barely suppressed anger, taking heavy swigs from a freshly opened can of lager.

They continued to try and watch the remainder of the recording, but it was obvious to Pete that his father's mind was elsewhere, judging by the agitated expression on his face. Feeling guilty for having ignited the latest flare up, Pete was choked with emotion at what he had just been witness to. It had rolled back the years to when he was eight years old, opening up the raw pain he had endured in the final months of their being a complete family, when the arguments were increasingly frequent, elongated, and loaded with unadulterated animosity.

For ten minutes they sat in silence, both pretending to be watching the venerable Bob Wilson predict the outcome of the day's football fixtures. Pete felt as if he was going to explode into tears at any second, and was using all of his resolve to hold himself together. He wished he could be tougher and more thick-skinned, and not feel as fragile as an eggshell. He was embarrassed by his own emotions, believing tears were immature and for babies, not teenage boys such as himself.

When the programme was over, his father left the room to go upstairs to the bathroom. Presented with an opportunity to escape the suffocating, highly charged atmosphere, Pete stood up from the sofa, grabbed his coat from the peg in the porch, and slipped out of the front door. He sprinted as fast as his legs would take him across the cul-de-sac, and darted through the narrow, creosote scented pathway at the non-access end of the street. Weaving around the stray dogs busily sniffing each other and defecating on the patch of waste ground, Pete continued onto the long, straight road that led to the town centre. He only slowed to a walking pace when he felt his lungs were fit to burst, and when he was confident enough distance had been placed between himself and his father to prevent him being caught up.

The act of silently absconding, of rebelling against the mental shackles imposed upon him by his warring parents, felt for those few moments as he made his way to the bus station amazing and liberating, instilling him with a personal sense of empowerment.

CHAPTER 5

The Heat Is On

Pete removed the cover from his snooker table, and ran his hand systematically across the six-foot long, green baized surface to remove any lingering specks of dirt and dust. He proceeded to place the coloured balls onto their individual spots, before gathering the reds into the black triangle and placing them in between the pink and black balls in readiness for his first frame of the evening.

Located within the cramped confines of the house's adjoining garage, Pete always found much needed solace within the solitude of the dimly lit room. With the rest of the family ensconced in the main part of the house, and more than happy to leave Pete alone to his own devices, he was free to enjoy hour after hour potting balls to his heart's content, immersed within his own world.

Fully opening the garage door to its full horizontal position to allow ample cueing room at the baulk end of the table, Pete took his opening shot of the evening. He was participating in an imaginary knockout snooker tournament, pitching himself against his most favourite and despised players in the quest to be the Embassy Snooker Champion of the World. There were so many players to choose from in the competitions Pete frequently played, but his regulars always included the likes of Steve Davis, Alex Higgins, Tony Knowles, Dennis Taylor, Cliff Thorburn, and Jimmy White. The latter had become Pete's favourite player in May of that year, during the pinnacle event of snooker, the world championship. Pete was enthralled as he watched the twenty-two year old from London fight with all of his raw talent against the robotic, seemingly invincible Steve Davis in the final.

Pete was obsessed, watching every frame of the first to eighteen match over two long days. In despair at the end of day one when Davis led twelve-four, Pete watched with amazement as White clawed back to trail thirteen-eleven the following day. The final session was real edge of the seat stuff, especially when the match was finely poised at seventeen-sixteen in Davis's favour. Pete was gutted when Davis clinched the next frame to retain his title. He felt the hurt of what he perceived as a grave injustice, and lived to see the day when sweet revenge over Davis would be gained.

When Pete was on top form, compiling impressive breaks and feeling that he couldn't miss a shot if he tried, the garage appeared to transform itself into the Crucible Theatre at Sheffield. The red bricked walls and shelves containing pots of paint, DIY accessories, and other miscellaneous household items, were replaced by a hushed, captive audience, entranced by his skill with a snooker cue, all doing their best to spur him on to victory. The sound of the occasional car passing by outside, or roar of a high-speed train at the rear of the back garden, was drowned out by the commentary provided by the television presenting team of 'Whispering' Ted Lowe and Clive Everton, waxing lyrical about the talent on display.

"What an audacious shot, Clive. The youngster has really gone for the jugular in this opening frame," Ted would comment, as a sunken pink secured the first frame for Pete.

"He certainly has, Ted. It will be interesting to see how the champion responds to such a drubbing."

Pete often pondered how incredible the life of a professional player must be, participating in tournaments week after week, travelling constantly around the country, and being stopped in the street for autographs, photographs, and a quick chat by an adoring public.

Bending over to play a safety shot up to the baulk end of the table, from the corner of his eye Pete was startled by the sight of a hooded figure standing motionless at the top of the driveway, peering into the garage, accompanied by a dog on its lead. Pretending not to have noticed the figure in the hope he would walk on by, Pete did his best to act as normal as possible, casually chalking his cue and taking his time over his shot selections.

Three shots later, Pete was fully stretched over the table in readiness for a game winning shot.

"Hello, Pete. I thought that was you," came a voice from behind.

Taken completely by surprise, Pete miscued his shot and nearly fell off the table. Composing himself, he turned around.

"You," gasped a relieved Pete, finding himself face to face with Jake Rigby, his identity revealed with the removal of his coat hood.

Jake Rigby had only joined Framlington Hall Comprehensive School that September. Nothing much was known about him, only that he had left his previous school, a fee-paying public school located in Yorkshire, to attend the state-run educational establishment. There was some argument among pupils as to whether his mother was local author Kate Randall, who had published two well-received novels to date. This idea was not given much currency initially, due to the difference in surnames, until one day Joe Hindmarch confidently announced the rumour to be true, explaining that Jake's mother preferred to publish her novels under her maiden name. Joe's mother was a Home Economics teacher at the school, and had overheard a conversation in the staffroom discussing this very point.

Labelled as posh by his classmates, due to the fact he was well spoken and perceived to come from a privileged background, Jake was still to make any firm friends at his new school. This situation did not appear to unduly worry Jake, as he completed the first half-term with a minimum of fuss, appearing almost content to amuse himself with his own company during breaks in lessons.

Pete had been sitting next to Jake in biology classes since the beginning of term, but the pair had scant opportunity to chat about anything other than the current experiment they were required to undertake in that day's lesson, under Mr Brown's overbearing style of tuition. He was an eccentric, no-nonsense individual, and even the boys who took liberties with other teachers behaved themselves in his presence.

Over the weeks, the initial frosty atmosphere between the two boys had thawed slightly, as they slowly got used to being in each other's company. In the short, sharp snippets of time before Mr Brown arrived for a class, and towards the end of their lesson, when they were packing up, Pete had tried to elicit more convivial conversation from Jake, always ready with a "Hi, how's it going?" or "See you next week, Jake."

At various times, Pete would see Jake standing alone on the schoolyard in between lessons, or walking home ahead of him at the end of the day, but his shyness prevented him from approaching Jake and engaging in banter.

"Sorry if I startled you, Pete."

Pete felt an initial flush of embarrassment that he had been caught unaware in his own little imaginary world of snooker. He glanced above the table, half expecting to find an incriminating comic strip bubble displaying his secret thoughts dangling in the air.

"Hi there, Jake," said Pete, attempting to disguise his annoyance at being interrupted, just as he was beginning to find his rhythm. "I'm just getting a bit of practise in," he said.

Jake's eyes opened wide with astonishment at the sight of Pete's snooker table.

"Wow, you lucky thing," he said, an incredulous look on his face. "I absolutely love watching snooker when I get the chance, but I've never actually played."

Pete's irritation at the unexpected intrusion into his own private sanctuary evaporated with this news. In that instant, as Pete took in the rapturous expression on Jake's face, he relaxed and felt comfortable in his presence. The ice between the two boys was well and truly broken. Pete felt a queue of questions forming an impatient line, replacing the blankness that usually filled his head when attempting to make conversation with people.

"Have you been watching the tournament this week?" asked Pete.

"Oh, not this week. I haven't been allowed."

"Why's that?" asked Pete.

"My parents are a bit strict with what I can and can't watch on TV."

"Don't you have a portable in your bedroom?"

"No, they aren't that keen on me watching it," replied Jake. "They say there's nothing to be learnt from watching soaps or quiz shows, so they like to filter what we can or can't watch. They are much happier if I have my nose in a book."

Pete thought Jake's parents must be really strange to prevent him from watching the television. He couldn't survive without his daily fix of *Top of The Pops*, *The Young Ones*, or *Auf Wiedersehen, Pet*.

"There's nothing wrong with reading, though," said Pete. "I love James Herbert, especially the ones about the killer rats."

"I've not heard of him."

"Whaaattt! You've never read any of his books? He is amazing. He writes all sorts of horror stories, real adult stuff. I've just finished reading his latest. I can lend it to you, if you like?"

"Maybe another time."

Running out of things to say, Pete could only think of one more thing to add.

"We can play snooker now, if you like."

An anguished expression of indecision screwed up Jake's face, as the tempting offer see-sawed in his mind.

"Oh, I'd really love to, but my parents will be wondering where I've got to if I'm gone too long with Jack. I'm taking him out a bit earlier tonight before all of the fireworks start. He gets scared stiff by all the explosions."

Pete had forgotten all about it being bonfire night.

"Anyway, Pete. Dinner is always ready at 6:30. I'd better get going. They'll be really mad if I'm late."

"Okay, Jake."

Pete thought it was bizarre to be sitting down for tea at so late a time. Pete usually had his made for him by his mother within an hour of returning home from school, and even if the house was empty, he was sufficiently adept at frying up some fish fingers or a burger.

"But I can ask their permission," added Jake as an afterthought, "and maybe arrange a game for another day."

"Yes, that would be great," said Pete.

"Well then," said Jake. "Best be off."

Pete walked with Jake to the top of the driveway. The smokiness in the night air suggested that the numerous bonfires dotted around the estate were beginning to be lit.

"Do you have a favourite snooker player?" asked Pete.

"Of course. It has to be Jimmy White."

Pete laughed. "He's mine, too. I can't believe Davis beat him in the final, especially after he fought back so well."

"Too right," replied Jake, beginning to walk up the street. "Even my parents were watching it by the end."

"Well, then. See you in biology tomorrow," said Pete.

"Okay. See you then."

As soon as the bell rang to signal the end of morning assembly, Pete dashed out into the bright but chilly November day with a spring in his step. He had numerous reasons to be cheerful. It was Thursday, meaning another week of school was nearly successfully completed and consigned to history. Secondly, due to maintenance works the changing rooms were out of action until the New Year, so Pete and his peers were spared the dreaded showers for the foreseeable future. Finally, and most crucially, the smell of the festive period was well and truly in the air. With only a month to go until the big day itself, the tickets for the school Christmas disco, scheduled for the penultimate week of term, were going on sale at lunchtime.

Pete was en route to that morning's French class. He wanted to get there as early as possible so he could grab a minute or two's chat with Frances before Mrs Watson started the lesson. Although he needed no additional excuse to spend time in her company, he wanted to try and establish, in as casual and offhand a manner as possible, so as not to arouse suspicion over his motives, whether she herself would be queuing for a ticket.

It had been a blessing when the gods had conspired to pair Pete up with Frances in French, but it had also been a curse, unleashing within him the most passionate mix of emotions and feelings he had ever experienced in his young life. On the one hand, he felt happy and in an optimistic frame of mind, but conversely he was also imbued with sadness, full of a burning ache and a deep yearning to be around her when they were apart. In films and books, Pete had often come across the term "crush" in the context of describing a person's strong romantic feelings for somebody else. Having spent nearly three months sitting in such close proximity to Frances, Pete now knew how appropriate this word was, as she had proceeded to place a beguiling spell on him. It had gotten so bad that Pete was suffering from bouts of insomnia, lying in bed awake until the early hours imagining potential scenarios that would allow him to win her heart, without having to go through the predictably awkward ritual of asking her out. Every outcome involved a Hollywood ending, his most favoured being to intervene and save her from a group of hooligans intent on robbing her, calmly dispatching them single-handedly with efficient martial arts skill, like the Karate Kid or Bruce Lee.

Life as her boyfriend was the paradise for which he strove, but there was a part of him that revelled in the turmoil and frustration he was going through. Pete had never felt so alive, or so involved in the moment. While this remained the case, he was still able to cling onto his dream, however faint the hope was in reality. Pete's major fear was that an unexpected predator would pounce and steal her heart while he stood scratching his head at the crossroads of indecision.

In the limited time available to him in class, Pete did his best to make small talk with Frances, and had managed to scrape together various snippets of information about her. The Smiths were her favourite band and were influential in her decision to wear non-prescription National Health glasses, in homage to Morrissey. Pete discovered she was a vegetarian, primarily because she hated the taste of meat, as opposed to any specific objections about the cruelty involved in meat production. Finally, in the future she hoped to complete a politics degree and become a member of Parliament, to join the fight against what she argued would then be the next generation of Thatcherites.

Pete was amazed that anyone could be as certain as Frances was of the course that their life was going to take, as he had absolutely no idea where his destiny lay. In his younger years, Pete had vowed that he would become a professional footballer, and had not contemplated the thought that he would be anything else. This aspiration was brutally shattered at the age of eleven when, upon entering secondary education, Pete discovered he had a struggle on his hands just to make the school team, never mind attain a level of greatness beyond. The painful lesson in life this taught him was still keenly felt, with the vacuum of ambition left behind still to be filled.

His secret mental dossier on Frances had been painstakingly built up over the weeks, as Pete was still smothered in awe whenever he attempted to discuss matters of a vaguely personal nature. It was ironic that conversing with her in the Gallic tongue possessed no such worries. With the dialogue textbooks as their script, they would turn to face each other in their chairs and verbally simulate typical daily activities as experienced by the French.

Pete enacted the part of Henri, next to Frances's role of Marion, his sister. Already in the current school term they had ordered a meal in a cafe, bought train tickets to Paris, made their way around the French capital, and attended a family wedding. Pete loved the fact that he did not have to get stressed about potential awkward pauses in the conversation, as it was all written down in black and white, and wished he could converse with her just as easily when the veils of their French characters were dropped.

It was in these moments in the weekly French classes that Pete thought he could detect an occasional unspoken connection between the two of them. This occurred whenever a cheesy line came up in the dialogue, such as a question or sentence that nobody in their right mind would dare utter in the real world. The pair of them would look knowingly at each other, and smile or gently laugh at the sheer corniness of the phrase.

Charmed by her uninhibited and carefree personality, Pete had once felt a compelling desire to slip in a quickly ad-libbed "Je t'aime," in much the same way as he had once felt the urge to leap from the window of his father's thirteenth floor flat several years ago, while pressing his whole body against the large pane of glass in the front room and staring at the toy houses and matchstick people far below. In both cases he managed to resist the temptation, knowing the moment would pass and disaster would be averted.

In his current haste to get to the classroom, Pete decided to risk the shortcut around the rear of the sports hall. Officially out of bounds, and an offence punishable with detention, this area also happened to be the unofficial territory of the smokers, a group known to hang around in between lessons. Most of those who chose to congregate there were counting down the days until they were legally permitted to be cut free from the umbilical cord of the educational system, with the odds on them achieving qualifications and going onto further education greater than the Labour Party's prospects of forming the next government.

Turning the corner, Pete jumped at the sight of approximately a dozen fifth formers up ahead, standing in a circle by the wall of the building. Noticing that a couple of the group had noted his presence, Pete didn't wish to lose face by turning back, so he maintained a fast walking pace through the carpet of fallen leaves lying on the grass verge, keeping his eyes to the ground and hoping his non-threatening attitude would allow him to successfully pass by. As he neared the thick cloud of cigarette smoke, the entire assembly turned to face him, forming a human wall to block his progress. A line of impassive, hard faces stared threateningly at him. With his heart pounding, Pete paused, hoping his internal fear was not so visibly etched onto his face.

"Well, well, well, boys," said the youth stood in the middle of his cronies. "Who do we have here?"

Pete had to do a double take when he saw who the voice belonged to. With his rudimentary crew cut hairstyle, mouth full of jagged, broken teeth, and small cluster of tattoo dots on his cheek, it could only be one person. Davey Carter was back.

If there was one person in the whole of school it did not pay to annoy, it was Davey Carter. The very mention of his name was enough to fill one with paralysing fear. To this end, like the majority of the pupils and staff at the school, Pete went out of his way not to incur his wrath. This had not been so difficult to achieve in the previous two years, as Carter's frequent suspensions ensured that his attendance record was barely over fifty percent.

Pete had heard all of the hearsay about Carter returning to school, but had just dismissed it as idle gossip emanating from his bunch of followers, keen to ensure their gang's reputation remained intact. The reason for his latest suspension, the vandalising of a teacher's car the previous July, had, as far as most of a relieved student population were concerned, put paid to his reign of terror for good. The headmaster's original line of thought had been to expel Carter, but thanks to the last minute intervention of his social worker and counsellor, he was persuaded to offer him one final chance.

"Davies," he began, jabbing an accusatory finger at Pete. "You're the kid who was caught thieving, aren't you?"

It was not the type of question Pete felt a simple yes or no answer could do justice to, but Carter was not the type of person who had the patience to listen to an elongated response.

"So what?" replied Pete, instantly horrified that his own tone of voice sounded a great deal more menacing than he intended.

"Bit of a hard man we got here, boys, a right little maverick. Well, let me tell you, Davies, that I'm the mush around here again. I'm back for good, and I call the shots. Plebs like you tow the line. You get me?"

Pete was confused as to what point, if any, Carter was attempting to make. More worryingly, Pete was distraught that his sole indiscretion at the end of the summer break was coming back to haunt him once again. To cross the border between anonymity and notoriety in the eyes of Carter, and be singled out for special attention, was a highly unwelcome development, particularly as it was now frustrating Pete in his attempt to see Frances before the lesson began.

"I get you," he answered obediently, hoping to placate Carter.

"But," continued Carter, clearly not finished with Pete. "It proves you've got some bottle inside you, something I never thought you had personally, which just goes to show how wrong you can be about someone. And, you had that new mush Brookes shitting himself, by all accounts. A right one-man riot. I think that deserves a chance to run with the big boys."

Pete was still failing to see where this was all leading to.

"Me and the boys hang out most nights. How do you fancy meeting up with us tomorrow night, for starters? Friday's are always good for a laugh. We usually get our kicks downtown at the weekend."

Now that it had been spelled out for Pete, he felt caught between a rock and a hard place. To instantly rebuff Carter's hand of friendship could prove fatal, particularly as there was nobody else in the immediate vicinity to ask for assistance should they decide to take rejection personally. By the same token, Pete did not wish to instantly agree. He had vowed to learn from the harsh lesson he had been taught after doing Liam a favour, and had no desire to become involved with a group of infamous troublemakers. Obviously, Carter thought Pete was somebody he most definitely was not.

With the band of thugs all eagerly awaiting Pete's response to Carter's proposal, he scratched his head and thought furiously for the most diplomatic reply.

CHAPTER 6

Wild Boys

Sitting at the kitchen table, Pete munched quickly on his breakfast of toast smeared in golden syrup.

"Would you like some more toast, Pete?" asked his mother.

"Yes please, Mum," he replied, dividing his attention between Nick Owen and Anne Diamond on breakfast news, and talking to Carla.

"Carla have toast too, Mummy."

"Finish that piece first, darling," she said to her daughter.

"Okay, Mummy."

As Pete's mother placed two more slices of bread in the pop-up toaster, she smiled at the rare picture of domestic bliss being played out in front of her eyes. She couldn't remember the last time her son had woken up unprompted on a school morning, never mind sit at the table and make conversation. Usually he would make a bowl of cereal and retreat upstairs with it to his bedroom. It made her feel content to see everyone getting along for a change, and she hoped that the convivial household atmosphere would carry on into the holiday period.

"Is my Fred Perry shirt clean, Mum?"

"Which one, son?"

"The white one."

"Did you put your pile of dirty clothes into the laundry basket for washing, when I asked?"

"Erm, I can't remember, Mum."

His mother sighed and bit her tongue, not wishing to shatter Pete's good mood. "Well, I'll check your room today, and get it sorted for the weekend."

"Mum," protested Pete. "It's the disco at school tonight. That's my favourite top."

"Oh, Pete," she chirped. "Why do you always leave things to the very last minute? If you'd told me yesterday, I could have had it done for today."

Her heart sank at the despondent expression on her son's face. She knew how much he liked to wear his favourite clothes whenever he went anywhere special.

"I'll tell you what, Pete. If you bring that dirty pile downstairs before you leave for school I'll see what I can do, but I'm not making any promises."

Pete's eyes lit up. "Oh brilliant, Mum," he said, springing up out of his seat. "I'll go and do that now."

"And check you have a decent pair of trousers, too. Leave them on your bed and I'll press them tonight for you," she shouted, as Pete's heavy footsteps rapidly ascended the stairs.

Pete's mother sighed. She could remember as if it was only yesterday how it felt like a matter of life and death before an important night out if your hair wasn't cut to your satisfaction, your favourite skirt had a stain on it, or you had a pimple on the morning of a big date. She didn't wish to be too hard on Pete on this occasion as it pleased her to see him beginning to make new friends, and not spending all of his time alone playing snooker or cocooned in his bedroom.

There was a palpable air of excitement outside the entrance to the school disco among the large crowd of teenagers impatiently waiting to be admitted. The girls, huddled together in small groups, were enthusiastically comparing and complimenting each other's choice of outfit, hairstyle, and make-up. The boys hovered in and around them, some silently viewing with amazement the transformation in their female peers, while others were doing their best to act ultra cool, chewing hard on gum and displaying machismo traits as they nervously chatted and fooled around.

For many in attendance, the disco offered a rare opportunity to make public the torch that was being carried for another. With such bold declarations came the risk of being publicly humiliated if turned down flat, and having to eat humble pie in the days and weeks to follow while nursing a bruised ego.

At one minute to seven, Derek Brookes, the teacher assigned the dubious honour of declaring the Christmas school disco 1984 well and truly open, peered out of a side corridor window at the sheer weight in numbers now gathered outdoors. He smiled and shook his head, knowing full well the throng would not be so keen to get inside the building the next morning when normal service had resumed.

"Ah, Mr Brookes."

The teacher spun around to find the caretaker, Mr Duckett, better known as Ducky, at his shoulder, a large bunch of keys jangling impatiently in one hand, and an empty black bin liner in the other.

"Come on then, Mr Brookes," said Ducky, continuing down to the main door. "The sooner we let them in, the sooner we can chuck the little sods back out in two hours."

Chuckling at Ducky's abrupt and brazen attitude, Mr Brookes followed.

"What's the plastic bag for?" called Mr Brookes to the caretaker.

"Confiscated beer cans," barked Ducky over his shoulder.

As the doors were unlocked and swung open, a jubilant roar erupted from outside. Mr Brookes raised a hand to quieten everyone down for a moment. "Please, everyone," he shouted. "Get into an orderly queue, don't push, and everyone will get inside a lot quicker. And have your tickets ready to give to Mr Duckett or myself."

As one, the teenagers obeyed the instructions, and were soon streaming through into the building, as strains of Wham's "Freedom" echoed down the corridor. The evening had well and truly begun.

"Evening, Pete," said Mr Brookes to the youngster, as he handed over his ticket.

"And we'll be checking you, laddie," exclaimed Ducky with pompous authority, overzealous in his searching of Pete.

"No prizes for guessing where I've stashed my beer, Ducky," teased Jake, handing his ticket over.

"What did you call me?" demanded the prickly caretaker, scowling at the disrespectful boy whose name he was yet to learn, before proceeding to subject Jake to a similarly thorough check.

"Give them a uniform," sighed Jake, holding his arms up submissively while looking sarcastically at the ceiling.

The pair entered the school canteen, transformed for the evening into a temporary tuck shop, the familiar smell of chips and pungent vinegar lingering in the air. A line of off-duty dinner ladies stood behind the open hatch, awaiting the first customers of the evening.

"Let's go and check the action out," said Jake. Wide-eyed with excitement, he headed towards the main hall, transformed for the evening from its usual humdrum existence into a maker and breaker of dreams.

"Just a minute," replied Pete, hopefully peering down the corridor that led to the cloakrooms for a sign of Frances. Pete had not uttered a word to anyone about his infatuation for Frances. Although he and Jake had been spending many evenings together, playing snooker and hanging out on the estate, Pete still didn't feel confident or trusting enough to share his deepest secret.

"Come on, Pete," urged Jake. "There's an ocean swimming with all kinds of fish through those doors. We can't waste a second longer."

Deciding he couldn't just wait there indefinitely like an obsessed freak, Pete followed Jake into the hall. With the main overhead lights switched off, the only source of illumination came from four sets of rotating multi-coloured lights, situated on top of the disc jockey's speakers on the main stage.

With the evening still in its infancy, the room was only a third full. While a handful of girls were dancing to the disco tempo of "Together In Electric Dreams," the remainder of the occupants were lurking in the shadows, around the chairs that lined the perimeter walls.

Opting to do the latter, Pete and Jake found a space at the back of the hall where all new arrivals could be noted, and watched the dancers energetically move and gyrate their bodies. With the sheer volume of noise making it impossible to engage in normal conversation, Pete listened patiently to a trio of tracks from Wham, Duran Duran, and Paul Young, before the disc jockey's gravel-toned voice made its first intervention of the evening.

"Okay, time for a little break from the latest chart hits. For the next few minutes, it's time for all you metal lovers to take your place on the dance floor and do your thing, starting off with Rainbow and 'I Surrender.'"

As a raucous explosion of thrashed guitar riffs took the place of white boy soul, it was too much for Pete to take. He gestured to Jake with his hand that he was thirsty as an excuse to escape the din. The majority of those present appeared to have similar sentiments, as the musical equivalent of a stink bomb proceeded to clear the room. Only a handful of boys, including Thames and Appleby from Pete's year group, remained behind, gleefully taking over the floor space, the sewn on patches adorning their sleeveless denim jackets proudly displaying their allegiance to acts like AC/DC, Rainbow, Quo, and Black Sabbath.

"I'm parched," said Pete, once the doors closed behind them, and they were able to hear each other clearly. "Just going for a can of pop."

"Okay, Pete. I'm bursting for the loo," said Jake, heading off down the corridor that led to the cloakrooms.

"What'll it be, love?" asked Betty, the elderly dinner lady, more used to dishing out ladles of mushy peas than taking money for crisps and pop.

"Erm," hesitated Pete, surveying the options. "Shandy, please."

"Don't be drinking too many of those, Pete," she joked, winking to him as she handed it over. "We don't want to be carrying you home, do we?"

While he sat at one of the dining tables and waited for Jake to return, Pete took a sip from his can and glanced down the corridor at the entrance to the disco. It was deserted, apart from Mr Brookes and Ducky standing around casually chatting. Pete noted despondently that it was nearly 7:30 p.m., and briefly pondered why it was that time had a habit of passing by at the speed of light when you wished it would last an eternity. Already a quarter of the evening was gone, and Frances was nowhere to be seen. Pete doubted whether there would be any latecomers so far into the evening, so could only assume that if she was present, then she could only be in the vicinity of the cloakrooms.

A hollow feeling of anti-climax began to seep through Pete as he began to contemplate the notion that all of his efforts had been in vain: hounding his mother to prepare his favourite clothes in time, the long soak in the bath pampering himself earlier that evening, and the time and expense of getting a new haircut the previous weekend.

One small consolation was the relief of avoiding the dance floor. For someone as self-conscious and shy as Pete, dancing was a traumatic act to perform, particularly when surrounded by so many people.

A further five minutes passed by and still Jake was nowhere to be seen. Pete felt marooned in no-man's land.

"Hope all of you metalheads enjoyed that trio of songs there," Pete heard the disc jockey announce, his voice slightly dampened by the dividing wall between the main hall and the canteen. "Please, I implore you all to get on the floor with U2 now as they give us 'Pride...In the Name...of Love.' And don't forget everyone, if you want to dedicate a song to someone, there is still a little more time to get those requests in."

Fed up with waiting around, Pete launched his empty can into the waste bin and stood up to venture down into the cloakrooms.

"Hi, Pete," shouted Helen Davenport, emerging from the hall and heading over to him. "You haven't seen Charlotte around anywhere, have you? She said she was nipping out for a drink. But she hasn't returned, and that was ages ago."

"Sorry, Helen," said Pete, a little taken aback by her appearance. Dressed in jeans and a baggy, white casual cotton shirt, she looked a completely different person from her daytime self. What most struck Pete was the change in hairstyle. Her usual brushed back style, tied into a ponytail, was now hanging loose and flowing.

"You haven't seen Jake, have you? I lost him a while ago, too," he said, feeling a little foolish for sounding like a child who had lost his parents in a shop.

"Well, I was about to have a look down there," she said, indicating the corridor leading to the cloakrooms. "I've heard it's all getting a bit wild, so it's more than likely that Charlotte will be in among the thick of it. Coming?"

"I was just about to look there myself."

"Great," said Helen. "Lead the way."

The opening stretch of the corridor was packed to bursting point with teenagers chatting away, but there was no sign of Jake or Charlotte. Arriving at the first stairway, Pete saw a flustered Ducky climbing up the flight of stairs two steps at a time with his skinny, lanky legs. He was craning his neck upwards like a human ostrich at the sound of barely suppressed giggles coming from the unlit first floor landing, out of bounds for the evening.

The thought of being up there in the shadows sent a shiver through Pete. A ghost, rumoured to be a white lady, was said to wander the empty corridors of the building at night.

Continuing onto the cloakroom at the far end of the corridor, Pete was staggered to see the five rows of wooden seat benches underneath the coat hooks all crammed with people. This explained why the main hall was nowhere near as full as Pete had expected it to be. In the very last row, snuggled together against the far wall, were Jake and Charlotte.

As he followed Helen over towards them, Pete felt a tinge of envy at the way the pair appeared to be so happy in each other's company, as if they had known each other for years. The thought that Jake would meet someone this evening had never crossed Pete's mind.

"Budge up," shouted Helen, grabbing Pete by the arm and stepping over the obstacle of outstretched legs. "Make room for two more."

Pete managed to squeeze beyond Charlotte and Jake, with Helen sitting on the other side of her friend. "Where did you get to?" asked Pete, wounded that his sole friend had wandered off and deserted him.

"Sorry, Pete," replied Jake, making light of his friend's dejection. "This little lady grabbed hold of me and wouldn't let me go. I was just about to come and fetch you. It's really happening in here."

Jake reached under the bench by his feet, emerging with a white disposable cup in his hand. He offered it to Pete.

"What is it?" asked Pete. It looked to him like pop.

"Vodka and Coke. It's fab stuff," replied Jake, taking a drink himself when Pete failed to take up his offer.

"Where did that come from?" asked Pete, unable to disguise the tone of disapproval in his voice. Pete knew that if Ducky discovered alcohol was being consumed on the premises, then that would be the night over for all of them.

"Morgan smuggled it in. He left a window unlocked on the first floor before the end of school today. When he arrived tonight, he sneaked back into the room, got his mate to throw up a piece of rope with a shopping bag containing the vodka tied to the other end, and hoisted it up. He's selling it for thirty pence a go from the toilets."

"No, I'll give it a miss. It's school tomorrow."

"Please yourself. That leaves more for me and Charlotte."

Jake turned around to resume his conversation with Charlotte, leaving Pete to scan the room for Frances. A few familiar faces, including Sam and his small clique of friends who always hung out together, were sat two rows away, but there was no sign of the elusive Frances.

Within a few minutes, Pete's bladder was at bursting point. He did his best to hold on as long as possible until his friend was ready to return to the disco, but with Jake still engrossed in Charlotte and showing no sign of moving from his seat anytime soon, Pete was left with no option but to push through the congested mass of bodies.

"Alright, Pete," greeted the imposing figure of Bryan Fawcett outside the entrance to the boys toilets. At six foot three, Fawcett was the tallest person in their school year. "Seen any teachers about?" he asked.

"No," replied Pete.

"Sweet. You'd better get in there fast. I don't think Giles has much drink left," he said, before rapping three times on the door, his little smirk as he did so going unnoticed by Pete.

Lacking the heart to say he was not interested in buying alcohol and simply wanted to enter in order to use the facilities for the purpose they were originally intended, Pete gave Fawcett a false grin of complicity and pushed the door open. Finding it was empty, Pete assumed Fawcett was just spinning him a yarn. Dashing over to the urinal, Pete smelt cigarette smoke in the air, which was not that unusual. It was only when Pete unzipped his trousers and was about to relieve himself that a disconcerting sound came from the bottom cubicle at the far end of the room.

It was the wild, unrestrained laugh of a female.

Alarming as that was given the location in which it had occurred, for Pete it was worse. Much, much worse. He recognised the person to whom the cackle belonged. It was Frances Bailey-Jones.

Swiftly redoing his zip, Pete turned around and looked at the cubicles. All three doors were closed, but there were further irrefutable clues that they were occupied: suppressed giggles, the slight shuffling of feet on the tiled floor, and a puff of smoke twirling up to the ceiling from the cubicle where the giggle had originated.

The head of Giles Morgan peered over the top of the middle cubicle. "Gordon Bennett, it's only Davies."

All three doors flew open and ten relieved people emerged from the cramped interiors, clutching a collection of white paper cups the same as Jake's. As he originally thought, the laugh had belonged to Frances, who had Lucy Small next to her.

"Bonjour, Henri," said Frances to Pete. With her pale skin flushed red and the usual serious, focused look in her eyes replaced with unrestrained abandon, Pete did not have to be Bergerac to be able to put two and two together. Unsure as to whether her greeting was genuine or just a mickey take, Pete's response was subdued.

"Hi."

"Bloody Fawcett, what's that dickhead knocking on the door for?" complained Morgan.

Bryan Fawcett opened the door, delighted by the semi-shocked expressions on the faces of his friends. "Got you all, suckers," he laughed.

It was only then that Pete understood. Fawcett was acting as lookout, with the instruction to do a warning knock on the door at the first sign of Ducky or a teacher.

"Guess you must be after one of my special Christmas potions, Davies?" presumed Morgan, gesturing to the bag in his hand.

With Frances looking on, Pete felt as if he had no option but to agree. He didn't wish to lose any face in front of her.

"You can have this one on me, mate. You look as if you could do with it after the fright we just gave you."

"Cheers," replied Pete.

As Morgan poured him a generous measure, Pete glanced at Frances, now sitting on a lowered cistern lid, taking a heavy draw on a cigarette and returning to her conversation. In an instant, it was as if Pete was invisible to her. Hovering around the cubicle entrance chatting to her were Lucy and a couple of sixth-form boys who, by standing up and blocking the open doorway, were effectively barring unwanted newcomers from getting too close to her.

Pete was deflated, not just because the version of Frances in front of him was the complete antithesis to the Frances Bailey-Jones he had come to know, who would usually run a mile from Morgan, but also because of the dismissive attitude she was displaying. Pete knew that to try and ingratiate himself into her conversation was pointless, and would possibly end by being physically ejected by the two older boys vying for her affections. As much as it pained him, Pete made his way back to Jake, gave him the freebie cup of vodka, and mulled over everything he had just witnessed.

The whole dance floor went mad when the outro of "Nellie the Elephant" blended into the beginning of "Agadoo." Pete leaned against the outer wall, watching Charlotte, Helen, and Jake on the dance floor. Charlotte was laughing hysterically at Jake's unsuccessful attempts to copy her dance moves. The trio had been dancing for well over half an hour. Despite numerous efforts to get Pete to join in, he had stubbornly remained on the periphery, no longer in the party mood. Frances was still to set foot in the hall, an indication to Pete that Morgan or one of the sixth-formers had been more successful in winning her heart than Pete and most others could ever dream of.

As "Do They Know It's Christmas" faded out, Mr Brookes took to the stage to address the exuberant crowd.

"Students of Framlington Hall, I'm afraid it is that sad time of the evening when the end is nigh. There are now only two songs left to play."

A universal collection of disappointed "aahs" echoed around the room.

"It has been my first experience of the school disco here at Framlington, and I sincerely hope it will not be my last. As tonight has been an unqualified success, I would just like to announce that, in my position as School Entertainments Committee Chairman, I have formally booked our good friends who have been entertaining us all this evening to return for a Valentine's disco to be held in, unsurprisingly, February."

Mr Brookes smiled as the expected cheers nearly raised the roof.

"But that is, of course, another day and another year. So, I think it's time for me to do a sharp exit and let the final songs commence."

"Thank you for that, Mr Brookes," began the disc jockey. "Thank you for having us, pupils of Framlington Hall. As always, we've had a great time. To finish the evening off in a moment will be Wham and the instant classic of 'Last Christmas,' but before that a blast from the not too distant past. This is Bonnie Tyler and 'Total…Eclipse…Of The…Heart.'"

While half of the crowd began to reluctantly shuffle towards the exit, those lucky enough to have a partner made the most of the additional floor space to smooch. Several boys, caught in the all or nothing zone, had to make an instant decision whether to finally summon up the courage to ask for a dance with the object of their affections, or to head for home and live to fight another day, with nothing lost and nothing gained.

Pete stood alone listening to the song of melancholy, believing that nothing Shakespeare wrote in his finest hour could possibly match it for describing how he felt at that exact moment, with his hopes and dreams lying in ruins.

With Charlotte and Jake clasping each other on the dancefloor, Helen headed over to the onlooking Pete. She cupped a hand over his ear and fired a question at him. Even at such close proximity, Helen's words were totally drowned out by the music. Shrugging his shoulders, he pointed to his ear and shook his head.

Helen smiled knowingly. She pointed to the exit, gesturing at Pete to follow. Standing in the canteen, Helen repeated her question.

"I said, would you mind walking me home? It looks as if our friends may have other plans for the rest of the evening."

"Yeah, no problem," replied a disgruntled Pete to a visibly relieved Helen.

"Great. I'll just get my coat from the cloakroom. Shall I fetch yours?"

"I never brought one."

"Oh my God, you'll freeze."

"I'll be okay. I'll wait outside the main door," said Pete. "It's like Piccadilly Circus in here."

"Don't leave without me," pleaded Helen.

Pete was actually secretly relieved at the prospect of having company on the way home. One of his biggest fears was walking alone at night, a phobia the new television programme *Crimewatch* had intensified in recent months. He made his way to the exit and waited for Helen to emerge. It was a clear, starry night, and bitterly cold. With a dusting of frost glittering on the ground, it reminded Pete of the kind of evenings he always used to pray for in his pre-teens in the run-up to Christmas, to imbue the holidays with extra magic.

"I really appreciate this," said Helen when she emerged from the building, her teeth chattering in the biting chill of the night. "My parents would kill me if they thought I had walked all the way home by myself. I mean, I know the estate is pretty safe, but, being parents, they do worry a lot, don't they?"

Unsure whether Helen was making a statement, or asking a question, Pete remained tight-lipped.

"They're happy for me and Charlotte to walk back together," she continued, "but I don't want to ruin her evening by being a gooseberry. I know how much she has been dying to ask your friend out."

Pete's heart sunk to rock bottom at this revelation, as he assumed Jake's feelings were mutual. Looking at the night's events from a purely selfish perspective, Pete had just got used to the idea of having a best friend to hang out with, someone to chat with and hopefully confide in at some point. To have a serious rival for Jake's attention so soon into their friendship was completely unexpected, particularly as his own romantic dreams had been dealt a severe blow.

"Did you not fancy anyone there tonight, then?" asked Helen.

"There's no one I like," Pete lied, a little too quickly.

"Oh," she replied, sounding disheartened.

Pete then realised the trap he had fallen into and attempted to dig himself out. "I mean," he began, desperately trying to formulate a reasonable excuse, "I like girls as friends, but it's impossible to say you really like someone until you get to know them first." He was rambling, but by the way Helen appeared to agree with him, Pete felt he had undone the harm.

"I suppose so," she said. "Still, you should have got yourself up onto the dance floor, instead of standing all alone and miserable. You might have met someone. You can dance, can't you?"

"There's no music I really like enough to dance to," replied Pete unconvincingly.

"None at all?" she asked in disbelief. "What about Wham? They're my favourite band. George is sooo gorgeous."

"My Dad says Andrew Ridgeley is the luckiest millionaire since Ringo Starr."

Helen turned to Pete. "Ringo who?" she asked, clearly puzzled.

It was Pete's turn to show genuine surprise. "You've never heard of Ringo Starr? He was the drummer with The Beatles."

"Oh, them," she said nonchalantly. "My Dad's got some of their records. They're ancient, Pete. You should hear the way they hiss and crackle when he plays them. Don't you listen to anything modern like Wham or Duran Duran?"

"I like 'Careless Whisper,' " Pete conceded, "and 'Freedom' isn't too bad."

"What about Paul Young? Oh, he's dead gorgeous. Culture Club are quite good. Boy George is really talented. Howard Jones and Nik Kershaw are brilliant, too."

Approaching the turn in to the estate, Pete asked where Helen lived.

"Brancepeth View."

"Great. That's more or less on my way. I'll see you to your door, if you like."

Helen smiled. "Thanks, Pete."

Pete had an ulterior motive for offering. From Helen's street, it was only a short jog to his own home, if he went through the cut by the field.

"Where do you live?" enquired Helen.

"Langdon Road."

"Ooh, right next to the railway line?"

Pete nodded.

"Don't the trains keep you awake at night?"

"It's not so bad once you get used to it," said Pete.

"Fancy me living so close to you and never seeing you around the estate," continued Helen, in chatty mode. "Then again, this place is so big, I don't even know who half of my neighbours are. You only ever get fleeting glimpses when they go to work on a morning and arrive back at night."

"How long have you lived here?" asked Pete.

"Six years. My father's a police officer. It's alright on the estate, just a bit boring at times. Nothing much ever happens around here. What about you?"

"I moved here about four years ago. I'm from Sunderland originally. I still go back at weekends. It's a bit, well, posh around here for my liking. The people are so different to what I'm used to. When I told my Dad I was living in the same street as a copper, he nearly had a heart attack."

Helen laughed. "I find the problem is the pensioners who have nothing better to do than peer out their windows when we play in the street, or come out and tell us off. All we're doing is playing blocky or kerby. Nothing that's going to cause a riot."

"I know what you mean," agreed Pete. "The way some of the people in my street look at me, you'd think I was from another planet."

"But you are from another planet," replied Helen, in all seriousness.

Pete instantly looked pained by Helen's statement.

"You should see your face," she said, maintaining her temporary facade for a couple of seconds before collapsing into hysterics. "Sorry, Pete. You've got to learn to lighten up. Don't take everything so serious."

Arriving outside Helen's home, the pair paused awkwardly at the top of the driveway.

"Thanks for seeing me home, Pete. I've enjoyed our little chat. You're funny."

"Thanks," said Pete modestly, inwardly enjoying the small compliment, even though he figured she was compensating for hurting his feelings a moment ago.

"Well, now we are better acquainted, don't be afraid to speak to me in French in future. There's more girls in the world than Frances, you know. Who knows, we may be seeing a lot more of each other if Jake and Charlotte get together after tonight. I'll need someone to talk to while they are being lovey-dovey with each other. Goodnight."

"Goodnight," replied Pete.

With Helen home safely, Pete felt uneasy and insecure on the dark street. Seemingly innocuous noises such as a faraway car accelerating, the meow of an unseen cat, and a house door slamming, spoke to him of sinister forces at play. Staring at the nearly full moon, Pete imagined ghosts, witches and zombies lurking in the shadows, waiting for a lone teenage boy to take a wrong turning into oblivion.

Instinctively, Pete broke into a steady jog, feeling like Sebastian Coe kicking for gold on his final lap in the Los Angeles Olympics. In the distance, beyond the frost-sprinkled playing field, was the streetlight illuminating the entrance to the shortcut to his street. Enjoying the sound of the crisp grass under his feet, Pete bounded towards the end of the field. Turning into the narrow pathway that ran between the two houses, he was surprised to find his passage blocked by a group of youths. Slowing to a fast walk, he was distraught to find himself face to face with Carter.

"Well, boys, look who we have here. If it ain't the boy wonder himself. Davies, we really need to stop meeting by accident like this. Of course, when you do get an official invite to hang out with us, you choose not to turn up at the agreed time. You'd rather be brown nosing that posh git Rigby than knocking around with the real men. What's the matter? Aren't we good enough for you?"

"N...No," stammered Pete, finding himself completely surrounded. "I'm sorry, but I couldn't make it that Friday night."

"All you had to do was come and say, Davies. The boys and me are out most nights. We'd have found another time for you. But no, you walk around school ignoring us, raising your nose at us."

"It's not that at all," protested Pete.

"Hold your breath, Davies. Okay, boys."

Pete found himself helplessly dragged by several of Carter's gang back towards the field. Once there, he was forcefully thrown to the ground. Pete hit the frozen ground sideways on, jarring his left shoulder. A searing pain shook him.

"Aaahhhh," he wailed.

"Okay boys, bring him over here," ordered Carter.

Each gang member grabbed an arm or a leg, and lifted Pete up off the ground. They walked over to where Carter was standing, ten feet away.

"You know what we do with pieces of shit, Davies," cackled Carter. "We drop them in it. Okay, boys, let go of him."

For the second time in less than a minute, Pete was unceremoniously dropped to the ground. He hit the grass with a thud. A hand gripped the back of his neck before he could stand up, and shoved his face into the earth. The foul smell and taste of dog excrement invaded his nose and mouth.

"There you go, Davies. Now you really can call yourself a brown nose," he said, before the whole gang ran off, whooping and laughing.

CHAPTER 7

Shout

Pete paused on Prebends Bridge, the centuries old stone arch bridge construction that crosses the River Wear in the shadow of the cathedral. He looked downstream at the seventeenth century boathouse and the Old Fulling Mill, two familiar buildings that stood on opposing banks, beyond which were the tall, bare trees that flanked the riverbanks of the waterway all the way down to Framwellgate Bridge.

Pete liked to come here often, to walk up and down the narrow footpaths and enjoy the peaceful surroundings, the perfect environment in which to clear his head and recharge his flat batteries. He was also drawn by the feeling of magic, particularly on cold, bright winter mornings like today, where ground frost covered the landscape and it felt like a scene from a bygone Dickensian age.

Pete glanced over to his right at the Victorian style street light that stood beyond the bridge, at the point where the footway forked off into two separate directions. Pete had heard from an old English teacher that this might have been the very spot that inspired C.S. Lewis to write his Chronicles of Narnia books. Pete liked to think this was the case, wishing he, too, could be whisked off to an amazing world packed with opportunities for fun and adventure, and escape the harsh realities of his own life.

It had been a difficult couple of days since the school disco. Pete had managed to avoid going to school that Friday, telling his mother that his left arm was too painful. He showed her the compelling evidence of black and blue bruising that ran from his shoulder all the way down his upper arm. Pete had been less than economical with the truth in his account of how he had come to sustain the injury, claiming to have tripped over and landed awkwardly on the way home. She fussed at him for being so careless.

Despite the physical pain, it was the mental injuries he had incurred that inflicted the greater damage. Pete was ashamed at what he had been subjected him to, and he was dreading the next time he came face to face with Carter. He had spent ages in the bathroom afterwards, first rinsing out his mouth, before thoroughly scrubbing and washing himself in the shower. If there was any consolation whatsoever to gain, it was that the offending waste was highly solidified, ensuring he was not heavily smeared. His shirt, however, was covered in the offending dirt, forcing Pete to wrap it up in a plastic bag and deposit it in the outside dustbin, to avoid further probing questions from his mother.

Besides Carter, Pete's other problems had been very much at the forefront of his mind that extended weekend, and he had given a great deal of thought to the latest developments with Jake and Frances. His overriding feeling was that he was friendless and back to square one again, just as he had been at the beginning of September. Pete felt as if he was standing static and isolated in his own life, while the rest of the world continued to revolve and change all around him.

On Saturday, Pete had been preoccupied with the fourth anniversary of John Lennon's murder. To mark the occasion, he spent a reflective day of solitude in his bedroom playing his favourite Beatles and Lennon records, wishing he could have met his idol, and cursing the person who had senselessly brought his life to a premature end. In an instinctive moment at the end of the day, just as he was about to go to bed, Pete had sunk to his knees and prayed for the first time since school assemblies in primary school.

"Please, John Lennon," he began in a hushed whisper, gazing through his exposed window at the bright moon in the night sky. "If you are really up there in the sky somewhere, and you can hear me, then please, you will know how much I need your help."

Pete felt a little ridiculous, but persevered. "I need you to offer me some advice. You're my only hope. I don't have anyone to share my problems with. So this is my prayer to you," he continued. "Give me a sign. Please. I just don't know where else to turn."

Pete remained on his knees for a few minutes, palms touching and eyes closed, awaiting heavenly intervention.

Nothing happened.

A minute later, his knees began to ache. Feeling slightly foolish, he stood up and climbed into bed, angry with himself for even thinking such a resolution to his problems could be found in that way.

"You're not thinking of jumping into there are you, bonny lad?" asked a vaguely familiar voice, bringing Pete back to the present.

Pete looked up from the river. Approaching slowly across the bridge, aided by a wooden walking stick, was Barney, the cathedral guide he had sat next to at Palace Green many weeks ago.

"Aye, it's a beautiful vision to behold," he commented, standing next to Pete while appreciating the view. "Especially at this time of year when the first frosts are appearing. I think God did alright by us when he created Durham."

A silence of thirty seconds ensued, long enough for Pete to wonder if Barney recognised him from their previous meeting, or if he was simply exchanging pleasantries. Barney was smartly dressed on this occasion, wearing a dark grey cashmere overcoat that was buttoned all the way up to his neck, sharply creased navy trousers, and polished black brogue shoes.

At closer quarters, Barney briefly looked Pete over. "We've met before, young man. But for the life of me, I can't quite put a name to your face."

"It's Pete, Sir. We met on your seat at Palace Green. I was reading the football reports."

Barney smiled as he recalled their meeting. "Of course. Silly me," he said, mildly scolding himself. "I'm just on my way home, young Pete. And it's Barney to my friends, none of this 'Sir' formality. I was wondering if you wouldn't mind walking back up the hill with me, just in case my angina comes on. I haven't been feeling myself today, you see. It's a long, lonely walk when you rely on one of these things." He gestured at his walking aid.

They walked at a snail's pace up the steep incline into the narrow walkway of the South Bailey, with Barney red-faced and wheezing heavily.

"Let's have it then, what's worrying you?" asked Barney gently, once the road levelled out and he regained his breath. "You're walking like your shoes are full of lead, with a face to make a clown redundant. It's," he glanced at his watch, "9:30 on a Sunday morning with Christmas coming, yet you're as miserable as sin. Which means," he concluded, like a lawyer drawing together a stack of damning evidence in a courtroom, but deriving no pleasure from believing himself to be correct in his hypothesis, "there's something troubling you, lad, isn't there?" he probed, with genuine concern.

Pete looked straight ahead, making it blatantly obvious the matter was not open for discussion. He was worried that in the cold light of day, Barney would think he was making a mountain out of a molehill.

"Oh well," continued Barney, when no response was forthcoming. "I'll let it rest for now, whatever it is. I don't want to feel like I'm getting at you, lad. I hardly know you, really. It's just that, well, I see a lot of my son in you. When he was your age, that is. And if he was ever upset about something, then I wanted to know about it. Bottling something up makes it ten times worse when it eventually explodes. Anyway, come on," he said. "I know a place we can go to. Rosie's Cafe. Just on the corner down the road here by Dunelm Bridge. Let's see if we're her first customers of the day."

Keen to change tact and lighten the dark mood that threatened to shroud the atmosphere, Barney began to recount one of his stories.

"When I was a youngster, which was a long, long, looonnng time ago," he started, accentuating the last "long" with a wide smile on his face, as if the very act of talking about his boyhood memories brought them alive once again, "they were the best times I ever had, even if there was a war on for most of them. Free as birds, we were."

"What was there to do in those days?" asked Pete, warming slightly to Barney's easy-going nature, with curiosity getting the better of him. Pete couldn't imagine what it was like to live without a video recorder, never mind a television set, and to exist in a world that excluded pop music and computer games, things that Pete took for granted.

Barney's eyes widened in joy at the cue from Pete to further divulge his past, the memories queuing up in his mind to be resurrected, as fresh now as they had been when experienced the first time.

"Anything and everything," he exclaimed, a wide grin on his leathery features. "Away from the city we'd go and out into the country. And there was so much of it to explore in those days. Fewer houses, and less noisy cars clogging up the lovely clean air. Just miles and miles of green fields, rivers, and woods. Like a crazed pack of lions, we tore up the land, getting into a few innocent scrapes along the way, I hasten to add, but nothing serious. Just the usual things young lads get up to. No two days were ever the same. We rode the crest of life's wave, not knowing where it was going to take us. We were young and fearless, and I dare say the same thing applies to youngsters today. So much has changed, but young lads never do."

A minute later, they turned right and walked down the cobbled lane towards Dunelm Bridge. "There's signs of life at Rosie's," said Barney. "I'm sure she'll have something to help keep the cold at bay."

Barney entered first, greeting the two fellow customers with a nod of the head and a ready smile. "You sit at that table with the view of the river, Pete, and I'll get us a bit of service."

Pete sat down and looked around the room. It struck him how small and cosy an interior it was, with a dozen four-seater pine tables crammed into the limited floor space. A blackboard mounted on the wall had the day's specials written on in chalk. The small windowpanes that Pete attempted to gaze through were weepy with condensation from the trapped heat.

Barney picked up a small hand bell on the counter and rang it. "Shop," he shouted.

From an open doorway behind the counter emerged the proprietor, drying her hands on a tea towel before picking up a pen and notebook. A small, heavily built woman in her late fifties, Rosie was a no-nonsense, down to earth character. The rolled up sleeves of her blue checked uniform revealed thickset forearms, visible testimony to a life of manual labour. They were the unashamed tools of her trade. Thick-rimmed glasses sat perched on the rim of her nose, magnifying her eyes with exaggerated prominence.

"How are you today, Barney, love? Feeling any better?" she enquired, hand poised to write down the order.

"Oh, I can't complain," replied Barney. "Every day's a blessing, Rosie. How are you?"

"A lot quieter now the students have returned home for Christmas, but it gives me a chance to prepare for the holidays. I'll make the most of it while I can. Your usual, Barney?"

"Yes please, Rosie, and," he paused, turning to Pete, "my young friend will have a…"

"A Coke, please," said Pete.

Rosie did a double take when she noticed Pete.

"And a Coke for my young friend, Pete," confirmed Barney, exchanging a brief, knowing look with Rosie.

"Two minutes, gents," said Rosie, snapping out of her brief reverie.

Barney shuffled over to Pete's table, leaned his stick against the wall, and carefully sat down opposite the boy. "Aye, Pete. Every weekend without fail, young Rosie serves me the best cuppa in town. In proper mugs, as well. Not those little posh china things where you only get two mouthfuls."

Right on cue, Rosie returned with their order, and placed the drinks onto the table.

"Now that's what I call first-rate service. Why, I've barely taken the weight off my feet. Pete, I'd like you to meet the greatest toastie maker in all of Durham. With a heart of gold to match."

"Oh yes, a title to be envied," said Rosie, rolling her eyes in mock flattery at Barney's introduction. "It's very nice to meet you, Pete," she said, before retreating once more into her backroom area.

"Are you looking forward to Christmas, Pete?" asked Barney. "It's a lovely time of year, especially in the city with all the festive lights around the streets. There's so much going on to keep me out of mischief too. The fair's next weekend, followed by the carol service. Nothing beats the sound of the choir singing in the cathedral."

Pete was astonished to hear an adult talk about the Christmas period with such enthusiasm. Most men in his family, especially his father, seemed to use it as an excuse to drink and eat to excess. The magic of the occasion had departed long ago for them.

"We're raising money for Ethiopia this year. It's a tragedy what is going on over there," lamented Barney, shaking his head in disbelief.

"I bought three copies of the record," said Pete, "and I gave one week's paper round money for Africa, too."

Barney's eyes twinkled as his face lit up. "You've a compassionate soul, Pete. I knew that the first time I set eyes on you. Please, don't ever change. That, too, would be nothing short of a disaster."

Pete felt a surge of pride at Barney's praise. It was comforting for him to be talking to an adult on an equal footing. Most other grown-ups usually made the fatal mistake of adopting a false, patronising tone. When Pete told his father about his contribution to Band Aid, he admonished his son for wasting his money, saying it was not Joe Public's job to try and save the world whenever there was a crisis, and what the hell did he think governments were there for. Pete had tried not to take his father's harsh words to heart, as he knew he was struggling to find a job in the run-up to the holidays, which made him short-tempered at times, but at times it did feel that whatever Pete did, in the eyes of his father it would always be wrong.

Pete and Barney chatted a while longer about the ongoing highs and lows of being a football supporter, with the older man glancing at his watch every other minute until he eventually brought the conversation to a halt.

"I'm sorry, Pete, but I really have to get going now. Mrs Barney has arranged for the tree to be delivered, and I have to be at home when it arrives as she is going out to visit a friend for the day. You stay put for a while longer and get properly warmed through. And don't go worrying about the bill. You can have this one on me." Barney finished off his drink, stood up, and steadied himself with the aid of his stick. "If you can make it, I'm sure I could get you into the carol service. It is an amazing evening. There'll be lots of children your age there."

"I'm not sure, Barney," Pete replied flatly. "My Mum has my little sister to look after in the evening, and I don't have anyone else who could take me."

"Hmm," said Barney thoughtfully. "That is unfortunate. But, if you can make it yourself, I will ensure you get home safely. Here," he said, producing a card from his coat pocket, "take this card with my work number on it, and you can get your mother to speak to me. I'm sure things can be sorted out. It would be a real shame to miss out. It's taking place a week today. Okay then, I'll be seeing you, bonny lad," said Barney, also bidding farewell to the other customers and Rosie as he headed for the exit.

Pete reached over to the window and wiped away the condensation with the sleeve of his coat. The world outside was beginning to stir at last, with half a dozen pedestrians bypassing each other as they made their way across the narrow Dunelm footbridge.

Chapter 8

Ghostbusters

Pete was walking by himself over to the Languages block. With only two days of the term remaining before the holidays officially began, the school as a whole was in a state of barely suppressed jubilation. Just before he entered the building, Pete was surprised to find Jake approaching him, as he was supposed to be over the sports centre getting ready for PE.

"Hi, Pete. I just wanted to let you know that I have a spare ticket for *Ghostbusters* tomorrow night. Would you like to go? My father will drop us off and pick us up afterwards."

Pete had been stubbornly holding out against Jake's charm offensive all week. No amount of apologies or attempts at humour had been successful enough to return the friendship to how it had been prior to the previous week's disco.

"Why don't you take your girlfriend?" replied Pete, displaying no hint of a thaw in his frosty attitude.

"I don't want to take Charlotte," sighed Jake earnestly. "I want you to go. After all, we've been talking about little else for weeks."

With the song from the highly anticipated blockbuster movie riding high in the music charts, the whole country had gone *Ghostbusters*-crazy. The song promo, containing a compilation of clips from the movie, had been regularly featured on *Top of the Pops*, whetting the appetite of the two boys.

Pete hesitated in the doorway, while dozens of people pushed past him.

"Come on, Pete," urged Jake, mindful he had to dash halfway across the school grounds. "I'm going to be late. Please."

Pete looked Jake in the eye, and after a couple of seconds he acquiesced. "Why not?"

"Yes," shouted Jake, punching the air in delight. "Right, got to go," he said, already running. "We'll pick you up at five tomorrow if I don't see you before. See you."

The gesture from Jake lifted Pete's spirits. All week long at school, Pete had been a figure of detachment, still reeling from and coming to terms with the events of the week before. The only thread of consolation was that his humiliation at the hands of Carter had not become public knowledge. This, as well as not wishing to be labelled a grass, were the primary reasons for Pete staying tight-lipped about his maltreatment. There had been some knowing smirks among Carter's gang whenever Pete came within range of them, but nothing more verbally damaging. Pete guessed this could only be because Carter was one warning away from expulsion, and the thug would be writing his own suicide note if he allowed word of his actions to reach a wider audience.

"Close the door please, Pete," asked Mrs Watson, as he finally entered the classroom.

As the class busied themselves with removing their coats and getting their textbooks ready, Frances greeted Pete brightly.

"Morning, Pete."

"Hi, Frances."

"Pete, I need to ask you a favour," she said.

Pete didn't attempt to disguise his surprise.

"But not now," she whispered, as the class began to settle down. "I'll catch you afterwards."

"Ah, there you are," said a visibly relieved Frances, when she spied Pete in the corridor. She was the last pupil to leave the French classroom and thought Pete may have got fed up waiting for her. "I'm on my way over to a school council meeting in the English block. Are you going that way?"

"Yes," he croaked nervously. Pete would follow her to hell and back if it meant he could win her heart.

"Super. It's just that, as you know, we have our French oral mocks in our second week back after Christmas. The problem is, as I've just been explaining to Mrs Watson, I'll be missing the first week of school as I'm away skiing with my parents. That means we don't have much time at all to rehearse for our test before the actual day, as when I return we'll have so many other exams that week too."

Pete and Frances were required to recite from memory a long passage where their French alter egos, Henri and Marion, had to go shopping for food for a family barbecue, followed by preparing the food and accessories before everyone arrived.

"Anyway, I was thinking, and I don't want to impose upon you, so don't feel obliged or anything," she rambled, "but if you could find time to meet up for French practice early in the New Year that would be such a benefit to us."

Pete wanted to leap into the air with joy. "Erm, yes. I can't see that being a problem, Frances."

"Great," she said. "So, shall we say Thursday, 3rd January, at 10 a.m. by the horse statue in the Market Place?"

Pete pretended to give it ample consideration before agreeing. If she had suggested Timbuktu and the only way to get there was by foot, he would willingly have set off there and then, and to hell with *Ghostbusters*, Christmas, and everything else.

"Right, that's a date then," confirmed Frances, beginning to walk off alone. "I hope you have a good Christmas."

"You too, Frances."

Pete stood still and watched her go, unable to believe how his world in the space of an hour had turned around completely.

"We have got to go and see that again over the holidays," beamed Pete, skipping down the cinema steps into North Road.

"That is what we should become when we leave school, Pete," said an equally enthusiastic Jake. "Forget working in a boring bloody bank or in a shop. We should become real-life spook zappers. What an amazing job that would be."

"I'm so pleased I came now, Jake. Cheers for asking."

"That's what friends are for, Pete."

The boys walked in the direction of the bus station at the top of North Road. Waiting for them somewhere in among all of the parked cars, and taxis awaiting their next fare, was Jake's father.

"There he is," said Jake, picking out his father's vehicle in the distance.

"How was it, boys?" asked Jake's father, as the boys climbed in.

"Great, Dad," exclaimed Jake. "We're going to become ghostbusters ourselves when we leave school."

Jake's father chuckled drily, pulling away from the kerb for the five-minute drive home. "If I don't get us home pronto, I fear your mother will make me your first customer."

"Wow, it's Mum's big dinner party tonight, isn't it?"

"Oh, it's not that formal, Jake. A little Christmas get-together of her work colleagues over supper, if the truth be told. Speaking of which, as usual your mother has completely overdone it on the catering front. We could feed the entire street from what she has prepared, so if Pete would like to join us for a bite to eat, then he is more than welcome."

Jake turned his head to Pete in the back seat. "You must come, Pete. Mum's celebrating her latest book being nominated for an award. She's prepared a real feast. There's gammon, and pork roast. And we get to drink wine."

"A little drop to go with your meal, Jake, and no more."

"Go on, Pete. Say yes. Please. It'll be fun."

"I'll have to let my Mum know, but if she agrees then I'd like that, Jake. Thank you, Mr Rigby."

"My pleasure, Pete. You can call her from our house."

"Evening all," greeted Jake's father, to the family members and houseguests assembled in the lounge. "The travellers return."

Pete removed his shoes and coat in the porch, before tentatively entering the room.

Jake's mother, a tall, thin woman with short, black hair neatly styled into a bob, wandered into the room from the kitchen. Brandishing an electric carving knife and wearing a kitchen apron, her features were flushed.

"Hello, Jake. Evening, Pete," she said politely, before turning to her husband. "Howard, I'm struggling in here. I'd really appreciate a hand, please."

"Of course, darling. Jake, please introduce your friend to our guests, and show him where he can telephone his parents. Excuse me everyone, no rest for the wicked," he joked, obediently following his wife into the kitchen.

"Edward. Libby. I'd like to introduce you to Pete, my best friend from school."

"Hello, Pete," smiled the grey-haired Edward, sipping from a glass of wine as he relaxed on the sofa.

"Edward is Mum's agent," explained Jake. "If he hadn't believed in Mum's work, she would still be posting manuscripts to this day."

"Oh, I think you're being a little harsh on your mother," said Edward in mild disagreement. "It was just a matter of time before the world realised what a talent she is, and I was just happy to be able to shine a light upon her."

"And this is Libby," continued Jake, "from Mum's book publisher."

The middle-aged woman stood up and courteously shook Pete's hand.

"And, Sarah, you know."

"Hello, Pete," said Jake's eighteen-year-old sister.

"Okay," continued Jake, clapping his hands together. "I'll just show you where you can ring your Mum from."

"Kate," said Edward, pushing his empty dinner plate slowly away from himself, "if you ever decide to give up writing, a second career as chef beckons. Seriously, that meal would give Delia herself a run for her money. If my ex-wife's cooking was half as good as this, we would still be married," he joked, patting his portly stomach. "Libby," he said, turning to his colleague. "I think we have made the right decision in choosing to eat here and not at a restaurant in town."

"I think cooking's loss is our gain, Edward," pitched in Libby. "Kate has dozens of books left in her yet, and I for one cannot wait to see what she comes up with next."

"I'll drink to that," interjected Howard, raising his glass.

Jake and his sister laughed. "Father," said Sarah, eyes wide in mirth, "it's empty."

Howard glanced at his glass, and then reached over to give the bottle of burgundy in the middle of the dining table a little shake. It was nearly depleted. "Good God, we're getting through these fast. Well, then, I'd best go and fetch some more from the revered wine cellar."

"You mean to say you have a proper wine cellar?" said Edward, his eyes lighting up. "I'd like a look at that, if I may?"

"He's pulling your leg, Edward," said Kate, smiling at her husband. "Unless you happen to have a keen interest in utility rooms."

With no room in his stomach for another forkful of food, Pete placed his cutlery in the middle of his nearly empty plate, silently concurring with the sentiments aired by Edward. He had never tasted food that exquisite in his life. The saltiness of the melt in your mouth cuts of gammon had been complimented by a rich, fruity sauce that he had liberally poured over his food.

"Can we have some more wine, Dad?" asked Jake, as his father swiftly re-entered, carrying a further two bottles.

"Go on then, just a drop more and that's your lot, otherwise at this rate I'll have social services banging on the door."

With the dinner guests' wine glasses topped up, the conversation moved away from Kate's hopes for her current novel, and what future projects were in the pipeline, towards current affairs in general.

"I see that Jenkins chap has been making a nuisance of himself again," commented Edward. "He's from this neck of the woods, I believe."

Edward was referring to the Bishop of Durham, David Jenkins, and his recent claim that the Miner's Union leader, Arthur Scargill, wished to create a government system modelled on East European countries.

"Ah, the bishop," chuckled Howard. "I just think he likes to wind up the politicians and create more publicity for himself. And a good job he's doing on both scores, by the look of it."

"Of course, in the process he's being quite clever by bringing a debate into a wider forum, that of the significance of the Church in today's society," added an earnest Libby.

"Well," said Howard, the alcohol allowing his headstrong, opinionated personality to rise to the fore, "as a devout atheist, I have strong opinions on religion full stop. I really don't think, coming to the end of a millennium, it has any right to meddle in matters that doesn't concern it. In my educated opinion, religion and politics should never be mixed. One has only to look across the water at the whole Irish mess to see that. Unfortunately, there is no simple answer to Ireland, or to the current strike. But Scargill isn't helping matters by not having a referendum."

"It's terrible to see the suffering," said Libby. "I heard an interview the other day, and the deprivation being suffered by families is shocking. It tugs at the heartstrings to see those poor children having to go without. What kind of a Christmas are they going to have?"

"A bloody miserable one," said Howard. "Thatcher will never back down now. You only have to look at the cost of sending police officers to those pit sites to defend the scabs to see how determined she is to crush Scargill. It must run into millions."

"The news is so depressing," added Libby, "what with all of this violence at home, and seeing all of those poor innocent children dying of starvation in Africa. One feels powerless, but I've bought this pop song that has just been released by this Geldof fellow. I have to admit, I've not heard of most of the singers, either. What's the world coming to when it takes a pop singer to bring such a weighty agenda to the table?"

"Well, someone had to do it. Our government was obviously going to carry on ignoring it. They were well aware of what was happening in Ethiopia," said Jake, contributing to the discussion for the first time.

Pete was surprised at the way the adults listened respectfully to his opinion.

"Well, yes, but they're only pop singers," maintained Libby. "What do they know about such matters?"

"Enough to care, and embarrass the Tories into some kind of response," retorted Jake.

"But Geldof seems such a foul-mouthed bully. Have you heard him on the TV? His language is shocking," added Edward, attempting to reinforce Libby's argument.

"What's your take on this, Pete?" asked Howard. "You are the music expert after all, according to Jake."

Unsure whether this last point was a positive or negative comment regarding Pete's influence on Jake's newfound enthusiasm for pop music, he was surprised to be invited into the debate. His opinion was so rarely sought. Fortunately, the Ethiopian crisis had been made the main topic of discussion by Mr Brookes in a recent English lesson. It was to the main summary, as outlined by Mr Brookes at the end of the class debate, that Pete now turned to for inspiration.

"Well," he began, slowly attempting to recall the words verbatim, "it's an emotive subject, seeing people dying on our television screens in front of our eyes while we eat our supper. But music is an emotive force, something that has the power to move millions of people. I think Geldof has been quite clever in publicising the African issue through a pop song. In purchasing the record, people are buying and investing into the issue. It maybe scares the government if Geldof makes the song a success, as he can be seen to be speaking for the millions who have bought it. It's power to the people," he concluded, pleased to have sneaked in a reference to one of Lennon's song titles.

Edward and Libby glanced at each other, clearly surprised by Pete's well-considered reply.

Jake's father nodded his head approvingly at Pete's articulate contribution, while gleefully clapping his hands together. "Well said, Pete. I couldn't have put it better myself. It appears the comprehensive school system is teaching our kids to think for themselves and to become moral citizens after all, Libby."

"Who's for pudding?" intervened Kate, sensing a political argument brewing and keen to nip it in the bud before emotions became overheated. Grating her chair abruptly across the floor tiles, she reached over to gather up the empty plates.

"So remember, Pete. If you need us for anything at all, I've written Norman and Jean's telephone number down. I've left it on the phone table."

"Okay, Mum."

"And if anyone knocks at the door, just ignore it."

"Yes, Mum."

"And…"

"For heaven's sake, Sheila," butted in Trevor, adjusting his tie as he came down the stairs. "How's the lad meant to learn if you fuss on before we've even left the house? Carla's asleep and shouldn't wake up. He'll be fine for three hours or so. We're only a ten-minute drive away. It's only a dinner party in Shincliffe, not the other side of the world."

"I know," said Sheila, pausing to smile at her son. "I forget how much of a man he's turning into."

"Can I have some of your lager, Mum?" asked Pete.

"That's for Christmas time, Pete."

"It's the holidays, Mum. If it's not Christmas time now, it never will be. And I am nearly a man," he joked.

"Oh, go on, then," she smiled. "Take one can and one only. Make sure you mix it with plenty of lemonade. I don't want you moping around the house hung over in the morning. You'll regret it when the Hoover is switched on."

"Okay. Thanks, Mum."

"Here's the taxi," said Trevor, peering out of the front window blinds.

"Okay, love," said Sheila to her son. "Have a good evening, and I'll see you soon."

"Bye. Have a good time."

Pete spent the first part of the evening creating a new music compilation tape for his Walkman player. At 10:30, he flopped down in the sofa, and switched on the television to watch the highlights of the evening's play from the Hofmeister snooker tournament. All day long, he had been eagerly awaiting the grudge doubles semi-final game between Jimmy White and Alex Higgins on one team, and Steve Davis and Tony Meo on the other. The inimitable Dickie Davies, with his celebrated grey slick of hair, opened the programme, informing the viewer they were in for an evening of entertaining snooker. Over the next two hours, Pete was not disappointed as he watched the entire match, ending with a close victory for the White camp.

With the time way past midnight, Pete was by now fighting to stay awake. Hoping his mother would be home soon, he switched off the television set and plodded upstairs to bed. Within minutes he was fast asleep.

"Wake up, Junior. Wake…up."

Disturbed from his sleep by the persistent voice, Pete lifted his head a few inches off his pillow and peered into the gloom. As his eyes slowly adjusted to the dark, Pete was able to make out somebody a few yards away, peering out the curtains of his bedroom window. It wasn't his mother or Trevor. Strangely enough, for someone with a deep-rooted phobia of burglars, this failed to set off alarm bells in Pete's head.

"Hello. Who is that?" he asked, feeling no fear.

"Hey there, Junior," replied the stranger upon being addressed, still looking through the window. "Nice cathedral, by the way. Is it always lit up like that at night? Very quaint. So English. Anyway, now that you're back in the land of the living," he continued, turning to face Pete, "I believe we have urgent business to attend to."

Pete sat up and leaned against his bedroom wall, wrapping his duvet around him so that only his head was visible. "What are you doing in my room, mister?"

The man tutted to himself and tetchily crossed his arms. "What kind of a greeting is that? You asked for help, didn't you, Junior? Or am I in the wrong neighbourhood? Let's have a look here." The man unfolded a piece of paper from his trouser pocket and began to skim read it. "Please, John Lennon…blah blah blah … Really need some help … blah blah blah … you're my last hope."

Pete looked at the man in disbelief. Could he possibly be imagining this? To test out this theory, he dug his nails as hard as possible into the skin on his own arm, certain the pain would quickly wake him up from his dream. "Ouch," he said, swiftly letting go.

The only other explanation, he thought sleepily, was that he was the victim of an elaborate prank by Jake, Carter, or his mother. Pete instantly kicked this idea into touch too, as he realised he had not told a single person about the prayer he had made.

Pete watched the man shove the sheet of paper back into his trouser pocket. With an unmistakable thatch of golden hair, and dressed in a pink suit with a matching sweater underneath, and wearing white shoes, the person in his room was most definitely not John Lennon. The most striking aspect of the mystery stranger to Pete was his voice, clearly marking him out as being of American origin.

"But you're not John Lennon," said Pete eventually, lost for any other kind of opening line.

"You don't say," replied the man mockingly. "Well, ain't that your tough luck, buster. But he's so in demand at the moment, I'm afraid, which is why yours truly has been sent to try and help with your problems. I'm a few weeks overdue, I know, but it gets like that sometimes. The main point is I'm here now. So, let's cut to the chase, Junior, as I'm on a tight enough schedule as it is. Let's have it. Come on, spill the beans."

"Well, it's like this. There's this girl in my class at school."

The man smiled knowingly, nodding his head. "There always is, Junior, there always is. Begin at the start."

The man listened as Pete ran through his feelings for Frances, interweaving this narrative with all of his secondary issues – the infamous day in Newcastle with Liam, and the knock on effect with his parents, school, and Davey Carter. When Pete finally stopped talking, the man let out a low whistle.

"Phew, there's more going on in your life than I imagined, Junior. To put it briefly, then, the girl of your dreams doesn't know you exist, school is absolute hell due to this Carter jerk, and your parents take every opportunity to re-enact *Kramer Versus Kramer*."

Pete nodded.

"I hate to say it, Junior, but there's nothing I can do about your parents' divorce. You know the old saying – you can choose your friends, but not your family. What you're left with once the pack is shuffled, you just have to make the best of. They may be the two biggest pains in the ass in the world, but they're two pains in the ass who love their son, no matter what you think. They just have funny ways of showing it at times. Give it time, their emotional scars will heal and you will reap the benefit."

The man paused briefly before continuing.

"The day your cousin robbed the store. I guess you don't need me to tell you that wasn't the wisest thing in the world to be getting caught up in. You don't exactly strike me as gangster material, so I guess you're learning your lesson the hard way that crime doesn't pay. Especially when your cousin gets off scot-free. However, Junior, if there is a positive side to this, it's that you showed some balls there. A lot of other kids would have confessed all in order to wriggle free from the blame. You didn't. You showed some loyalty, however misguided."

Pete heard a car engine running outside and the slamming of car doors, followed by the unmistakable laugh of his mother. "I think my Mum's arriving home," he informed the stranger.

"No pressure to finish then, huh, Junior. Right, this other guy who keeps getting in your face. You get idiots like that in all walks of life, they're ten a penny. You just have to learn to stand up to them. Easier said than done, I accept that, Junior, but he won't always be bigger than you. He just sees you as an easy target. If you have the courage to stand up to him and show him you're not afraid, he'll think twice about getting at you."

The sound of a key being slid into the front door lock, followed by the high-spirited voices of Trevor and Sheila, blew life into the silent house.

"Jeez, my time's nearly up, Junior. This girl, Frances. Are you sure it's not just a crush? If it is, I can guarantee it will pass. They are as common as pimples. Give it a few weeks and you'll wonder what all the fuss was about."

Pete was unconvinced by this final piece of advice.

"Hmm, I can see by the look on your face that you don't want to hear that. But that's love for you, Junior. It's tough, whether you're seven or seventy-seven. It's an amazingly powerful force. Trust me, I've had my fingers burnt on more than one occasion. But, let's not be so defeatist. Miracles can happen. All I can suggest is, and I apologise if you have thought of this solution already, you talk to her and let her know how you feel. She's not a mind reader. She could be sat next to you thinking she is the last girl in the world you would ever want to date."

"Really?" Pete hadn't looked at the situation from that angle.

The man lifted his arms in exasperation. "Hell, Junior, how do I know? It's up to you to find out. Stand up and take a hold of the situation. Assert yourself."

Pete heard his mother's footsteps climb the stairs, pausing on the creaky floorboard outside his bedroom door, listening to hear if he was asleep. He lay back down and closed his eyes in pretence of slumber, until the landing light was switched off and she went back downstairs.

Re-opening his eyes, Pete could see no sign of the man he had just been speaking to. His eyes began to feel heavy, and he shut them until he was fast asleep.

CHAPTER 9

We All Stand Together

Pete got off the bus and set off on the short walk to the home of his aunt and uncle. With a two-day stay at his father's at an end, Pete had arranged with his mother to be picked up on neutral territory. He preferred this arrangement as it made negligible the possibility of a fresh war of words erupting.

It felt strange for Pete to be walking through the scene of so many good times, particularly as so much water had passed under the bridge since his last visit. As he turned into their street, Pete was not surprised to hear the sound of music emanating from the home of his relatives. The annual end of year party at their house was always a lively affair, with family, friends, and neighbours popping in at their convenience to drink, chat, and party. It usually commenced late afternoon, and would continue through the night until the last guest standing closed the front door on their way out into the dawn chill of a new year.

It was nearly four months to the day since Pete had last seen his cousin. In the interim Pete had not received a single phone call or letter, with the only snippets of information regarding Liam's progress gleaned third-hand from Pete's mother, following one of her frequent coffee sessions with his Aunt Angela. Although he had badly missed Liam's presence in the initial days and weeks following his departure, Pete had grown to accept the situation and no longer felt in such a confused state of transition. Now that Liam was finally home on leave, however, Pete was eager to see him once again.

The catch on the front door was up, allowing Pete to enter without knocking. Already a handful of early revellers were getting into the spirit of the occasion, as the *Grease* soundtrack blared from the speakers.

"Pete," shouted Uncle Ronnie, descending the stairs. "How are you doing? Do you want a drink?"

"No thanks, Uncle Ronnie. Is Liam around?" asked Pete.

"He was here a minute ago, son. Try out the back, he's probably having a tab."

In the kitchen, Pete's Aunt Angela was busily preparing the evening's buffet, an inviting spread of sausage rolls, open bread buns of various toppings, crisps, nuts, and pork pies.

"Hello, Pete. Your Mum just rang to say she'll be here soon."

"Thanks, Aunty."

"If you're looking for Liam, he's in the backyard."

"Thanks."

"Now then, fella," grinned Liam, as Pete entered the yard, closing the door behind him.

Liam was leaning against the sidewall, bathed in the light from the kitchen. His appearance was markedly different from the last time Pete had seen him. His hair was shaved off, and his face appeared thinner and more defined. Pete stood there awkwardly, unable to think of anything to say. Several seconds of silence passed.

"How's your Christmas been?" asked Liam, breaking the silence. "Did Santa Claus bring you everything you asked for?" he lightly mocked.

Pete resented the question, with the hidden insinuation that he was still a child.

"I got money for my main present," replied Pete, "as well as some bits and pieces."

"Have you seen your Dad?"

"I've just come from there."

"I saw him a few days ago. Bumped into him in town, so bought him a few pints and repaid him the two hundred quid I owed him for stumping up to get me off the hook, plus a little extra for his trouble."

Pete was puzzled by this statement, convinced that his father had only given the store manager half that amount.

"He's alright, your old man," Liam continued, "especially for helping me out with that bit of bother. He told me the ins and outs of what happened to you. Bloody unlucky that you ran into a teacher from your school. The chances on that happening must have been a million to one. I bet your face was a picture when you saw him in class, though," he laughed.

"It wasn't funny, Liam. I was bricking it."

"I know, I shouldn't laugh. I'm proud of you, actually, for not grassing me up. Your Dad said it was pretty tough for you at school for a while. I'm sorry for that." Liam pulled out a wad of notes from his back pocket of his jeans, and unrolled two notes. "Take these," he said, handing Pete the money. "It's the least I can do."

"Ta, Liam," said Pete, stuffing them into his coat pocket without looking at them. "What's the army like, then?"

At the mention of his employers, Liam's smile faded. He looked up to the clear, dark sky. "It's alright," he shrugged. "Not exactly as I'd planned, but few things ever are."

"What do you mean?"

Liam cast a glance to the house before continuing. "Listen, Pete. I'll let you into a secret, but I don't want you breathing a word to anyone, especially my mother or the old fella. It's been little short of a nightmare. I'm just putting a brave face on it, as they are proud as punch. It's all they've talked about since I came home on leave. How can I tell them what it's really been like, and then expect them to put a front on for all the family and friends?"

Liam paused to take a heavy draw on his cigarette.

"The bloody sergeant there, he makes your life a misery. Picking on you all the time, always on your back for the smallest thing. A speck of dirt on your shirt, boots not being shiny enough, even for missing a hair when shaving."

Pete couldn't believe the tale of woe Liam was describing. He never imagined Liam in the role as victim. He had always been the strong one.

"That's not the worst of it, either."

What could be worse, thought Pete to himself.

"The other lads there. Cockneys, mainly. They hate me. Hate my accent, the way I act and look. I can't put a foot right in their eyes."

"You have no mates at all?" asked Pete, incredulously.

"Oh, I've got mates. A few Jocks, a couple of lads from Yorkshire, but the Cockneys, the Cockney mafia we call them, they run the show in our quarters. What they say goes."

"Can't you tell someone about them?"

"Grass? More than your bloody life's worth, mate. I've had enough beatings already. Black eyes, dead legs,

Chinese burns. I don't want to risk any more. I don't think I can take anymore. Anyway, I've made my bed now, so I have to lie in it."

"You can always leave if you hate it."

Liam gave Pete a cold stare. "Quit? I'm no quitter, Pete. And what is there to come back to? The dole queue, that's all there is up here for people like me. Or end up with a lass up the duff, with your name on the council house waiting list, like Stevey."

"Stevey's going to be a Dad?"

"Didn't you know? Aye, it was that lass he went with a while ago, can you believe. That's his life knackered before it's even begun. He'll be eighteen when the kid's born."

Liam dropped his butt onto the ground and stood on it. "A word of advice, Pete, and an apology is due, I think." Liam paused, struggling to find the correct words to begin. "I'm sorry for those times when I was horrible to you, especially about living in a posh house. Truth be told, I guess I'm jealous. But I just want you to promise me that you'll stick in and work hard at school, and don't end up leaving with barely two qualifications to rub together like me. You've got the brains and you're at a good school, so do your best, mate."

Pete was so shocked by Liam's unexpected candour that he could only nod in reply.

"Right, Pete, let's go inside. I'm bloody freezing."

"Come in, Pete," beamed Jake, ushering his friend into the welcoming warmth.

Pete slipped off his shoes, hung up his coat and went into the lounge.

"We've got the house to ourselves, Pete. My parents are away until Wednesday, and Sarah won't be home until late. No Charlotte, either. Tonight is strictly a lad's night only. Oh great, you remembered to bring them," said Jake, eyeing the plastic carrier bag by Pete's side.

Taking the bag from Pete, Jake removed the selection of albums and quickly looked them over. "*Plastic Ono Band*, *Abbey Road*, *Imagine*, *Revolver*, and *Rubber Soul*," he said, excitedly reeling off the titles, before hesitating like a child on Christmas morning undecided about which newly unwrapped toy to play with first. "Which one shall we put on first?"

"If we play them in chronological order," suggested Pete, "*Rubber Soul* was the first to be released, in 1966."

"That sounds good to me, Pete. You're a walking encyclopedia about the Beatles, aren't you?"

Jake set side one away, and the boys sat down to listen to "Drive My Car."

"Good choice, Pete," he said, as the first track finished. "That was a fantastic song."

"It gets better, Jake," replied Pete, relieved by his positive response. He had dreaded his friend turning up his nose at the choice. "Actually, Jake, I'd like you to have this record, as a birthday present for yesterday."

"For me? Wow, thanks."

"I was in Sunderland earlier today, and bought myself a copy as well from the second-hand shop."

"Oops, I nearly forgot," said Jake, rising up off the sofa and disappearing into the kitchen, returning a minute later with two full half-pint glasses, and a wide grin on his face.

"What's that, then?" asked Pete, noticing the golden hue of the glass contents.

"This, my good friend, is Norway's finest cider. A head thumping six percent."

"Is that strong?" asked Pete.

"Strong enough for our purposes, Pete," he giggled. "I've got a two-litre bottle for tonight to see out the old year in style, as well as an extra special surprise for later in the evening," he added intriguingly.

Pete had limited experience of drinking alcohol, only in small amounts when mixed with lemonade, and always under the watchful eye of his mother or father. To have free access to such a large quantity, free of all parental shackles, was an enticing prospect.

The two boys played the collection of records all the way through, with an inquisitive Jake asking Pete a whole range of questions about the career of The Beatles. Just before midnight, Jake briefly went upstairs.

"And for my second and last trick," he said upon his return, one hand concealing something behind his back. "Ta daa," he announced, showing Pete what he was holding like a magician pulling a white rabbit from a black top hat. Pete examined the three white, cigarette shaped objects on the palm of Jake's hand.

"Cigarettes?" Pete asked.

"Of an illegal nature, yes. To be more precise, Pete, they are technically known as joints," he proclaimed, with knowing authority.

"Wow," said Pete. He was aware of the influence of drugs on the members of The Beatles, but had never partaken in any shape or form himself. Pete had never even smoked a full cigarette. A simultaneous wave of anticipation and fear shook him at the thought that he was in the presence of real, actual drugs.

"Where did you get them from?" asked Pete.

"Ask no questions, tell no lies," replied Jake. "Let's just say I have connections," he added mysteriously.

The sixty-second countdown to the New Year had begun on the silent television screen, with the camera alternating between the crowds that had flocked to Trafalgar Square in London, and Big Ben, its pointer tantalisingly close to the hour.

"Quick, Jake. Get the stylus ready."

When the countdown reached zero, and Happy New Year was flashed up onto the screen in bright red text, Jake placed the needle at the beginning of track one. The boys had decided to swap the traditional chimes of the famous landmark with the altogether more funereal tolls at the beginning of "Mother," the first track from Lennon's first solo album.

"Goodbye 1984. Welcome 1985!" shouted Jake, turning the dimmers down to a dull setting. "Right, Pete," he said, putting one of the joints into his mouth and striking a match. "Let's start the party."

Pete watched apprehensively as Jake took a long draw, eyes closed as if in a state of hypnosis, deriving maximum enjoyment from it before exhaling slowly through his nose. Jake reached over to Pete and handed him the rolled item.

"Use your empty glass to flick ash into," suggested Jake, flopping back into his seat.

Feeling Jake scrutinising him intensely, Pete braced himself for his first taste of narcotics, quite unsure what to expect. He held it to his mouth and took a quick, tenuous puff before handing it back to Jake.

"No, no," said Jake, "you're doing it all wrong. You need to suck it in, hold it a while, and then breath out through your nose. Go on, have another go."

Pete attempted to follow Jake's instructions. A second later he was bent double, racked by a coughing fit as he choked on the smoke. He felt as if he needed an extinguisher to quell the fire in his lungs.

Jake was rolling all over the sofa in hysterics. "You're supposed to hold it, not suck it in all the way," he managed to say through attacks of laughter.

Pete tried again, with more success this time.

"These lyrics," began Pete, on a train of thought a few minutes later, suddenly feeling uninhibited and compelled to talk with someone interested enough to be prepared to listen, "perfectly capture and communicate how I feel about the divorce of my parents. I don't know of any other singer who writes songs like this. You know, Jake, I spent days, months, years even, living in the ever decreasing hope that my parents would get back together, things would return to normal, and life would be one long road of happiness."

Jake nodded understandingly as Pete spoke. With every word, Pete felt the emotional chains that had been tightly wrapped around him for as long as he could remember begin to slacken and unravel. His negative feelings were replaced by a wave of emancipation.

"But," continued Pete, "I woke up one day and realised that things aren't the same as in the movies. There is no happy ever after, and the sooner I realised it and accepted it the better. That's why I really enjoyed the dinner party here a few weeks ago. It was great to see a whole family gathered together, enjoying each other's company."

Pete was not prepared for what Jake said next.

"Don't judge a book by its cover, to use an apt metaphor."

"What. You have problems, too?' asked Pete.

Jake's face flushed red. "Yeah, but I'm trying to put them behind me. This school was supposed to be my fresh start."

"There were rumours about your mother when you started at school, whether she was the writer Kate Randall, and also about you getting expelled from your previous school."

"The public school scandal, you mean?"

"Yes. Were you kicked out?"

Jake paused to stare down at the carpet, wrestling with the complex emotions he was struggling to express. "Yes," he said finally.

"Which school was it?"

"I boarded at a school in Yorkshire. I was allowed home at weekends, but the weekdays were grim. I never want to go through something like that again. It was a prison."

"Surely your parents only wanted to give you the best start in life, so that you can go on to a good university and get a really top job," Pete responded, playing devil's advocate.

"Maybe," he conceded, "but to get the best start in life I wasn't prepared to be rogered."

"Rogered?" asked Pete, not fully understanding where Jake was leading.

"Fucked up the arse at lights out," said Jake, bluntly spelling it out. "Some of them weirdos don't want to know the first thing about girls, and I include some of the teachers in that, not just the kids. All they want to do is dominate you physically and mentally, and that means in every way. That is how they get their kicks. But I wasn't having it. One of the pervert teachers tried it on with me once. Philpott, his name was. I tried to ignore him at first, but he kept persevering, not taking no for an answer. In the end, I grabbed hold of his wandering hand, trapped it between the slats of the bed frame and my mattress, and jumped up and down as hard as I could. That taught him a lesson he won't forget in a hurry."

Pete found this disclosure difficult to believe, particularly in a public school where you should expect to feel safe. "But that's wrong, getting expelled for that," protested Pete, firmly back on Jake's side. "Surely that was an act of self-defence."

Jake gave a wistful smile. "No, that's not the reason I was expelled. What Philpott tried to do to me came out in the wash after an unofficial inquiry, but the school wanted to brush it all under the carpet, have me and Philpott shake hands and conveniently put it all down to a misunderstanding."

"So why were you expelled, then?"

"Well, because I told the headmaster that if he thought I was going to forgive and forget with Philpott, then he was a bigger cunt than Philpott would ever be," explained Jake, his invective loaded with deep, burning resentment.

Pete was speechless.

"My parents were summoned the next day after my little outburst," continued Jake, "and I was ordered by the school to pack my things and leave. Pete, I was so relieved, and I thought that would be an end to the matter. But for weeks afterwards, maybe even now, I was made to feel by my parents as if it was my fault entirely. I just don't understand why I should be blamed for defending myself. What was I supposed to do? Just go with the flow, accept the unpleasant stuff as par for the course, keep my mouth shut for the next few years and come out of it a stronger person? That's what parents are like. They just want everything to be plain sailing, ignoring the first signs of aggravation you cause them. Well, balls to that. I wouldn't have lasted another month. I had to cross the line to force the school's hand."

"What would you have done," asked Pete, "if they hadn't thrown you out?"

Jake shrugged his shoulders. "I don't know. Run away, possibly. I have a half-brother in London. I could have stayed with him until I was old enough to look after myself. Maybe I would have…" he began, before allowing the thought to trail away.

"What time is it?" asked Pete after an awkward pause, keen to lighten the mood a little.

"Nearly 12:30. Shall we have another smoke?"

"I don't want to sound like a killjoy," began Pete, "but is there any chance of a coffee? My head's spinning a little."

"Good shout. I'll just go and put the kettle on. Sarah will be home soon, too. I don't want her to find us both comatose."

"Thank you," said Pete.

"There was one thing I've been meaning to ask you, Pete," said Jake, upon returning from the kitchen with two steaming cups of black coffee. "Now seems as good a time as any, seeing as we are coming clean about stuff with each other. Why were you in such a bad mood with me after the disco? Was it really because of Charlotte?"

Put on the spot suddenly, it was Pete's turn to feel awkward. "Well, a little," he said sheepishly, "but not for the obvious reason that I was unhappy about being left on my own. Something happened to me on the way home. In my head I blamed you because if you had been with me, I wouldn't have walked that way home, and what happened wouldn't have happened."

"I don't follow. Helen told me that you walked her home, and she said later that everything appeared normal."

"After I left Helen," explained Pete, "I bumped into Carter and his mates."

"I'm starting to not like the sound of this Carter. So what happened, exactly?" pressed Jake.

Pete quickly ran through the events of the evening as he remembered them.

"They did all that to you?" said Jake in disbelief. "What did your parents say?"

"You're the first person I've told, Jake. I was too scared to tell anyone. Plus, what good will grassing him up do? It's my word against his."

Jake looked up to the ceiling, his face a mask of anger. "Carter's a bloody idiot, and he's gone too far this time. What will it take for him to stop acting like Rambo? At least your cousin will sort him, won't he?"

"No, as I'm not going to tell him."

"Well then, that just leaves the two of us. Carter may have the muscle, but we have the brains, Pete. It's time for us to fight back, to stand up and be men. I'm not sure how, but give me time to think about it between now and school. Revenge is a dish best served cold, after all."

Pete shivered at the prospect of instigating conflict with Carter, and hoped Jake's display of bravado was just talk.

"Let's get out of here and go for a walk," said Pete, the cup of coffee removing some of the fuzziness from his mind. "I want to see what 1985 looks like."

CHAPTER 10

Closest Thing To Heaven

The majority of the housing estate roads were barely passable due to the heavy overnight snowfall, leaving Pete with no option but to walk the two miles into the city centre. He embraced the prospect of the half-hour journey on foot as a labour of love, as opposed to viewing it as an obstacle. Pete was on cloud nine as he stepped out into the freezing morning, with every step taking him one step closer to Frances. He had been pining terribly for her since the end of term, and wild horses weren't going to keep him away today.

Making his way slowly along the narrow, winding footpath of Hopper's Wood, currently buried under a foot of virginal snow, Pete was enchanted by the spectacle that the wintry elements had created. It wouldn't have surprised him if at any moment he were to bump into Mr Tumnus, such was the resemblance to the mythical wonderland of Narnia.

Pete was beginning to regret not dressing appropriately for such testing conditions. Without giving any prior consideration to the negative aspects of the bleak weather, Pete had dressed in his burgundy Fred Perry T-shirt, navy sta-prest trousers, and black Harrington jacket. Wellington boots were passed over in favour of a pair of training shoes. Sacrificing practical clothing in favour of more fashionable items was now causing him a great deal of discomfort. He was shin deep in snow; the bottom half of his trousers were soaked; and his feet were frozen cold.

As he neared the rendezvous point, Pete grew increasingly nervous. An assortment of questions were flying around in his head, the chief one being would Frances be waiting for him by the statue in the Market Place? Or would she have fallen victim to the elements, opting out of travelling into town in case she was unable to make her way home should the conditions worsen. If Frances did arrive as arranged, Pete was undecided whether to come clean about the depth of his feelings for her, or to adopt a more surreptitious approach and play matters by ear. In a perverse way, a small part of Pete hoped Frances failed to show up, taking the matter out of his own hands.

It was 9:50 a.m. by the church clock when Pete arrived at the statue in the Market Place. He had ten minutes to spare, but did not succumb to the temptation to warm up in a nearby shop until the designated time, in case she appeared in his temporary absence and assumed he was not coming.

As the clock announced the hour, Pete looked all around him for a sight of Frances. Apart from the occasional, determined shopper, the town was a victim of the weather with most people sensibly choosing to stay safe and warm at home.

By 10:10 a.m., Pete was slowly resigning himself to the fact that his efforts had been in vain. This left him with the difficult decision of how much longer to remain outdoors in sub-zero temperatures before admitting defeat.

At 10:25 a.m., feeling extremely frozen and miserable, he decided to call it a day. Walking to the newsagent's shop to get warmed through, Pete had just begun to browse through the latest issue of *Smash Hits* when he felt a tap on his shoulder.

"Surprise," smiled Frances when he turned around. She had a red woollen hat pulled down over her head, and a matching scarf wrapped around her neck. All that was visible was her apologetic face. "I am so sorry, Pete. I was waiting for ages for a bus. None came, so I had no choice but to walk in. It only takes fifteen minutes, but I was convinced I was going to miss you. I'm so pleased you're still here."

"It's not your fault, Frances," said Pete, not prepared to apportion any blame in her direction whatsoever now that she had arrived. "You're here now, that's all that matters."

"I don't know about you, but I am in dire need of a piping hot drink. I am so cold. Shall we go to Treats? I'm sure the staff won't mind us doing our work there. It should be really quiet today."

A first floor cafe located in Silver Street, thirty seconds walk from where they were standing, Treats was popular with city centre workers, shoppers, and students, for its selection of savoury and sweet pastries, mouth-watering home-baked cakes, and hot beverages. Pete had visited on several occasions with his mother, and without hesitation always ordered the deluxe hot chocolate drink, topped with frothy cream.

While Frances went to order their drinks, Pete sat down at the window table overlooking the pedestrianised street below.

"The lady's going to bring them over," said Frances, joining Pete a minute later. "I suggest we have a chinwag for ten minutes while we have our drinks and get warmed up, run through our French homework, and then have another drink before we go on our way. Is that okay with you, Pete?"

"Fine," he replied. By his estimation that amounted to an hour or so in her company, even longer if he could think of something to chat about. Pete was so scared that he would bore her, and that she would be on her way home in the shortest time necessary.

"Oh, I love this time of year," she said, removing her coat, hat and scarf. "The optimism of a new year, and the days like a fresh canvas just waiting to be filled in. Did you have a nice Christmas?" she enquired.

"Yes, thanks. You?"

"Oh, it was fantastic. It was the turn of my parents to play host to all of our relatives, so it was a bit hectic. But fun. They've all gone home now, so I'm just enjoying the peace until my holiday."

"When do you go?" asked Pete.

"The day after tomorrow. I can't wait," she said, unable to disguise the excited tone in her voice.

The cafe assistant brought over two large mugs of hot chocolate to their table.

"Thank you so much," said Frances politely.

"You're welcome, my dears. Enjoy."

"Whereabouts in Europe are you going?" asked Pete, picking up the thread of the conversation.

"Champex-Lac in Valais, Switzerland. The pistes are fantastic this time of year. Have you skied before, Pete?"

"Not on snow, I haven't. I had a lesson at the artificial ski slope in Sunderland once. It was a bit of a disaster, actually. I spent more time sliding down on my backside than doing any actual skiing."

Frances laughed. "You just have to practice, that's all. Speaking of which," she said, taking a sip of her drink, "shall we begin to run through the test? If we get another snow flurry anytime soon, then I must head off, otherwise I'll be like a walking snowman by the time I get home."

Half an hour passed, during which time they worked through the required passages three times without any major problems.

"Well, I think that's enough work for one day, Pete," Frances said, peering outside. "The weather appears to be in our favour, so I'm sure I can manage another hot chocolate."

"I'll get them," said Pete, rising from the table.

"There's something I'd like to say to you, Pete," began Frances, upon his return to the table.

"Yes," said Pete, a little confused as to where Frances was heading.

"That night at the disco and my behaviour towards you. I'd just like to apologise," she said.

"There's nothing to apologise for, Frances," lied Pete.

"Well, I have to disagree with you there. I'd overdone it a tad with the drink. If I came across as a bit of a bitch, then please forgive me. I wouldn't want you thinking I always act like that."

As she looked at Pete with her apologetic expression, he sensed a sudden air of vulnerability about her. Pete felt an urge to reach over, squeeze her hand, and tell her it was fine. Instinct told him that this was his moment to reveal his true feelings. "It's fine, Frances," he said awkwardly. Trapped by his own indecision and shyness, Pete failed to act on his impulse.

"Two more hot chocolates, my dears," interrupted the assistant, placing the drinks in front of them. "That's my takings doubled for the day," she joked.

The brief disruption to their conversation broke the spell of intimacy that had briefly descended upon them. The moment was gone, lost forever. Frances regained her composure, her usual, bubbly character returned, and the pair spent the final twenty minutes of their time together drinking their hot chocolates, with Frances doing most of the talking and Pete listening attentively.

"What time is it?" asked Pete, sitting up and rubbing his eyes, annoyed that the bedroom light had been switched on in the middle of the night. It had taken him hours to drop off to sleep, as his mind had been preoccupied with thoughts of Frances, following their meeting earlier in the day.

"Time you began to give your head a shake, Junior, and wake up to the opportunity you managed to blow today."

His eyes rapidly adjusting to the bright light, Pete recognised the man with the golden hair and pink suit from his previous visit. "You don't have to tell me," admitted Pete. "I know that was the best chance I've ever had to ask her out."

"Best chance! Junior, you had her gift-wrapped on a plate," said the stranger. "It was perfect. What stopped you?"

"I was scared."

"Scared of what, Junior? Of acting like a man instead of a mouse? Jeez," he said in exasperation. "She took you into her confidence. She trusts you. You were halfway there, Junior, but she can't spell it all out for you. You have to do some of the work yourself."

"So what's my next step?" asked Pete.

The man scratched his head. "There's nothing you can do for a week or so, now she's going away on holiday. Use the time wisely to think of a fresh set of tactics."

"You make it sound like a game," Pete observed.

"It is a game. The game of life, and you only get one turn at it. It's your roll of the dice next, your turn to make some of the running. What you'll learn, Junior, is that broads don't just come to you, especially the really special ones. So get your thinking cap on and come up with something that makes you a bit different, and sets you apart from the herd."

"Like what?"

The man held his hands up, nonplussed. "This is your shout, Junior. The only advice I can offer is to try and create some mystery about yourself; something that arouses her curiosity and grabs her attention. Women like that."

"Okay."

"Good. Now grab some more sleep, Junior, and I'll see you around."

"Wait," said Pete. "Are you … are you who I think you are?"

The man allowed himself a wry knowing smile. "Just call me Barry. As I said, Junior, I'll be seeing you."

CHAPTER 11

No Retreat No Surrender

"Have you written your message for the school mag yet," asked Jake, as the friends made their way home from school at the end of a typically cold day in late January. "The deadline for handing them in is tomorrow at the latest."

Jake was referring to the window of opportunity that had arisen to submit a romantic dedication to the forthcoming Valentine's edition of the school magazine.

"No, not yet. Have you?"

"Yes. I'm handing it in tomorrow. It's more than my life's worth not to. It's all Charlotte's gone on about in the last couple of weeks. She's obsessed with love at the moment, and if I don't declare my affection publicly, I'll be well and truly in the doghouse."

"What makes you think I like someone, anyway?" Pete asked cagily.

"Oh, come on, Pete. I can tell you carry a torch for Frances. It's obvious."

Pete blushed. He knew it was pointless attempting to hide anything from Jake. "I've tried," he began, in reference to Jakes's question, "but whenever I try to write something, I just can't find the words, or my Mum will be hovering in the background wondering what I'm up to, or Carla comes into my room and starts mucking about with my records. I just don't have any privacy at home. There's always someone looking over my shoulder," he complained.

"Why not come to my house now," suggested Jake cheerily, "and I'll give you a hand at writing something. My parents won't be home until later as they go shopping on a Wednesday. That should be long enough to finish the job."

With the clock ticking until the closing date, Pete felt Jake's offer was too good to turn down.

"Right. That's the kettle and central heating switched on," said Jake. "Give me five minutes to make the coffee, and we will have the perfect atmosphere to compose a killer verse."

Pete did not share Jake's optimism. He had a feeling it was going to take more than a cup of Nescafe and a Kit Kat beside a warm radiator to awake the bard in him.

Twenty minutes later, Pete was feeling the heat, both physically and metaphorically. He was finding it no easy matter to create a literary stanza that did justice to his affections for Frances, within the required twenty-five words or less. It felt to Pete like a competition prize tiebreaker, where you had to state with a paucity of words why you should be the person chosen to embark on the holiday of a lifetime or drive away in the latest model motor car. The irony of the correlation between his attempts at winning the heart of Frances, and coming out the victor in a contest hit Pete right between the eyes. He figured that, as he had never won anything in his life to date, why should he begin now?

Popping the final piece of biscuit into his mouth, Pete looked forlornly at his blank piece of paper, before throwing his pen down in frustration.

"Hey, don't be so defeatist," said Jake, with half an eye on *Countdown*.

"It's okay for you," said Pete. "You already have a girlfriend. You don't have to run the risk of humiliation and having the entire world laugh at you."

"You're right," said Jake, sitting up straight and adopting a serious manner. "Let's look a little closer at the task in hand. First, it has to be clear enough to ensure that Frances knows it is intended for her."

"Okay," said Pete, writing down 'Frances' on the paper. "It's a start. One word down, 24 to go."

"Secondly, it has to strike the right tone. Too serious and she'll run a mile, but too jokey and Frances will think it's a wind-up."

The whole exercise was beginning to feel like homework to Pete, rather than the bit of fun he had been anticipating. "Sounds more like a job for Shakespeare," Pete noted.

"You're not wrong there," Jake agreed, thoughtfully chewing the tip of his biro. "Finally," he added, "and this is the tricky part. It has to offer clues as to the sender's identify, without revealing it completely. Right, let's get to work."

After a great deal of bouncing potential phrases off each other, scribbling down what were deemed to be the best, crossing out unnecessary words, and ordering and re-ordering the words that remained, the boys ended up with as honed a verse as they could manage in the limited time available to them.

"That's it," Pete said. "I'm about as happy as I'm ever going to be with it."

Jake took the sheet of paper from him. "I'll read it aloud slowly," he said, "and we can try and imagine it is Frances reading it for the first time. Okay?"

Pete agreed.

"For Frances – your smile lights up my day; makes me feel so alive. My feelings for you are not a crime. Be my Valentine."

Jake finished reading and nodded his approval. "Yes, that gets my vote. It gets away from the clichéd 'roses are red' drivel that most people write."

"Just one more favour, Jake."

"What?"

"Could you pop it into the submissions box at school tomorrow when you hand yours in?"

"No problem. How could I deprive your beloved of reading the verse you have covered in sweat, blood, tears, and Kit Kat crumbs?" he laughed.

Pete joined in with the laughter, more in relief that he had managed to produce something for the magazine than total satisfaction with his efforts.

Having finally done something positive to set out his feelings for Frances, a brief surge of empowering confidence ran through him. It was an alien feeling, which in that brief instant transformed Pete from a shy, insecure fourteen-year-old who experienced palpitations at the mere thought of displaying romantic inclinations, into someone with a palpable vision of clarity that made him believe anything was attainable. It was as if Pete had been trapped for years in a room with no doors, before one magically appeared, through which lay a path stretched out as far as the eye could see. All Pete felt he had to do was to walk down the path and take with one swoop what he felt was rightfully his. All that now remained was to wait for the Valentine's issue to be printed, and hope the sentiment worked its magic.

Now that the dreaded verse was accomplished, Pete sat back in his seat, keen to bring up with his friend something that was beginning to bug him. "Jake, do you ever see weird things, like people who aren't there?" he tentatively asked.

Jake gave Pete a searching look, unsure if his friend was pulling his leg. "Like ghosts, you mean?"

"Possibly. Or just people who have conversations with you."

"Like an imaginary friend?"

Pete nodded solemnly.

"Phew," said Jake, scratching his head, wondering where this unexpected direction in conversation was leading. "According to my parents, I had one when I was three or four, apparently. Not that I can remember him that well. Cedric, I think his name was. Why Cedric and not Bill, Ted, or Tom, I couldn't really say. Why do you ask?"

"No reason," Pete replied casually.

"Hey," said Jake excitedly. "You haven't been talking to a ghost, have you? That would be cool. So *Ghostbusters*."

"No," said Pete, in his most convincing "don't be silly" tone, while he frantically thought of a reason as to why he would wish to broach such a strange topic out of the blue. "Carla said she had been talking to an imaginary friend the other day, that's all. She says he keeps appearing when no one else is in the room. It's been freaking me out a little when I'm home alone. I guess she's watched too many My Little Pony cartoons."

Pete's stomach was beginning to rumble, a not too subtle reminder that it was way beyond his teatime. His mother would also be wondering why he hadn't returned home from school yet.

"I'd best be getting off, Jake," said Pete, arising from the sofa and walking into the porch to pull on his coat and shoes.

"Before you go," began Jake, "there's something I haven't told you."

"What's that?"

Jake had a wide grin on his face. "I think I've found the perfect opportunity to get back at Carter; something that will shut him up once and for all," he announced.

"What do you have in mind?" gulped Pete, content to have allowed the dust to settle on any plans for revenge. Carter had not picked on him at all since the return to school after the holidays, and Pete was more than happy for this state of affairs to continue.

"Loose lips sink ships," Jake said, tapping the side of his nose. "Just you be ready tomorrow night at 8:30 sharp. We'll teach him a lesson he'll not forget in a hurry."

"It's nothing dangerous, is it?" asked Pete. "I can't afford to get into anymore trouble with my parents or the teachers."

"There's nothing to worry about, Pete," Jake said confidently, in an effort to reassure Pete. "You get yourself home. I'll explain further tomorrow."

"Are you going to explain what this is all about?" demanded Pete the following evening as he stood outside on his driveway. He had been dreading this moment all day. His stomach was knotted with nerves at what Jake had in store for him.

"I'll explain in a little while," said Jake. "We need to get moving. We have a busy hour or so ahead of us."

Jake swiftly led Pete all the way through the housing estate to its western boundary.

"Are we nearly there yet?" asked Pete, when they arrived at the final street, beyond which lay a mixture of fields, undeveloped wasteland and factory units.

"Not quite. Another five minutes. Come on," urged Jake, leading them down the isolated, half-mile long main road that connected Newton Moor to the village of Pity Me. When they arrived at Front Street, Jake led them down Taylor's End, an unlit, hundred-yard long dirt track, flanked on both sides by overhanging hedges.

Jake turned to Pete when the track terminated at the top of a steep embankment, and they were unable to walk any further because of the dense undergrowth that acted as a barrier between them and the dual carriageway that lay beyond.

"This is it."

"What on earth are we doing here?" Pete demanded.

"Okay, Pete. Let me ask you one question. What is Carter notorious for at school?"

"You mean apart from being a thug and a pain in the arse?"

"Apart from that."

Pete thought a moment. His mind was blank.

"I'll put it another way. If you wanted to acquire some adult night-time reading, who would you go to?"

"Carter, probably."

"That's correct. Even I know he is the school's porn king."

Carter was reputed to boast a collection of some 300 adult magazines that catered for all persuasions – straight, gay, bi, kinky – and ran a highly profitable business hiring out and selling his goods to a list of insatiable customers. What was less well known was where he kept his stock. Through the grapevine, it was known that they were not stored at his home, due to the impracticalities of secretly hoarding such a large collection.

"Imagine if it had come to my attention where Carter is currently hiding his stash," continued Jake. "Then, think again of his expected reaction should said goods be found and destroyed."

"You know where they are hidden?"

Jake's smile told its own story.

"How did you find that out?" asked Pete.

"It's a bit of a long story, so bear with me. Charlotte told me about a conversation she overheard between Sam Bainbridge and one of his friends in her geography class. Sam was bragging that he had arranged to meet one of Carter's bozos for a business transaction at this very spot. So, after you went home yesterday, I decided to come over here and hang around in the video rental shop up on the main road at the designated time, and keep an eye out for Sam or Carter's gang. Once they appeared, I stood at the end of the track and watched with my old bird-watching binoculars. I knew they'd come in handy one of these days. It was too dark to see a great deal, but it was obvious the magazines are hidden somewhere in amongst the bushes and trees. It's a good location. Let's face it, who else is going to go wandering around here? Between the two of us, it shouldn't take too long to find them."

"We're going to steal them? But we don't have anywhere to put them," protested Pete.

"Better than that. We're going to have a little pyre. Send his whole business up in smoke." Jake showed Pete a small can in the plastic bag he was carrying.

"What's that?" Pete asked.

"Just a little petrol to make sure the job gets done properly. Here. Grab this torch and let's get looking. This place gives me the creeps."

They made their way into the darkest reaches of the highway verge undergrowth, stooping to avoid the overhanging thorny branches. From the bottom of the embankment came the constant noise of cars speeding past. With both spotlights trained on the ground, the boys were looking for anything that resembled a large container.

"Ouch," shouted Pete, as a thorn on a thin branch scratched at his cheek.

"We should spread out a little," suggested Jake. "You go right and I'll go left."

Pete did as he was told, and slowly made his way along the verge, sweeping the undergrowth with the beam of his torch. A long five minutes crept by, to no avail. Beginning to believe they was wasting their time, and a little scared at being alone in such a remote spot, Pete switched off his torch and headed back to the path at the top. There was no sign of Jake.

"Jake," he hissed. Silence. "Jake."

Nothing again. Then, the faint snap of a branch, followed by rustling and heavy breathing emanating from the gloom within, interspersed by the sound of something being dragged on the ground. Pete's heart missed a beat when Jake unexpectedly popped out of the bushes.

"Give me a hand," Jake asked, struggling to drag a large, brown leather suitcase out into the open. "Surprise, surprise. Look what I've got," he boasted.

Free of the undergrowth, Jake crouched down and snapped open the locks. Pete trained the flashlight on the interior. Tightly packed inside were the foundations of Carter's illicit empire.

"Bloody hell," exclaimed Pete. "It's true."

"Are you ready to see Rome burn?" cackled Jake. He removed the cap from the container, before liberally splashing the liquid all over the contents. Taking a box of matches out of his coat pocket, Jake removed one and handed it to Pete. Jake took one for himself, lit it and dropped it into one end of the suitcase.

"Your turn, Pete."

Pete nervously struck the match on the side of the box, and threw it into the opposite end. It, too, ignited immediately, and within seconds, the fire began to greedily devour their ill-gotten gains.

Jake and Pete briefly watched, mesmerised by the orange dancing flame.

"Let's get going, Jake," said Pete, aware that the fire, so close to the route of busy traffic, would be easily visible.

Jake took hold of a large stick he had emerged with from the bushes and cautiously used it to push the lid back over the exposed interior until it was closed again. "That'll stop the fire doing any additional damage, and buy us a bit of time to put some distance between the scene of the crime," Jake said, before prodding the case into the middle of the track, well away from the shrubbery. "Come on," he said, throwing the stick away. "Let's get out of here."

Safely back on home territory, Pete began to relax. "That was great," he said. Revenge had never tasted so sweet to him.

"That'll teach the bastard a lesson he won't forget in a hurry," agreed Jake.

"We'd best be getting home, Jake. If someone has called the police, we're bound to be suspected if they catch up with us."

"We're not quite finished yet," said Jake.

This statement surprised Pete, who failed to comprehend what else they could gain by remaining out on the estate streets. "But we've done what we set out to do, Jake. I've got my revenge. What else do you have in mind?"

Jake pulled out a plastic bag that had been concealed inside his jacket, opening it to reveal approximately twenty A5-shaped magazines. "I removed these little darlings from Carter's suitcase before I met back up with you," Jake said.

"What are we going to do with them?"

"Follow me," ordered Jake. "If you thought the fire was good, just wait until you see what's next," he added mysteriously.

CHAPTER 12

How Soon Is Now?

Even by Framlington Hall standards, it had been an unusual week, full of unexpected twists and turns. The major talking point had been the immediate expulsion on Monday morning of Davey Carter, the news of which was greeted by the majority of pupils with uninhibited glee. His departure lifted the dark cloud that had been squatting over the school in recent months.

There was a great deal of speculation initially regarding Carter's abrupt exit, particularly as his gang closed ranks and remained silent on the matter. Over the next couple of days, more and more snippets of gossip emerged, until a semblance of the facts was pieced together to adequately describe what had transpired. It became known that at the beginning of the week over a dozen indignant residents from Newton Moor had personally attended the school to seek an audience with the headmaster. Included within this group were police officers, a councillor, and several teachers. All had one thing in common. At some point on Friday evening, they had been the recipients of an explicit, adult magazine, posted by hand through their letterboxes. The front covers were all rubber-stamped with the same details:

Property of Davey Carter, c/o Framlington Hall Comp.

Hauled in front of a hastily convened governors meeting, Carter was lambasted and dragged over the coals for his alleged indiscretions, before being shown the door permanently from school, his nine lives well and truly expired.

In the days that followed, Pete and Jake kept their heads down and held their nerve, keen to remain anonymous figures in the background and not have any accusing fingers pointed in their direction.

The news got even better two days later with the announcement of a wave of one-day teacher strikes, scheduled to commence the following week. The opportunity for further authorised absences was something to be applauded, as far as the pupils were concerned. It was only the next day, when the downside of the extra days off was revealed, that many were left with a bitter taste in their mouths.

From the moment Ducky the caretaker began pinning up the announcement on the notice boards around the school, the devastating news spread like wildfire.

"It's what?" wailed Pete, unable to believe what Thames had just read out to the group of students congregated around the declaration in the corridor of the English block.

"Cancelled," repeated Thames, turning away from the notice board.

"They can't do that," a voice shouted from behind.

"They bloody can, and they have," chipped in Jake.

The rumours had been flying around the school all morning that, due to the current wave of industrial action, all non-curricular, out of school hours activities would be cancelled forthwith, and now it had just been made official.

Pete was dumbstruck. The one opportunity he had been relying on for weeks to ask Frances out had been blown right out of the water.

"But why, Sir?" protested Helen to Mr Brookes, when the class moved on to their English lesson.

"I'm afraid that, unfortunately, the school disco is an unfortunate victim of the current set of circumstances."

"But all it takes is one teacher to be present on the night," Charlotte said, backing up her friend. "That's not asking too much, Sir."

"If it was my decision then I would willingly do it, but, as I'm part of a union, my fellow members will not allow me. My hands are tied, I'm afraid," protested Mr Brookes, keen not to create a "them and us" divide between the staff and pupils, or be seen as the bad guy in recent developments.

"You're just the same as the rest of them," said Sam furiously. "We thought you were different, Sir."

Mr Brookes absorbed the criticism. "I'm sorry that you feel that way, Samuel, but you must understand, everyone must understand, that there are other issues at stake, such as health and safety. If there was a fire, God forbid, and a pupil was seriously hurt, the school wouldn't have a leg to stand on legally. Then there are other considerations, such as the building would need to be tidied up afterwards. Without Mr Duckett to assist…"

"Bloody Ducky, the teacher's pet," someone shouted. Several of the class laughed at this cheap comment.

"Without Mr Duckett to assist," repeated Mr Brookes, keen to make his point, "the building will be in no fit state when school commences the following day. Now please, we have a lot of work to get through today, so can we begin?"

The atmosphere was muted among the pupils queuing up to buy the Valentine's issue of the school magazine on the afternoon break. Without the disco the following Thursday to look forward to, the shine had been taken off its publication.

Pete and Jake were waiting in line for their copy, and once they obtained one, they found a quiet location in which to read the dozens of dedications printed in crude black type. As they were in no particular order, Pete scanned the numerous columns of hopeful, sarcastic, earnest, and bordering on vulgar odes, desperate to lay eyes on his own handiwork. "I can't see my ad," he said finally.

"It must be there somewhere," said a prickly Jake. "I definitely posted it in the box," he insisted, snatching the magazine out of Pete's hands and intently studying the messages, running down the ads with his index finger like a hardened gambler swiftly studying the form of racehorses. To his amazement, Jake, too, failed to pick it out.

The omission of his verse was a shattering blow to Pete, particularly as there was only one other Frances-related dedication. This struck Pete as strange, as a girl of her undoubted popularity should have expected to receive at least half a dozen dedications. For all of Jake's protestations to the contrary, Pete couldn't help feel his friend had betrayed him. What he couldn't fathom was why Jake could have acted so callously, particularly when he had been so encouraging in the creation of his verse. Mad as hell, but not wishing to fall out with Jake, he decided a period alone to cool off was the best course of action.

"See you later," said Pete sulkily, making his way over to his final class of the day.

Pete was relaxing at home with a cup of tea. With everyone out shopping, he had an hour or so free to himself to watch a video. Switching on the video player, he pressed play to see if what was already in the machine was worth watching. The opening credits of *Barry Live in Britain* rolled, before leading into the first song.

"Okay, Junior, so things haven't turned out as you wanted."

The voice belonged to Barry, sitting in the seat by the window. "Good choice, by the way," he continued, nodding at the concert playing on the television. "Is it yours?"

"No way," Pete blurted out. "It's my Mum's."

"Your Mom has great taste, Junior," Barry replied, refusing to be offended. "I bet she wouldn't believe it if she knew I was sitting here talking with you."

"I'll bet," agreed Pete.

"What's that you're drinking? I'm so thirsty."

"Tea."

"Wow, you Brits really have a thing for proper tea, don't you? Can I try it?" he asked.

"Be my guest."

Barry leaned over and lifted the mug to his lips and took a couple of sips, closing his eyes to savour the taste. "Oh, yes. That's the real deal, Junior. You don't get tea this good back at home."

"It's Ringtons."

Barry carefully placed the mug back on the coaster on the coffee table. "I'll make a note of that for the next time I tour these shores. So, getting down to the real business. What are you going to do next, now that Plan A has been shot out of the sky?"

Pete shrugged his shoulders, watching as the first song finished and the crowd gave a rapturous reception.

"Come on, Junior, it's not the end of the world. Sometimes things have to go wrong to put you on the right path. Like I told you the last time we met, all you have to do is think out of the box – try and be a bit more original than your nearest rival."

"The magazine and disco were my big chances, and both have been a disaster. I can't ask her out now."

"There'll be plenty more opportunities, Junior. You just gotta make sure you're standing on the court when the ball gets hit in your direction."

Pete was getting annoyed. "Do you always have to talk like that?"

"Like what?"

"Like telling me things, but in a jumbled up way."

"Listen, Junior, I'm here outta the good of my heart. I'm getting fond of our little chats, but don't overstep the mark."

"Sorry."

"Ah, that's okay. I can understand your frustration. But the path of true love is never straightforward. That's why there are so many songs written about it."

"So, can you tell me what to do next, or give me some kind of clue?"

"That's for you to work out, Junior. You still have Valentine's Day next week, and that's too good an opportunity to miss. Try to let her know how you feel. And if you don't want to tell her to her face, try and do it in a more enigmatic way. Give it some thought and see what you can come up with. I gotta dash. I really needed to be somewhere else like five minutes ago."

With Barry gone, Pete remained in his chair, thinking over everything they had just discussed. Pete acknowledged that Barry was right to some degree. He had to attempt to grab Frances's attention. But how? The only enigmatic example that sprang to mind was the daredevil from the Black Magic chocolate adverts. Pete would love to be as brave and daring as him, parachuting out of aeroplanes and climbing castle walls, just to leave a gift on the end of his intended's bed. Knowing his luck, Pete guessed he would either get trapped attempting to climb in through a window, disturb the next-door neighbour's dogs, or be discovered by a hysterical father who took action first and asked questions later.

The following week, Pete had a spark of an idea. Absent from school due to a heavy cold, he was listening to Radio One while reading *The Machine Gunners*. At 11 a.m., "Our Tune" came on, the section of the Simon Bates show where one listener's personal story of unrequited love or tragedy is read out by the host, followed by a song chosen by the listener that is personal to them and best expresses their emotions and feelings.

Pete threw down his book and smiled as his eureka moment began to gain substance in his mind. It occurred to him that if he couldn't himself put into words how he felt about Frances, then perhaps the next best thing would be to include an audio tape of songs with his Valentine's card. How so much simpler to let music do the work for him. It all suddenly made perfect sense to Pete, because throughout the long months of carrying a torch for Frances, he had begun to feel as if many of his favourite songs could have been written for his predicament. As he experienced the emotional highs and lows of his own unrequited love, his music formed the soundtrack to his life, acting as a solace, particularly when he was at his lowest ebb. When Pete felt all alone or as if he was going crazy, a seven-inch piece of black, circular vinyl had the power to give him the strength to believe he shouldn't feel embarrassed or ashamed about his feelings.

While the idea was fresh in his mind, Pete removed the Valentine's card that was hidden inside his album storage box. After a great deal of deliberation, he wrote his inscription, mindful of the necessity to change his style of handwriting:

"To Frances, from an admirer from afar!"

On the sticker of a blank cassette tape, he simply wrote: "PLAY ME!"

Restricting himself to two songs only, he spent the remainder of the day considering all possible candidates for inclusion. Pete's only self-imposed rule was to omit Beatles-related songs, as he feared that would reveal his identity straightaway to Frances. Eventually, he arrived at a shortlist of five, before finally whittling them down to the required number of songs: "Words" by F.R. David, and Bonnie Tyler's "Total Eclipse of The Heart." Pete chose them purely because he felt every word of every line expressed everything he wanted to say to Frances, if he could only muster the courage.

Pete's liking for songs, particularly ballads, that many of his peers would instantly dismiss as uncool was a secret he kept close to his chest, a guilty pleasure to be enjoyed only within the confines of his own bedroom, or via headphones on his Walkman cassette player. It was the influence of his parents' musical tastes upon him as a young child that he blamed for cultivating a fondness for such tunes. His mother's infatuation for Barry Manilow and Abba, and his father's passion for crooners such as Frank Sinatra and Andy Williams, had left an eclectic, indelible mark on Pete.

Valentine's Day itself proved to be a huge anticlimax when Pete discovered Frances herself was absent from school, although his deflation was tinged with a slight element of relief that he didn't have to sit next to her for a whole hour in French waiting for the subject of anonymous cards to be raised as a topic of conversation.

Over the ensuing weeks, Pete noticed a discernible change in Frances's personality. Her bubbly nature was extinct, and there was no jokey, good-natured banter between them in class. She had become subdued and distant, always appearing to be thinking about someone or something else. She appeared to have lost weight, too, with her figure becoming worryingly emaciated and her facial features drawn, developing dark bags under her eyes.

When Mrs Watson lectured in their French class, Frances assumed a pose of indifference, electing to haphazardly scribble away on the cover of her exercise book. Pete wondered if she had guessed the identity of the sender of her anonymous Valentine's card and was choosing to vent her displeasure with Pete by assuming a cold disposition. He couldn't summon the courage to raise the subject in case it created more bad feelings between them. The thought that Frances could ever feel negatively about him was Pete's greatest fear.

As the teachers' strategy of random strike days and working to rule rumbled on into spring, the prospect of a school disco taking place anytime soon receded. Denied such a platform on which to make known his desire for Frances, Pete kept his continuing infatuation a secret, neglecting to even mention to Jake his current unorthodox pursuit. After the fiasco of the non-appearance of Pete's verse in the school magazine and

Jake's perceived role in it, Pete had gone into a heavy sulk. By the time his mood simmered down after a couple of days, Pete decided to let bygones be bygones but not before vowing to himself that in future he would act with furtive discretion where Frances was concerned.

In early April, feeling that the momentum of his campaign had been derailed somewhat, but encouraged by signs of Frances returning to her old self, Pete chose to get his mission back on track by sending Frances a second cassette tape. Just like the first occasion, Pete took his time in selecting a further two songs that he felt would do justice to his current emotional state, eventually choosing "Could It Be Magic" by Barry Manilow, and "How Soon Is Now" by The Smiths. Pete included the briefest of notes with the songs:

"From your Valentine admirer. Two more songs to say what I struggle to say myself."

CHAPTER 13

Pride

The highlight of Pete's week was his regular Saturday morning visit to a youth club, held in a community centre in the city. After the Christmas carol concert in December, Barney had mentioned to Pete that he ran a club for youngsters, and asked if he would be interested in becoming a member. Pete's response had been lukewarm until Barney mentioned some of the activities that were available, the decisive factor being free access to a full-sized snooker table.

Pete's new routine had come at the expense of his visits to his father, which became more sporadic. This created fresh conflict between his parents. Every Thursday evening his father would ring up for a five-minute chat with Pete. For years, the conversation ended the same every week:

"I'll see you after school tomorrow, son."

"Okay, Dad."

In recent months, Ian Davies had become accustomed to his son making excuses as to why he couldn't visit that weekend, to his extreme annoyance. The previous Thursday, Ian lost patience and asked Pete to put his mother on the phone.

"Sheila? It's Ian. Is there something wrong with Pete? It's nearly a month since I last saw him."

"No, I don't think so. Not that he'd tell me if there was. He just enjoys popping down to his club on a Saturday."

"Now and then I don't mind," remarked Ian, his voice rising as he began to get increasingly exasperated, "but he should be with his father on a Saturday. I'm not happy with this arrangement. Will you have a word with him, and try to get him to come and stay at mine tomorrow?"

Sheila thought it was typical of Ian to play the slighted father when it suited him. "Don't shout at me, Ian. It's got nothing to do with me. Maybe if you made the effort to drive through and pick him up after school there wouldn't be a problem. But he's getting older now, Ian. He has new friends, new interests. We can't keep telling him what to do with his life."

"I might have bloody known you'd take his side in all of this. If he turns out to be a fairy when he's older, we'll all know who made him so soft."

"Ian, don't start with me, please. Arguing will get us nowhere. Surely you've learnt that after all of these years."

"Don't get all snotty and high and mighty with me, Sheila. When it comes down to it, you're still a Sunderland lass, born and bred. Just because you're living somewhere posh doesn't give you the right to adopt that tone."

"Ian, it is pointless talking when you're in this mood. I'm putting the phone down."

"Sheila. Sheila." The line rang dead. "Bloody hell," he fumed.

Pete set up the snooker balls in the youth club for his last frame of the day.

"Can I take a few shots, Pete?" asked Barney, hobbling in with his walking stick from the main room.

"If you can manage okay, Barney."

"I'm sure I can play for a little while, if you don't mind me taking my time walking around the table."

"That's fine, Barney," Pete said, keen to impress him with some of his skilful shots.

"So then, Pete, how are things with you?" asked Barney, after breaking off. "I have to say these past few weeks, you've seemed a lot happier. Not the shy, silent boy I first met at Palace Green last year."

"I'm okay," replied Pete, blushing. He hated to be reminded of the person he was then. These days, Pete felt more outgoing and optimistic about life. He attributed some of his change in outlook to the youth club, and not just because it allowed him the opportunity to indulge his love of snooker. It had become the one time of the week that afforded him his own space to relax and just be himself, away from the sometimes suffocating presence of his parents and school.

Pete had made several new friends at the club, and Barney was great fun to be around. Pete had also got to know his wife, Gwen. She would circulate among the youngsters to check how they were, asking if they were thirsty or hungry, and taking an interest in what they had been up to that week. To Pete, it felt like one big happy family, something he felt had been denied to him for a large chunk of his life.

Pete knew he still had some personal issues to address; he still had his bad days when his dark moods would unexpectedly hit like an intensive storm and life seemed hopeless, but he was slowly learning to cope with these episodic attacks, discovering they were controllable if he remained patient long enough for his normal mental stability to restore itself.

"Good shot," said Gwen, entering the games room just as Pete potted a long red. "Looks like there's only going to be one winner here, Barney."

"I used to be so much better," protested Barney good-naturedly. "It's my eyes. They're not as good as they once were," he said, winking at Pete.

"I know, honey, I'm just kidding with you. I just came to let you know that it's nearly noon."

"Thank you, dear. We'll just finish off our game, and then call it a day," Barney said sadly.

Gwen paused to watch the two friends play for a few seconds, and it very nearly brought a tear to her eye. She knew how much her husband doted on the young boy, and to look at the pair now was like opening a window on the past, transporting her back in time twenty years to the sixties, to when her husband and teenage son would happily spend hours together. Gwen had wanted to discuss with Barney the uncanny resemblance between Pete and their own son on numerous occasions, but an opportune moment never seemed to arise, leaving her to conclude that perhaps it was best not to resurrect old, painful memories, not when her husband's health was so poor. She wanted the remainder of her husband's days to be filled with as much joy and happiness as possible.

"Pete," said Barney, when the game was over. "I'm going for a walk to Palace Green once I've locked up. I have something to tell you, if you have time."

"Okay, Barney," said Pete, not suspecting anything out of the ordinary.

"What a difference in weather from the first time we met, Pete," began Barney, as he sat down in his usual seat on Palace Green. "Do you remember? Rain spitting down, and so chilly and miserable with nobody around. Now look at it. The place is vibrant and alive, with people everywhere."

Barney paused to look all around him: law and music students were milling in and out of the university library, with visitors going to and from the cathedral, and clusters of people relaxing on the green, enjoying the warm May sunshine.

"I'll not beat about the bush, Pete. Today is quite a sad day for me. Well, to be honest, after today, I'm afraid I may never set eyes on the old cathedral again. I have to go away, you see."

Pete was flabbergasted. He looked at Barney with disbelief. "You're moving? I thought you loved it here?"

"Yes, Pete, you are so right. If it were up to me, I would stay here forever. However, life is what happens while you make your own plans, and I'm afraid that I am quite ill."

He paused to turn to Pete, who looked back a little fearfully at what Barney was going to say next. Instinctively, Barney knew the best way to break the news, and how economical to be with the facts. He didn't wish to upset the youngster any more than he had to. "Well, Pete, as you can see, this damned stick has become my unwanted constant companion this year. Hence, I am unable anymore to deal with the demands and strains of showing visitors around our glorious cathedral."

"They're getting rid of you, after all the years you've been here?" exploded Pete. "That doesn't sound very fair, Barney."

Barney held up a calming hand. "No, Pete, you don't understand. It is a decision that I've had to take myself.

I think the time is coming for me to go somewhere to be looked after by people who are qualified to care for someone in my weakening position. I'm afraid the strain is beginning to show on Gwen, and I don't want her spending all of her time fussing and clucking over me. She deserves some time and freedom to herself."

Pete was emotionally choked, preventing him from responding further to Barney's bombshell. They sat in silence for ten minutes watching the world go by, broken only when the cathedral bells chimed to signal the hour.

"I feel more bad about the youth club closing than I do about myself. I'll really miss it," said Barney finally.

"Me too," agreed Pete, before firing a question. "Will I be able to come and visit you, Barney?"

"Let's play that one by ear," said Barney, staring straight ahead. "Where I'm going is not really a nice environment for youngsters to visit, if they don't have close family there. There's a good chance I'll not be my usual self, either. I would hate you to see me like that."

Pete looked glumly down to the ground.

Barney struggled up to his feet. Pete stood up too, not knowing what to say or do. As Pete began to stutter and mumble an incoherent question, Barney smiled and slowly put a finger up to his lips.

"Shoosh there, Pete. I hate goodbyes, too. Let's just call it farewell for now. You never know. In another time, another place, we may meet again."

He extended a hand out and firmly shook Pete's hand.

"It's been a pleasure, Pete," said Barney, before slowly heading off in the direction of Dun Cow Lane.

CHAPTER 14

I Feel Love

The first Sunday in July found Pete hanging out at Charlotte's house, together with Jake and Helen. Her parents were away for the day, so it had been decided to spend a leisurely day watching the Wimbledon tennis final on television, interspersed with spells of sunbathing in the back garden.

With Jake and Charlotte's relationship showing no sign of running out of steam, the quartet had taken to spending most evenings together that summer. At first, Pete had been reluctant to be in the company of the two girls, but quickly grew to appreciate their qualities. Helen, in particular, had become a good friend to him, and he found it surprisingly easy to confide in her about most matters, apart from Frances.

As he sat in Charlotte's back garden, Pete had a great deal to mull over. The worst scenario possible he could ever imagine had arisen the previous Thursday at school. Stories had begun to circulate around school that Frances had been out on a date, and nobody in her circle, least of all herself, was denying it. The boy being linked to her was David Corker, a close friend of Sam. The very thought of somebody else desiring Frances aroused extreme jealousy in Pete.

What was peculiar, though, was that Pete could not bring himself to actually hate Frances's alleged new beau. This was because Pete had always found David to be everything Sam wasn't. He was friendly, polite, a little shy, and had similar interests to Pete – music and snooker. Pete occasionally chatted with him in school and always found him to be perfectly amicable, although they weren't what you would call proper friends.

This latest development, combined with the realisation that the end of term was fast approaching, had led to Pete making the uncharacteristically drastic decision to change his appearance in an effort to appeal to Frances. With would-be hairdresser Charlotte offering her unproven hairdressing services, he had decided to have gold streaks put into his hair while Charlotte had the house to herself.

"There's nothing to worry about at all, Pete. I'm going to study hairdressing in a year's time, so I know what I'm doing," she confidently declared.

This reassured Pete. The added bonus was that Charlotte offered to do it for free. To have gone to a hairdresser's would have cost Pete a small fortune.

"Right," said Charlotte, sitting Pete down on an old stool in the garden after he had dampened his hair. "This should only take a few minutes. Keep still so I don't spill any of the dye onto your clothes."

Charlotte methodically applied the prepared dye mixture onto his hair, before covering his head with a transparent plastic cap. "Easy peasy, lemon squeezy," she said. "Now all you need to do is sit with the cover over your hair for a couple of hours. After that, I'll rinse it with the shower nozzle and, hey presto, you'll be a dead ringer for Andrew Ridgley and Simon le Bon."

Pete went into the house to watch the *EastEnders* omnibus, while Charlotte, Jake and Helen had a water fight in the garden. The first hint that things may not have gone according to plan emerged when Jake came inside to ask if Pete wanted a drink of Coke. The startled expression on his face immediately set off alarm bells in Pete's head.

"What's wrong?" asked Pete nervously, unsure if Jake was attempting to wind him up.

"Nothing," he said, doing his best to keep a straight face.

Jake disappeared quickly, only to return a few seconds later with the two girls. Helen instantly raised a hand to her mouth, failing to stifle a shocked gasp. Pete was beginning to worry.

"Come on, gang. I need to know what the joke is here. Has it come out a mess?" Pete asked, looking for some semblance of reassurance.

"No, it's erm, looking cool," replied Charlotte. "It's just not quite...erm...as you wanted it."

These were not the words Pete wanted to hear, as he began to regret ever letting Charlotte convince him she would do a professional job.

"Okay, Pete. Let's get you rinsed off," urged Charlotte. "Upstairs in the bathroom. Now."

With his head bent over the bathtub, Charlotte washed Pete's hair for several minutes, before switching off the shower nozzle and handing him a towel.

"Get me a mirror, please," requested Pete.

Charlotte disappeared into a bedroom, returning with a handheld circular mirror.

"Before I give it to you, you have to promise not to lose your temper with me," pleaded Charlotte, her face a mixture of amusement and horror.

"Okay, I promise," replied Pete, beginning to empathise with how Frankenstein must have felt before seeing his image for the first time. "Now give it to me."

Pete lifted the mirror up to see how the job had turned out. He was speechless. His safe, reassuringly normal dark-brown hair had vanished, replaced by a shock of cartoon-esque bright orange-yellow. He thought he more resembled a character from the board game Guess Who? than an A-league pop star.

"Oh no," Pete wailed. "Mum is going to bloody well kill me! How could this have gone so horribly wrong, Charlotte?"

A million thoughts began to swirl around Pete's head. How am I going to get out of this predicament? Will this demolish my hopes of winning Frances's heart? How can I survive school looking like a baby-faced punk rocker?

"I can't go home like this," Pete said. "Charlotte, put it back the way it was," he demanded, unable to disguise the desperation that had crept into his voice.

"It's not as easy as that, Pete. I'm so, so sorry. You should be able to dye it back, but I don't have any in the house and all the shops are closed. It's Sunday. But you said yourself, your Mum has a good sense of humour. I'm sure she'll see the funny side."

"Oh my God," shrieked Pete's mother, when he finally plucked up the courage to make his way home several hours later. "What on earth have you been doing?"

"Mummy," said Carla standing beside her, scrutinising her brother. "Why Pete's hair funny colour?"

"Mum," began Pete, attempting a charm offensive. "It's not as bad as it looks," he said unconvincingly, his words sounding false and hollow like a bad film script.

"Not as bad as it looks," she fumed. "You promise me your hair was going to have highlights, and return looking like a bloody albino! Didn't I tell you to go to a proper hairdresser's? Didn't I? You just don't listen, and now look where it's got you. You look ridiculous. Get out of my sight. I need to think."

"What's an albino, Mummy?" asked Carla.

Pete languished sheepishly in his bedroom for the remainder of the evening, dreading morning coming around when he would have to reveal his new image to the entire school.

Pete woke up with a knotted stomach. It was ironic that the Monday blues had returned at a time of year when they had usually long since been dispelled with. Pete rolled reluctantly out of bed and went into the bathroom. He observed his appearance in the mirror. The sight was no more comforting than it had been the previous day. He grabbed the hairbrush and tried every different hairstyle he could think of, but it was futile: bar shaving his hair off, he was going to have to ride out the storm that was sure to erupt the minute he set foot onto school grounds. His mother had decided his punishment was to attend school and run the gauntlet of ridicule that would undoubtedly be thrown in his direction by a thousand unsympathetic teenagers. She told Pete it would be character-building, and make him think twice in the future before acting so rashly. As he dressed for school, Pete felt like a condemned prisoner on death row about to make his way to the electric chair.

From the minute he entered the schoolyard, it was obvious to Pete that his radically changed appearance was going to be the major talking point of the day. Wherever he went in the first hour, people stopped to point and stare, with small clusters of pupils laughing raucously and hurling insults. "Canny colour. What is it? Lighthouse amber or golden sunset?" shouted one youth.

By first break time, the news had seemingly rippled through to everyone. Pete was positive that no one would be immune from the news of his freakish appearance, from Mr Pleat, the headmaster, down to Ducky the caretaker.

"Welcome class, and good morning," said Mr Glanville at the beginning of his maths class. "You will be pleased to know that we will be taking things a little easier now that the end of year mini-exam from last week is done and dusted. No doubt you are all dying to see how you performed, so I am planning to mark them as soon as possible, before seeing each of you individually to go through your work and offer areas of improvement. But before we begin, can I just say that exam stress obviously manifests itself in different ways. Just look at Pete's hair, the worry has changed his hair bright blonde!"

Unsurprisingly, the class erupted at Mr Glanville's wit.

By the end of the morning, Pete was beginning to feel less sorry for himself and slightly emboldened. In a perverse kind of way, he was almost enjoying the attention being thrown his way, and was beginning to wonder what the big deal was. For the first time in his life, he felt like an individual. Even a couple of sixth-formers who he had never spoken to during all of his years at the school stopped to say hi, and told him not to take any notice of the mickey takers. They thought he looked cool. That made Pete feel slightly better. To his credit, Jake stayed by the side of his friend for a large part of the day, support that Pete appreciated.

"Well then, how was it?" his mother asked at teatime, fully expecting her son to confirm her suspicions: that it had been hell, and he would admit he would never be so stupid again as long as he lived. Having had a full day to get used to Pete's new image, his mother's anger had gone off the boil and she was now able to see the funny side.

Pete stayed silent. Although by the end of the day people had stopped staring and laughing, and he himself was beginning to get used to it, he would be pleased to get rid of it.

"Lucky for you that I stopped off at the chemist's on the way home from work then, isn't it, and bought this," she said, handing Pete a small box with a head and shoulders photograph of a woman on the side. It was hair dye.

"Will this do the trick?" Pete asked.

"Well, it won't be like it was before you messed about with it, but it will look a lot better. But let this be a lesson to you. Promise me you won't mess about with your hair again. It was nice enough the way it was. I don't know what you were thinking of."

Yeah, Mum, that's why I did it, Pete thought, biting his tongue. He hated the perception he had of himself: normal Pete, boy-next-door Pete, boring Pete, wouldn't stand out in a crowd Pete. But what Pete had learned the hard way in the past day was that no matter how hard he tried to portray an external image to the outside world, it didn't alter the person he was inside.

To his immense relief, Pete's second new hairstyle in as many days obliterated the outrageous disaster of the first one inflicted upon him by Charlotte. The smile of relief that crossed his features when he looked in the mirror was as wide as the bridge over the River Wear in town. Immediately heartened by his near-normal appearance, Pete left the house to walk to Charlotte's house, the usual rendezvous point on an evening.

"I guess that's our Charlotte's hairdressing career over before it's even begun," declared Charlotte's mother, as she invited Pete inside. "Eee, she feels really bad about what happened. Go on up, they're all waiting for you in her room."

Charlotte, Helen, and Jake all cheered ironically when they witnessed Pete's new hair colour. Pete laughed, able to now see the funny side.

"Aahh," said Charlotte. "I was just beginning to get used to it. It was nice."

"I'm pleased it's gone," countered Helen. "You looked like a right thug."

"Okay, everyone. I just want to put the whole episode behind me now," Pete said, pleased to feel like a normal human being once again. "Where are we going to go tonight?"

"The park?" suggested Jake.

"Oh, good thinking, Jake. We haven't done that for at least, oh, 24 hours," teased Charlotte.

"Okay then, clever dick. What did you have in mind?"

"How about the park first, followed by a bag of chips between us to end the night with?" suggested Helen, always keen to keep everyone happy. "Whose turn is it to buy them tonight?"

"Yours," bellowed Pete and Jake in unison, tearing through the door and heading for the stairs.

CHAPTER 15

Don't You (Forget about Me)

Pete woke up earlier than was normal for him on a school day, and had showered and dressed by 7 a.m. A nervous, restless ball of energy, he was unable to eat any breakfast, consumed by a mixed feeling of excitement and trepidation. The reason for his hyped up behaviour was that his self-imposed deadline for resolving the drawn-out saga with Frances had finally arrived. Pete had vowed to himself at the beginning of the month that by the end of the day, on Friday 12th July, the weeks of emotional torment that had been bouncing around in his head like a tennis ball over a net of uncertainty would finally be resolved one way or another. Having felt for months like a terminally ill dog that needed to be put out of its misery, Pete desperately needed closure one way or the other. He very much doubted his heart could survive entering the long void of the extended summer break without a resolution.

This particular day had not been randomly plucked out of the air by Pete, but was chosen as it potentially offered the perfect opportunity for him to reveal to Frances that he was the phantom Romeo who had been regularly sending her cassettes to express his pent-up feelings. The occasion was a pre-Live Aid concert house party that Lucy Small was believed to be hosting that evening. To his consternation, however, Pete had not been invited, and he didn't expect that situation to change so close to the party. He had never been part of the clique that had slowly been growing at school, comprising Frances, Lucy, David, Sam, Thames, and Appleby, amongst others.

He did have a small chance to change this state of affairs and legitimately garner a highly coveted invite from Lucy or Frances, as today they were all attending a Year Four history day trip to the cathedral. Failing this, Pete did have a backup plan. Originally suggested by Jake, and for which Pete himself had deep reservations, it was simply to gatecrash the party. To do this, though, would first require them to know basic facts they were currently lacking, such as Lucy's exact address. To this end, Jake had promised to do some digging at school while Pete was on the trip, with the pair agreeing to convene at Jake's house straight after school to pool their findings.

The atmosphere was jovial and light-hearted as the pupils congregated at the pre-arranged meeting place at Palace Green, in front of the cathedral entrance. Pete had bumped into Joe Hindmarch on the estate bus to the city centre, and the pair chatted about the day that lay ahead as they made the short walk to the peninsula from the bus station.

Mr Feehan and Mrs James, the history teachers of the classes involved, had arrived promptly and were busy handing out the day's itinerary and instructions to pupils as they arrived. Looking down the sheet, Pete was dismayed to discover that he was not listed as being a member of either Frances's or Lucy's working groups for the day, thus denying him valuable time in which to achieve his objective.

After a brief tour of the interior of the cathedral, the main party split up into their smaller working groups in order to commence their tasks for the day. After an hour spent gathering information in the Galilee Chapel, home to the remains of Bede, Pete's group moved into the nave, where they continued to work until lunchtime.

Pete wandered off alone down the cobbled lanes into the heart of the city. Returning with a corned beef pasty, a bag of pickled onion crisps and a can of Coke, he found a vacant bench in Palace Green on which to eat his lunch and contemplate what lay ahead that afternoon. He hoped Jake was having more luck than he was, otherwise it looked as if the day was going to fade out with a whimper, rather than the crescendo of fireworks he had originally anticipated.

Having eaten his food, Pete watched as a cluster of tourists slowly ambled up Owengate towards the cathedral, judging by their accents that they were a party of American tourists. The lead group, consisting of a middle-aged husband, wife, and two children, looked on in amazement at finding themselves in such close proximity to the building. The plump, tanned male, adorned in knee length, garish yellow shorts, white polo shirt tucked snugly into his waist, red baseball cap, and with a camera hanging loose around his neck, turned to the group trailing in his wake.

"Jeez, guys, would you just get a look at that?" he remarked to his entourage.

His wife paused momentarily to gape open-mouthed, before turning around to pass comment to a petite, elderly woman, hunched over a walking stick as she struggled to negotiate the uneven road surface.

"Ma'am, ma'am," she shouted. "Do you see that?"

"So quaint," replied the more senior of the two, squinting in the sunlight.

Pete was curious as to what part of America they originated from. New York? Maybe Florida, New Orleans, or even Texas. All were places of mystery he had only ever seen in films or read about in books.

Pete stared down at the scores of ants scurrying aimlessly on the ground between his feet. One solitary insect that caught his eye had become separated from the main group. He watched as it scuttled along for a couple of inches before pausing. Stooping even closer, Pete wondered if the lone ant sensed his presence, and was curious to know what it was thinking, and whether it was aware of a world so different to its own going on around it. Adjusting the trajectory of its journey, the ant dashed to catch up to its companions.

Scrunching up his rubbish and placing it in a nearby litterbin, Pete headed back to the cathedral. Passing through the knocker door entrance into the cool inner sanctum, Pete returned to the front row of seats located in the main nave area of the cathedral where his group had been working before lunch, and where they were due to reconvene after the break. All he found were the group's A4 writing pads, pens and pencils, but no fellow pupils, which was hardly surprising as he was twenty minutes early. With time to kill, he headed off in the direction of the cathedral shop. As he made his way through the cloisters, Pete was surprised to find Frances and Lucy walking towards him, their laughter reverberating around the corridors.

"Hello," greeted Frances pleasantly. "Where are you off to then, all on your lonesome?"

"Oh, I thought I'd go and look in the bookshop."

"Well, me and Lucy are going to meet some of the others at the top of the tower. Want to come?"

Pete couldn't believe his luck at being invited, and quickly nodded his head in agreement before the opportunity was lost. Within seconds, all three were ascending the tower steps. Just over eight minutes, and 332 steps later, a fatigued Pete found himself standing on the exposed summit, gingerly peering over the edge at the miniature sized cars, and people the size of ants far below.

Lazing on the small-seated area was Frances's set of friends, the group that Pete had so far been excluded from. David Corker was eating the contents of a brown bag. He politely offered some to Pete.

"What are they?" asked Pete, accepting a generous portion.

"Sunflower seeds," he said. "They are incredibly good for you. Full of vitamins."

Masking his disappointment that it wasn't a strawberry bon bon or a cola cube, Pete chewed silently on the handful in his palm. They tasted to him like wood chippings.

Sitting next to David was Sam, who eyed Pete's fresh presence with suspicion, making no attempt to put the newcomer at ease or incorporate him into the conversation.

"David," asked Lucy, clinging onto and swinging around the flagpole situated in the centre of the tower's flat roof. "Which records are you bringing tonight?"

"Oh, are we meant to bring music? I thought you already had enough for the party."

"I do. But I don't think everyone will want to listen to my Smiths songs for the entire evening. We'll all be slashing our wrists."

"Oh, right," said David, smiling. "I've never given it any thought, actually. Are you bringing any, Sam?"

"A couple of my Now albums, if you like."

"Great. That should be enough. I don't mind anything from the charts."

"As long as it's not Duran Duran," interjected Sam.

"And what's wrong with them, exactly?" asked Debbie Heyward, arching an eyebrow.

"They're poncey," Sam said.

"Oh God," moaned Debbie, who never failed to get wound up by Sam's opinions. "Yes, Sam, and so are Wham, and Frankie Goes to Hollywood," she said sarcastically. "Just because they choose to be individuals and wear make-up doesn't make them wusses. This is the eighties, you know."

"What about you, Pete?" asked Frances. "What music do you like?"

"Erm…The Style Council, Tears for Fears. That kind of stuff," he replied, feeling a tingle of anticipation course through him at being included in a conversation connected with the party.

"Oh, they would be perfect for tonight. I quite like them. Do you have any of their albums?" she asked.

Pete was stunned. Had he just be asked, in a roundabout way, if he was bringing music tonight? Before he could respond to Frances's question, he was rudely interrupted.

"Paul Weller," snorted Sam indignantly. "He's one of those leftie loonies, isn't he? Yet he's probably richer than most Tories. What a hypocrite."

Pete bit his tongue and said nothing, not wishing to begin a petty slanging match in front of Frances.

"And Billy Bragg," continued Sam, his cantankerous nature coming to the fore. "What is he all about? He can't sing. Just him and that silly guitar. Give me Dead or Alive any day of the week."

"Do you need a hand with carrying the drink up the hill from the off-licence, Lucy?" asked David, keen to derail Sam from one of his rants.

"No, thanks. Seb is going to drive down to the off-licence and buy it for us." Seb was Lucy's sixth-former brother.

"Cool, that's the hard part sorted out. I'll bring you my contribution for the drinks later on," replied David. "All we need to agree upon now is a start time. How about 7 p.m.? Is that good for you, Lucy? It is your house, after all."

Lucy confirmed the meeting time was fine, with a nod and a smile.

"Cool," said David. "Frances?"

"Yes. Fine by me."

"Debbie?"

"Bring it on," she laughed.

As David worked his way around the group of friends, Pete realised that after Sam and Thames, he was next in line to be asked. This was it, he thought. His invite looked nailed on.

"Bloody hell, it's Feehan," interrupted Appleby, pointing at a figure in the distance. David stopped talking and everyone stood up to look. Appleby was right. The unmistakable figure of their teacher, dressed in his fawn coloured shirt and black trousers, was strolling up from the Market Place into Saddler Street, with Mrs James by his side.

David glanced anxiously at his watch. "Oh no, we're late by five minutes. If Feehan finds out, he'll go bonkers. Come on."

As one, the group dashed to the stairway entrance, in the process nearly bowling over an elderly couple who had just made the weary climb to the top.

With the first flight of stairs only wide enough to permit one person at a time, the youngsters were forced to gradually feed themselves back into the tower. Panicked cries and giggles rang out around the stone walled interior as they spiralled downwards like a slow moving human train, their initial pace of descent frustrated by the limited space available to them.

Pete felt a hand on his shoulder, and a voice imploring him to go faster. Glancing over his shoulder, he discovered Frances was right behind him, close enough for Pete to feel her breath on the nape of his neck.

"I'm going as fast as I can," he replied, enjoying the complicit and comical nature of the moment.

Once they were halfway down the tower its girth widened considerably, allowing them to filter downwards at an increased speed.

"Cutting it fine there, Pete," whispered Joe, as Pete sat down on the chair where he had left his notepad that morning. "Feehan would have had you hung, drawn, and quartered if he'd discovered you were late."

"I know," said Pete breathlessly. He picked up his pen and pretended to be locked in a relaxed state of studious thought, just as Feehan and Mrs James entered the building. Pausing to undertake a swift headcount to confirm that all of Pete's group was present, the teachers headed off to check up on the other pupils working at various locations around the cathedral.

Pete was rueing his misfortune. He was positive that David had been poised to include him in the group conversation regarding the best start time for the party later on that evening. Pete cursed Appleby for spotting Feehan when he did and cutting David short. He would have happily accepted a dressing-down from Feehan for being late in return for the greater prize of an evening in the company of Frances. What was doubly galling was that Pete had not even found out Lucy's home address, so he couldn't even try and pluck up the nerve to turn up by himself and bluff his way inside. Now the moment had gone, and Pete couldn't see how between now and the end of the day he was going to make any further progress.

CHAPTER 16

Love Is A Battlefield

Despite Pete's failure to acquire an invitation or ascertain the whereabouts of Lucy's home, Jake had been doing his own detective work, with more impressive results. Chatting to Morgan in that morning's PE class, Jake discovered that Morgan knew Lucy's home address, and that he too had heard rumours that some kind of party was due to take place later on that evening. Despite numerous attempts to wear Morgan down and glean the much-valued golden information from him, Jake was initially unsuccessful. Morgan had the upper hand in the negotiations that then took place, making it clear to Jake that he was only prepared to share his knowledge on one condition: he wanted to tag along with Jake and Pete that evening. Furthermore, to ensure Jake remained true to his side of the bargain, Morgan promised to divulge his information only once all three youths were physically near the house.

Although Pete was extremely grateful for Jake's tenacity in generating a lead on his behalf, he could see how turning up mob handed might pose problems. There was also the obvious disadvantage of involving Morgan. Pete cast his mind back to the dozens of PE lessons over the years where Morgan had revelled in dishing out brutal, crunching tackles in games of football and rugby upon many of those due to be in attendance tonight.

In more recent times, there had also been the humiliating episodes involving Thames and Appleby in the changing rooms. Pete knew that by turning up at the front door with Morgan by his side, he risked being tarred with the same brush by the partygoers. Morgan was also a loose cannon, infamous for his unpredictable antics and temperamental outbursts, and for giving the impression that even he sometimes never quite knew what he was going to do next. Realistically, Pete didn't expect the front door to be even opened, never mind have the opportunity to try and sweet talk themselves inside.

Despite all of the disadvantages Morgan brought to the table, however, there were no other alternatives available. Pete decided to throw his natural caution to the wind, believing the ends more than justified the means.

The three boys had arranged to meet on the silver railway footbridge at 6:30 p.m. for the walk into the city centre.

"Come on then, Morgan," implored Jake, as they strolled down the gently winding pathway to the farm, doing his best to avoid swallowing any of the midges swarming around his head. "You can tell us the address now."

"Not until we arrive," teased Morgan smugly, enjoying holding all of the aces in the pack.

"Are we going to try and buy some drink beforehand?" asked Pete, keen to obtain some dutch courage. He felt as if he had a million nervous butterflies fluttering around inside his stomach as the moment of truth drew near.

"Too bloody right," declared Morgan. "I know the best off-licence to go to. It's the one just before the bus station. I always get served," he bragged.

"Right lads. Cough up," ordered Morgan thirty minutes later as they neared the shop in North Road. Pete and Jake both handed over a pound note.

"I could only get fifty pence myself," confessed Morgan.

"Fifty pence!" snorted an exasperated Jake. "Could you not even scrounge a pound?"

"No," said Morgan, shaking his head. "My mother's keeping a tight hold of her purse at the minute."

"I'm not surprised, if you keep nicking from it," added Jake mischievously.

Morgan shot Jake an angry look and turned around to menacingly confront him for his flippancy. Spotting the danger immediately, Pete intervened swiftly to pour cold waters over the potential for fisticuffs. A bust-up was in nobody's interests, least of all his own.

"Calm down a minute, lads. I'll put in Morgan's shortfall," said Pete, willing to sacrifice his bus fare home to keep the peace. "That makes us all even steven."

"Cheers, mate," beamed Morgan, instantly forgetting the minor flare up with Jake and getting back to the problem at hand.

"What will that get us, then?" asked Jake. "Eight cans of Kestrel? I think that comes to three pounds."

"I'm not keen on Kestrel," stated Morgan. "It tastes like piss. I say we go for a small bottle of spirits. We will get drunk faster, and it will improve our patter with the girls."

"But with cans, we can dish them out more fairly," Jake reasoned, keen to get his money's worth and not have Morgan consuming more than his fair share. "What do you think, Pete?" asked Jake.

With Morgan also looking to Pete for his opinion on the matter, it appeared he had been allocated the casting vote. Ever the pragmatic coward, and aware that it was vital to keep Morgan on side for a while longer, Pete sided with him. "I guess a small bottle would make us less conspicuous on the streets, as opposed to walking around with heavy bags of lager."

"That makes sense, I suppose," agreed Jake. "The last thing we need are the pigs giving us a load of hassle."

"Okay, lads. I'll meet you underneath the viaduct in a minute," said Morgan, as he confidently strode towards the off-licence.

"Try and get vodka," shouted Jake.

After five minutes of waiting on the bench under the railway bridge, Morgan had still not shown up. Pete and Jake were beginning to get nervous.

"What's he playing at?" muttered Jake, not trusting Morgan as far as he could throw him. "If he's done a runner with our bloody money, I'll kill him," he stated with mock bravado, well aware Morgan could easily demolish him with one hand tied behind his back.

"He'll be here," Pete said, as much to reassure himself as Jake.

"Look, here he comes," said Jake a minute later, pointing down North Road.

Both boys strained to see what Morgan was carrying.

As Morgan neared, Pete's heart sunk. "He doesn't appear to have bought anything," he moaned.

"They mustn't have served him. What a bloody bullshitter," spat Jake.

As Morgan approached them, the boys read his expression of misery. "Sorry, lads," he said flatly. "No joy, I'm afraid."

"What are we going to do now?" asked a despondent Jake. "You can't go to a party without a drink. They're no fun when you're stone cold sober."

Suddenly, Morgan's face cracked into a mischievous grin. From his rear jeans pocket, covered by the tails of his chambray shirt that were hanging out over his waist, he unearthed a small bottle of vodka to flash teasingly at the boys, before breaking into a run. "Fooled you, lads," he howled, unscrewing the bottle and taking a swig.

Pete and Jake looked at each other with euphoric disbelief before sprinting after Morgan, impatient to get their hands on the illicit contents of the bottle.

The trio decided to head up to Wharton Park as it afforded plenty of secluded spots in which to imbibe their intoxicating liquor while plotting their next move.

"This'll do," said Morgan, perching on a swing at the deserted play area, situated at the top of the hill. "Just make sure you keep one eye out for the poofters. Not forgetting the prowlers and nutters that come out at night up here. Kids hanging around playgrounds are meat and drink to them lot."

"They don't hang around up here, do they?" asked Jake anxiously, suddenly seeing danger lurking within every area of deep undergrowth. He took a quick surreptitious mouthful from the bottle, before passing it to Pete.

"We'll be alright. There's three of us if any of them try it on," declared Morgan assertively.

"I'm not planning on staying here long enough to find out," said a visibly unsettled Jake, sitting down at the top of the slide. "As soon as we get this down our necks, we're on our way."

"Too right," seconded Pete, enjoying the afterglow he was experiencing from his first mouthful. "There are parties and kicks to be had out there somewhere," he gushed optimistically, surveying the rooftops of the city from their vantage point, "and we're going to find them," he declared, enjoying the feeling of promise in the evening sunshine.

Half an hour later, they were still rooted to the play area. With the vodka freshly consumed, Morgan was buoyantly striving to achieve maximum elevation on the swing, Jake was thoughtfully smoking a cigarette on the roundabout while slowly spinning it around, and Pete was laid out on the grass, eyes closed and head spinning, wondering in his inebriated state what Frances was up to at that exact moment, and pondering what fate had in store for him that evening.

With each minute that continued to pass, Pete began to feel the fundamental reason for them being in Durham was slowly being forgotten, in the process eroding their impetus and focus. "It's nearly 8 p.m., lads," he shouted, galvanising himself into action, while attempting to psyche himself up into an "it's now or never" frame of mind. "Do you think we should head off to Lucy's house now? We can't stay here all night."

"Give me five minutes," said Morgan.

Stirred by Pete's request, Jake flicked the butt of his cigarette onto the ground and slid off the roundabout. "Just going for a leak," he said, heading off in the direction of the nearest bushes.

"Good idea," Pete said, standing up and following his friend.

Morgan allowed his momentum on the swing to slowly decrease until he was able to plant his feet on the ground and get off. "Okay," he said, when both Pete and Jake had returned. "Let's go, lads."

They set off back down the grassy slope a good deal more lightheaded and uninhibited than they had been upon entering the park, and walked down the steep flight of concrete steps that brought them back out at the top of North Road, by the telephone box and public toilets.

"Which way?" asked Pete, as Morgan hesitated on the pavement.

"Follow me," Morgan replied, purposefully leading them over the quiet main road to the entrance of Western Hill. This was an affluent area of the city, with its long line of prestigious two and three-storey terraced townhouses stretching for a quarter of a mile, with the first two hundred metres of properties positioned on a lung-shattering steep incline.

"Is this the street?" asked Pete.

"Yes."

"Which one is it, then?"

"I'm not sure what the house number is," replied Morgan.

"What do you mean, exactly?" Pete asked, knowing things had been too good to be true where Morgan was concerned.

"I know she lives on Albert Street, is what I'm saying."

"But you don't know the house number? That's great, isn't it," wailed Jake.

"Listen, Rigby, if it wasn't for me, you two would be putting pins into maps to guess where to go tonight. At least I've given us a fighting chance."

"So what do we do now?" asked Pete, again exercising his unofficial role as peacemaker.

"I can tell you two have never crashed a party before," boasted Morgan. "It's not that difficult. All we have to do is listen for the sound of records playing, or lots of talking and laughing. It's a warm night, so they're bound to have the odd window open. Plus, it's more or less a straight road, so if there are people arriving or hanging around outside we'll be able to clock them."

Pete had to silently agree that Morgan, for once, appeared to be talking a good deal of sense. Maybe he did have a wealth of experience getting into parties uninvited.

"Assuming we do find the house," Jake asked. "What happens then?"

"Just leave the talking to me," Morgan replied. "My charm will get us in, don't worry about that."

Even though the majority of the thirty or so people congregated in Lucy's house were good friends at school, a tense, restrained atmosphere had unexpectedly prevailed during the first hour of the gathering. Aided in no small part by the sheer volume of alcohol being thirstily consumed, the negative vibes were now slowly beginning to dissipate. The small clusters of same-sex groups were beginning to relax and intermingle with each other. Most were content to chat, a few couples had begun to dance to the high tempo rhythm of "You Spin Me Round," while a couple of partygoers were already lost in their own worlds, slumped on the various bean bags that were scattered around the front room. Lucy had also just drawn the thick velvet curtains hanging in the front room, shutting out the bright light from outside. Together with the freshly lit candles and burning incense sticks, this helped create a more conducive ambience.

In the back kitchen, Lucy was leaning against the long kitchen bench smoking a cigarette, while attempting to estimate how many unopened cans of lager, cider, and bottles of spirits were stacked on the kitchen table.

Although not sixteen years of age until September, Lucy easily passed for an adult, both in outward appearance and maturity of personality. Quiet but confident, she was well-spoken, as befitted her solid middle class upbringing, and already was self-educated in languages and politics to such a standard that she would not be overwhelmed were she to commence studying at undergraduate level.

To many of her peers, Lucy was considered a figure of intrigue. No one at school had ever seen her with a boyfriend or ever known of one, and the rumours as to why were varied. A popular one was that she had a secret boyfriend who was married and in his thirties; another one that occasionally did the rounds was she was a lesbian; or, that she was abstaining from sex until marriage. These and others were never denied or acknowledged by Lucy herself, for whom rumour-mongering was water off a duck's back. She was a firm believer in the Oscar Wilde sentiment about it being far worse not to be talked about than to be a figure that attracted gossip.

"It's really warming up now," said Frances, entering the kitchen.

"They always take a while," replied Lucy. "Particularly when it's broad daylight outside. Just doesn't feel natural, somehow. Fancy a ciggy?"

"Oh yes, please," smiled Frances, taking one offered to her, even though she herself had an unopened pack.

"So, you and David, you're definitely an item now, are you?" enquired Lucy, an impish grin on her face.

"Hmm, sort of," replied Frances hesitantly. "We've just been on the one date up to now."

"Where did he take you?"

"It was that restaurant near to the cathedral."

"Not Hanratty's?" said Lucy. "That place costs an absolute bomb. David must like you an awful lot," she continued, not letting on she knew a great deal more.

"Yes, I think he does. He is such a gentleman and quite shy with it. Do you know, he was standing there on Palace Green with a dozen red roses when I arrived."

"Bless him."

"And he must have been so embarrassed, the poor love, judging by how red he was. Yes, he is really sweet, although a bit fussy over some of my habits. He's got a bit of a downer on my smoking, for example. But I've told him, he's got to take me warts and all."

"Oh, he's keen, Frances. It'll take more than a few cigarettes to scare him away. I wouldn't worry about that," said Lucy, silently recalling the hours in English classes in the weeks leading up to their getting together, when David had spoken about nothing else but Frances. She enjoyed being a shoulder to lean on. "Oh, did you ever ask him about the letters and tapes?"

"Oh, no. I don't want to humiliate the poor lad further," said Frances. "It must have been him, though. He did admit that the verse in the school magazine was his, although it was a little clichéd."

"Don't knock it, love. It's not everyone who inspires poetry in others," Lucy said, drawing on her cigarette quickly, and exhaling smoke through the left hand side of her mouth. "I would be rather flattered."

"I am. It's nice after some of the idiots I've had the misfortune to have crushes on these past few years."

"Ooh, tell me more," said Lucy.

"Sorry, but they're all in the past now. What I need at this precise moment in time is a nice, clean cut boy like David."

"You know, Frances," began Lucy thoughtfully, "David and I have been really good friends for many years now. Our fathers lecture in the same university department and we're always at each other's houses for dinner parties and the like. I hope you don't resent our shared past."

Frances shook her head. "David has explained. I completely understand, Lucy. There's absolutely no reason for boys and girls not to be platonic friends."

"That's cool. I just wanted to clear that up. But please, I do know how much he likes you, so try not to break his heart."

"I wouldn't have come this far, Lucy, if I wasn't fond of him. Anyway, have you got your eye on anyone?" Frances asked, keen to change the subject.

Lucy dismissively shook her head. "No, the boys here are all very nice and everything, just a bit immature for me. I don't mean that in a nasty way, you know. They are good fun."

"What about Sam? I think he has his eye on you."

"Yes, but he's a bit…"

At that moment the current song playing in the front room ended, with the ensuing brief silence filled by the grating voice of Sam, booming down the corridor. He was running through his full repertoire of Young Ones impersonations, the scripts of which were as well known to the current crop of teenagers as the songs of Lennon and McCartney were to previous generations. On this occasion, Sam was attempting to mimic Neil the hippie. Sam's poorly delivered imitation was followed by his own shriek of laughter, before becoming mercifully lost within the opening bars of "Everybody Wants To Rule The World."

"...a bit eccentric, even for my tastes," finished Lucy, rolling her eyes. "I guess I go for the strong, silent types more."

"Maybe you have a point," agreed Frances. Both girls glanced at each other for a split second before bursting into laughter.

"Hi, darling," said David to Frances, entering the kitchen and wondering what the joke was about. The way he allowed his gaze to linger on Frances made it blatantly obvious to Lucy just how smitten he was. "Hi, Lucy. Just popped in for another drink, if that's okay with you?"

"You don't have to ask me, David," replied Lucy, used to the over-polite and slightly pompous demeanour he displayed when he was extremely nervous. "You get another. I dare say you paid for at least half of them."

"Well, yes. But they are for everyone. Lord, there's no way I could consume, or expect to consume, that much alcohol."

Lucy smiled softly. "Just enjoy yourself, dear. It's a party remember. Happy summer days are here again."

David chose a can of lager and snapped back the ring pull, slightly spraying the bench.

"Whoops, a bit frisky this one," he said, slurping at the erupting froth. "I'm, erm, going back to chat with the others. Coming?"

"In a minute, David," said Frances. "Just as soon as I've finished my ciggy."

"Me too," said Lucy.

David smiled, and gave them the thumbs up. "Right then, see you soon," he said, leaving the two girls alone again.

"Actually," said Lucy to Frances, "I think I'll grab some fresh air and go and get a pack of cigarettes before the shop down the road closes."

"Want me to come with you?"

Lucy smiled. "Thanks, but I'll be okay. I think somebody else needs your attention more at the moment. I'll be back in two minutes," she said, stubbing out the butt of her cigarette in the ashtray, before grabbing her purse and heading down the hallway to the front door.

The boys were no further along in their quest, despite having wearily paced up and down the whole of the street twice.

"Bloody hell. Bar knocking on every door, we'll never find out where it's at," moaned Jake, sitting down on the pavement at the top of the hill.

Pete shared his frustration, knowing Frances was within spitting distance of where he was standing, but at the same time existing in a different world that so far excluded him. "Let's have a quick rest, then we'll walk back down again," he said, refusing to give up so easy.

"You two can go," Jake said. "I need to give my feet a rest."

"Come on, Jake," pleaded Pete. "We need all our eyes and ears to help find it."

Jake sighed, before raising himself up onto his feet. "Come on then. But if we don't find it this time, then I'm going back home."

"Boys," interjected Morgan, "shut up for one minute. Do you see what I see? Look. There is a God."

Pete and Jake obeyed Morgan and followed his gaze. Coming out of a brown front door, not twenty metres away, was Lucy.

"Lucy," shouted Morgan, dashing down the pavement to head her off. "Do not move," he ordered.

Lucy waited as Morgan, swiftly followed by Pete and Jake, descended upon her.

"Hello, boys," she said, unflustered by their sudden appearance.

"Lucy. Please, please, please can we come to your exquisite party?" pleaded Morgan, dropping down to his knees in front of her and placing his hands together in mock prayer. "We're good lads. We promise to behave ourselves."

Lucy looked down at Morgan with an amused look on her face. "Sure. Let yourselves in. The door's not locked. I'm just going for a pack of cigarettes."

"Really?" said Jake, braced for instant rejection.

"Why not?" she said. "There's loads of people inside. Three more aren't going to make much difference."

"You two lads go on in," said Morgan, linking arms with Lucy as if they were an old married couple. "I'm off to the shop with Lucy."

Lucy folded over in hysterics, before the unlikeliest of couples proceeded to march down the hill.

"You heard her," said Jake disbelievingly to Pete. "Let's get in there and party before she changes her mind."

Pete was greeted inside by Appleby, who was sitting at the bottom of the stairs in the hallway, talking to Thames about the latest spectrum games due to be released. The sound of Frankie Goes To Hollywood, together with a good deal of exuberant whooping and shouting, was emanating from the first room on the left down the corridor. Pete and Jake swept in to find nearly two dozen of their school colleagues crammed in. Half were dancing on the makeshift dance floor, while the remainder were sitting on bean bags or simply squatting down on the floor with their backs against the wall. Most acknowledged the pair with grins of recognition, as the music was cranked up to such a high volume that normal conversation was impossible. Catching Pete's eye, David came over to gesture if he wanted a drink, before pointing in the direction of the room situated at the far end of the downstairs corridor.

Pete turned to see if Jake wanted a drink fetching, only to find he had been willingly dragged into the crowd of dancers. Before he left the room, Pete scanned the faces for Frances, but was surprised not to pick her out. He easily found the kitchen where the treasure trove of alcohol was being stored, and helped himself to a lager. His head had cleared a little after the initial rush from the vodka, and he wanted to try and keep it that way. However, Pete didn't want to lose face in front of all the others, and decided that it wouldn't do his image any harm to be seen casually sipping from a can.

Heartened by the warmth everyone had shown to him upon his entrance, Pete asked Thames where the toilet was.

"Upstairs somewhere," he replied.

Deciding it couldn't be that difficult to locate, he eased past Appleby and climbed the stairs. The first floor landing contained three unoccupied bedrooms, a storage cupboard, and the required bathroom. Pete was just about to enter when he noticed a light switched on in the room situated on the second landing. At the sight of the person inside, he quickly scurried up to make his presence known. The girl was standing with her back to him, gazing out of the open window.

"Hello, Frances," he said, standing in the open doorway.

Shocked at being unexpectedly disturbed, Frances span around. "Jesus Christ, Pete. You nearly gave me a heart attack," she said, holding her hand to her chest. "I never expected to see you here."

"I was just, erm, looking for the loo," he replied, sidestepping the real meaning of her question.

"Come in and take a seat. I was just getting away from the din for five minutes."

Pete entered and sat down in a wicker chair in the corner of the room, guessing that he must be in Lucy's bedroom, judging by the Morrissey, CND, and polar bear posters on the wall.

"It's a beautiful night, isn't it?" she said, popping her head out of the open window to stare at the blue and red tinged sky.

"Yes," replied Pete.

"I love summer nights like this, when it never seems to really get dark at all. The world seems a much better place."

Pete didn't respond, still not quite believing the scenario he had stumbled into. For months, he had imagined being involved with Frances in such a set of circumstances, but now it was reality Pete was finding it difficult to think of anything of substance to say. He felt as if he had been transported to heaven, and never wanted to use his return ticket back to earth.

Frances turned around to face Pete, leaning her back against the windowsill. Framed against the open window,

Pete thought Frances the most beautiful portrait that had ever been painted.

"So, why have you come?" she asked. "I didn't think this would be your scene."

"Well…erm…" he began, falteringly. Pete realised this was his golden opportunity, the one he had dreamed about for so long. "When I was with you and the others on the tower earlier today, I thought that, you know, I was kind of invited."

Pete could see Frances rewinding back in her head to earlier on in the day. "Oh yes, I remember now," she said, without actually confirming or denying the validity of Pete's explanation.

"And then, we all had to dash back downstairs when we spotted Feehan," continued Pete, picking up the thread of the story. "I never found the right moment to ask again, we were so busy. Actually, that's wrong. I was too embarrassed to ask in case I had gotten the wrong end of the stick, and then I would have felt a right idiot, about as much as I do now, truth be told. It's just…" he paused, struggling to find the appropriate words to express himself and do justice to what he wanted to communicate, "…I really enjoyed being with you … with you all. Everyone here is really friendly, and not loonies like some of the lads from school."

"It's okay, Pete," smiled Frances. "I wasn't demanding that you justify yourself. It's nice to see you. I'd much rather you were here than idiots like Morgan."

"Well…erm…I actually came with him."

Frances shot him a look that, if humanly possible, Pete felt would have turned him to stone.

"And Jake," he added, as if that would cushion the blow of his first admission.

Frances let out a deep sigh, sat down on the side of the bed, and buried her head in her hands.

Pete instantly knew he had dropped a clanger. A huge, all-singing, all-dancing clanger.

"Oh shit," he began, "if it's a problem, then I can go, and I'll take Morgan and Jake with me. I didn't want to bring him, but only he knew where Lucy lived. Or so I thought at the time. He lied about that."

"Hah. Now that I can believe," she said with conviction, lifting her head up to reveal streams of tears flowing down her cheeks, and reddened eyes.

Pete was puzzled more than ever. "Are you … are you okay, Frances?" he asked hesitantly.

"Oh, yes, now I'm fine, but I wasn't so long ago. Remember the time when I was off school for a week in February? No, of course you don't, why should you? Anyway," she said, faltering slightly with the strain of attempting to finish off what she had begun to confess, "I wasn't technically ill. Your friend, Morgan, he got me … he got me … pregnant."

Having finally shared her secret with someone, Frances's face sank back into her hands as she continued to sob heavily.

Pete was shell-shocked. By the frankness of her admission, and Morgan's involvement. It made Pete's own secret feel a great deal more insignificant and juvenile. In an instant, everything Pete had been living for was turned upside down, with his illusion of Frances shattered forever.

"Does he know?" Pete eventually asked.

"Of course he doesn't know," she sniffled. "And that's the way it's staying. I had to have an abortion. It's been difficult enough rebuilding my life without letting that little bastard do any more damage. Pete, I've told you because it's been eating away at me for months, and will probably haunt me for the rest of my life. I trust you enough to know you won't tell a soul."

"Of course I won't," assured Pete.

Frances shakily removed a cigarette from her pack. Lighting it, she took a draw and handed it to Pete. Still completely stunned by Frances's revelation, he accepted. It was the first time since New Year's Eve that Pete had smoked, a lifetime ago now, on that hazy headed night.

After an awkward silence lasting several minutes, Frances half-heartedly attempted to steer the conversation away from her confession. "That was a hoot earlier today, wasn't it?" she said.

"What was?" said Pete, still numb.

"Running down the tower. We'd have all been given detention if Feehan had caught us skiving."

Pete smiled as he pictured the look of wild abandon in her eyes when he turned around to see who had touched him on the shoulder. He knew that for the rest of his life, until the day he drew his final breath, whenever he recalled the first real love of his life, he would return again and again to that image of her. It was how Pete would always remember her.

"What are your plans for the holidays?" asked Frances, composing herself further. "My parents are taking us all to the South of France for three weeks. This time on Wednesday, I'll be there. I'm so relieved to be escaping Durham for a while."

"I don't have anything on the horizon," lied Pete, deciding not to mention the week's holiday in Skegness earmarked for August, a world away from the glamour and exclusivity of Frances's exotic coastal resorts. "I'm just going to hang out with Jake, catch up on some reading, and see a few films. *A View to a Kill* is out soon."

"I'm looking forward to seeing that. Have you seen the Duran Duran video on the Eiffel Tower? It's so amazing. Simon looks really cool in that French beret he wears."

Pete half-smiled at this second surprise. Although nowhere near as dramatic as her first, it revealed how much Frances was changing. Once a devout indie music lover, her tastes were obviously broadening to include a wider range of pop music.

"That was a radical move for you this week," said Frances, stubbing out the cigarette she had been sharing with Pete, and instantly lighting a second. "Dying your hair peroxide blonde. What made you decide to go for something so different?"

Pete cast his mind back to the horror of the previous Sunday afternoon. "That was down to Charlotte getting her dyes mixed up," Pete explained. "I was only meant to have gold streaks."

"Even so, it certainly made you stand out from the crowd. I quite liked it," Frances admitted. "It suited you."

Pete did a double take. "You liked it?"

"Yes. Not many boys your age have the nerve to try new things out."

A pause in their conversation reminded Frances that a party was still in full swing downstairs, and that David would be wondering where she had got to. "I'd better be going down after this," said Frances. "I've barely spoken to David all evening."

Pete's heart sank a little at the mention of his name.

"What do you think about him?" she asked. "Truthfully."

"Well," began Pete. "I don't really talk that much to David at school. He has his friends, and I have mine. He seems okay, I suppose," Pete conceded.

"It was David who actually suggested inviting you today when we were in Durham, but by then you had gone home. Sam really went off on one, ranting on about how it should be close friends only and all that bullshit. He can be a dickhead at times, he really can." Frances stubbed out her half smoked cigarette and stood up. She headed for the door.

"Wait," called Pete. Even though he didn't quite know what to feel about Frances in the light of the revelations of the past few minutes, Pete still felt the urge to get everything off his chest and confess to Frances that he was the mystery sender of the tapes. It felt like the appropriate moment, now that it was so blatantly obvious his actions had been in vain from the very start anyway. "There's something I need to tell you too, Frances. To come clean about."

"What's that?"

Pete hesitated, the gravity of what he was about to own up to, combined with some alcohol induced giddiness, affecting his ability to place one word after the other. Unable to look her in the eye, Pete gazed down at the carpet. "It's just … that … well … something I should have … wanted to tell you a long time ago," he muttered, struggling to articulate his feelings.

Pete suddenly felt an urgent call of nature tugging on his bladder, the perfect opportunity to compose himself before coming clean. "Give me a moment, please. I'll be right back," he requested, dashing down the stairs to the first floor landing.

Pete and Frances had been so bound up within the solemn nature of their conversation that they had failed to realise that things downstairs were also not going entirely to plan. The unexpected introduction of one person, a human grenade, had completely soured the atmosphere.

"Well, well, well. What have we got here, then?" shouted Davey Carter, bursting into the hub of the action and pinching the backside of Debbie as she was dancing. "A little underage drinking and romance, is it?" he cackled, slobbering like a rabid animal.

Like a car tyre punctured by a sheath of broken glass on a highway, the mood of the teenagers was rapidly deflated. Lucy turned down the music to a more reasonable level in order to be able to make herself heard as she prepared to lay down the expected rules of behaviour to the unpopular late arrival. Second-guessing what Lucy was about to say, Carter responded first.

"Come on, people. Don't mind me. I'm just here for a good time, too. Seb, mate. Grab me a beer, will you?"

"No problem, Davey," replied Seb Small, running off to fetch a drink from the kitchen with all the eagerness and obedience of a well-trained canine.

In demonstrating he was there as an official guest of the host's brother, and not in any illegitimate capacity, Carter was clearly revelling in the opportunity to wander carte blanche around the house, and in the reaction of fear elicited due to his notoriety.

Carter approached Sam, who had just lit a cigarette. "Give us a go on that, Charlie boy," he demanded, expectantly holding out a hand. "Charlie boy" was a nickname Carter had always used to mockingly address Sam with at school, in relation to his slightly overgrown, protruding ears that were as prominent as Prince

Charles's. Sam instantly acquiesced and handed it over to Carter, his usual cockiness replaced with blatant discomfort at being singled out by Carter.

"Bloody hell, Seb," hissed Lucy, collaring her brother in the corridor upon his return from the kitchen. "What are you doing bringing him back with you?"

"Hey, sis. Be cool. Don't get your knickers in a twist. Dave's okay. People get the wrong end of the stick with him. Just give him a chance."

Her brother was the same age as Carter, and was going through one of his rebellious "hanging out with the bad boys" phases, as her father so neatly concluded after being introduced to Carter for the first time.

Lucy sighed, and followed her brother into the front room, hoping her presence would encourage the others not to be intimidated by Carter, and help them get back into the spirit of the occasion.

"Charlie boy, where's the bog at?" asked Carter. "I'm dying for a piss."

"Lucy," said Sam. "This rat needs to leave right now," he said indignantly.

"Oh, Christ," cursed Lucy, anxiously fiddling with her hair and fully expecting Carter to knock Sam's teeth out at so blatant an insult. "Up the stairs, first landing," she said, swiftly intervening to prevent world war three breaking out.

"Cheers, Lucy," said Carter, exiting the room.

Carter's temporary absence gave Lucy a few precious moments breathing space in which to think about how to recover the situation. A mini-conference began among the gathered throng.

"What are we going to do?" wailed Thames, no stranger himself to persecution at the hands of Carter and his mates.

"Ask him to leave, and call the police if he refuses," added Debbie, having warily retreated to the sofa.

"And find a house full of kids drinking and smoking," said Lucy. "That's not going to improve matters for anyone. Seb, you have to find somewhere to go for the rest of the evening. Take him for a drink to The Colpitts until we're done here."

"I'm skint, sis. So is Dave."

"Here," said Lucy, digging into her jeans and pulling out a five pound note. "Take this, and when he returns from the loo make yourselves scarce."

"Cheers, sis," said Seb, marvelling at the unexpected fluctuation in his finances.

Freshly relieved, Pete washed his hands and splashed several handfuls of cold water onto his face in an attempt to sober up a little and revitalise himself. Exiting the bathroom, he was distracted by the sound of movement, and cupboard doors and drawers being noisily opened and closed. As it originated from the bedroom next to the bathroom, Pete decided to investigate, pushing the door wide open and peering into the gloomy half-light. His fingers found the light switch, and clicked it on to bathe the room in light.

Caught in the act of stuffing jewellery and money into his trouser pockets, a surprised Carter froze, staring guiltily at the sight of Pete standing in the doorway.

Without quite knowing what to expect, and now wishing he hadn't acted so hastily upon his suspicious gut instinct, Pete stared silently at Carter, knowing he had one of two choices available to him. On any other day, at any other point in his life, the coward in Pete would have been guaranteed to triumph over his honest nature. Pete would have turned right around, walked away, and stayed silent on what he had just witnessed. Today, however, reinforced with a little dutch courage from the vodka and lager, and still reeling from what had just been disclosed to him by Frances, Pete was prepared to stand up and be counted.

"Put them back," ordered Pete, with nothing more than the weight of morality on his side.

"Bloody hell, Davies. Leave it out, mate," said Carter, regaining some of his composure. The tone of Carter's voice suggested he still considered Pete to be an easy touch, who wouldn't for one minute dare to lock horns with him. "I thought you were the hippy's mother or father. Amazing what these toffs have lying around the gaff," remarked the unrepentant thug. "A right little Aladdin's cave."

Pete stayed where he was, blocking Carter's exit.

"You ain't seen nothing, okay?" said Carter, as he walked towards Pete. "Not if you value your life."

Pete resolutely stood his ground. "Not this time, Carter. Now put whatever you have in your pocket back, otherwise I'm calling the police."

Unused to being challenged, particularly by someone he considered vastly inferior to himself, Carter gave Pete a hard, appraising stare, like a champion boxer at a pre-fight weigh-in who has suffered weeks of verbal abuse from the young pretender to his crown. After what felt like hours to Pete, but was only a matter of seconds, Carter removed the items he had pilfered and threw them onto the bed.

"Anything else?" asked Pete.

"No, Sherlock. Feel free to check if you don't believe me," replied Carter, raising his arms to acknowledge his point.

Pete preferred to keep his distance. "If I find out anything is missing, I will have no qualms about going straight to the police, and to Lucy's parents. You're on probation, aren't you? I would love to see you banged up inside."

Carter interpreted Pete's threats as provocation, and a red mist descended upon him. He advanced quickly at Pete, and pushed him out onto the landing. Undaunted, Pete retaliated by unleashing a venomous verbal assault.

"You know what, Carter? You're just a worthless piece of shit. In fact, what I feel about you is beyond contempt, it's almost pity. You were happy to just take the piss all the way through school, never wanting to work or to make life easy for people. You were just a thorn in the side of everyone you came across. So tell me, how does it feel to know that not one person, out of around a thousand kids and teachers, felt one bit of remorse after you were kicked out? That's some talent you've got there, Carter, to have a whole school hating you."

Carter paused in the doorway, glaring at Pete in what could only be described as a state of paralysed bemusement, clearly unused to having people point out home truths so bluntly.

The unfolding situation was quite unique in that Pete had no previous experience of asserting himself in such a candid manner. Something had snapped inside of him, revealing a previously hidden inner demon that was unafraid to vent his spleen, surprising even himself by his fearless desire to let Carter know the depth of his contempt.

"Just what have you been doing since I last saw you?" continued Pete. "Sitting on your arse and drawing the dole is my bet. That's your future, Carter. Nobody in their right mind would want to employ you. So why don't you do us all a favour, eh, and just kill yourself?"

Carter finally responded to Pete's invective with the only means at his disposal, launching himself at Pete and grabbing him by the throat. The momentum carried the pair backwards to the wall at the top of the flight of stairs, leaving Pete slighted winded from the force of the impact.

"Remember," hissed Pete, pinned to the wall by Morgan's unyielding grip, but determined to land one more verbal punch, "all of your mags that were posted through letterboxes? That was me, Carter. Getting my revenge. How does it feel to be outdone?" Pete began to laugh hysterically at the look of astonishment on Carter's face.

As Carter recalled all of the problems and hardships he had endured for nearly half a year because of that one act, his shock was replaced by rising anger and the sudden impulse to inflict brutal, physical damage upon the instigator. A volley of unrestrained fists and insults rained down on Pete, forcing him to crumple down to the floor.

Wrapping his arms around his head to protect himself as much as possible, Pete realised the only option available was to fight fire with fire, and go on the offensive. Without opening his eyes to betray his intentions, Pete lashed out with his left leg until the base of his foot found its target: the unprotected shins of

Carter. Successfully landing a couple of blows forced Carter to temporarily recoil. Seizing his opportunity, Pete sprang up to his feet, inadvertently hitting Carter underneath the chin with his rising head. Off-balance, a dazed Carter grabbed hold of Pete and, with the pair entangled, they rolled down the thirteen stairs to the hallway floor.

By sheer good fortune, Pete ended up on top of Carter at the bottom, cushioning him from the worst of the impact. Coming off second best, Carter's head smacked against the floor with a sickening thud, leaving him in an unconscious heap on the floor.

The sound of the commotion had begun to draw people into the hallway, as Pete gingerly rose to his feet.

"Carter was stealing from one of the bedrooms," explained Pete, as signs of life emerged from Carter, groaning and sluggishly rubbing his head. "I stopped him."

"Come here, dear," said Lucy softly, grabbing Pete's hand and ushering him towards the front door. "Please, leave now before he fully comes round. He'll be like a bull in a china shop in a minute. Get Jake to help you home."

"Get going, Pete," said Morgan. "I'll guard the door to buy you some time."

Once Jake had helped Pete through the door, Morgan slammed it shut. They heard the sound of a bolt sliding into place, and a key turning.

The friends set off back down Western Hill, until they reached the junction at the top of North Road.

"Which way now?" asked Pete groggily. "Shall we catch the bus?"

The bus station in the city centre was a minute's walk away to the right, while the opposite direction would set them on the long road home.

"This way," said Jake, pointing away from the city. "If Carter follows us into town, the first place he'll check is the bus station. If we go this way, we can turn off the road at the top, and take a shortcut through the woods."

With his body aching all over, Pete was in no mood to argue as they half ran up the slowly ascending road until they reached the roundabout. Cutting across the road lanes, the pair found the rural footway that led straight into the heart of the woods.

Pete and Jake parted company by the allotments on the estate, once Pete had managed to convince Jake he was well enough to walk the final quarter mile home unaided. All was silent on the streets as Pete hobbled home, weary and yearning for his bed. With the sun nearly set for another day, and the light almost faded, a sliver of red sky far away on the horizon hinted at another pleasant day to follow.

"Hey, Junior. How you feeling?"

Pete was joined by Barry for the final few hundred yards before he arrived home. "Not too good at the moment, truth be told, Barry," remarked Pete.

"I have to take my hat off to you, Junior, you really gave a good account of yourself tonight. That punk didn't know what hit him."

"He'll kill me the next time he gets hold of me."

"Don't be so sure," countered Barry. "You fired a telling warning shot across his bow. He'll think twice before he messes with anyone else, you mark my words."

"I guess you know about Frances, too?"

"I know how you must be feeling, Junior. Pretty rough, I bet. It must have come as a hell of a shock?"

"You're not kidding. All those months I spent dreaming about her, and the person I thought she was, only to discover I don't really know her at all."

Barry nodded his head in agreement. "That's the knocks life throws at you, Junior. Sometimes there's more to people than you originally thought. Don't judge her too harshly, though. Frances isn't a bad kid. She's had it pretty rough too, lately. She's not the first to make mistakes in life, and she sure as hell won't be the last. We all do it, young and old. Nobody's immune. We wouldn't be human, otherwise."

Pete paused at the top of the driveway to his house.

"I just dropped in to say my goodbyes, Junior. I've got a feeling things are going to be a lot better from here on in for you, regardless of how much you might not believe that at the moment. Whatever life throws at you in future, the good and the bad, you're a hell of a lot better equipped to deal with it than you were the first time I set eyes on you."

Barry put out his hand. Pete shook it. "It's been a pleasure, Junior."

"Is this the last time I'll see you?"

"Well, Junior, I wasn't planning on returning anytime soon. That's no disrespect to you, but I'm a busy guy with things to be getting on with."

"Of course," said Pete.

"But never say never, Junior. Maybe one day in the future, if I get the opportunity, I might just be able to make a flying visit. You can make me a cup of that Ringtons tea. Shall we leave it at that?" offered Barry.

"Okay."

Pete turned and walked up to his front door.

"One more thing, Junior," shouted Barry, still standing on the pavement.

Pete turned around to face him. "What?"

"You might wanna put a steak over that eye in the morning," he laughed. "You're gonna have one hell of a shiner."

CHAPTER 17

A New England

The final Monday of the summer term was the annual school sports day. The school was blessed with perfect weather conditions, and with normal lessons dispensed with for the day, there was an infectious atmosphere of conviviality among the pupils and teachers.

In sharp contrast, Pete's mood was flat and lacking zest. Following his escapades the previous Friday, he had decided to keep a low profile and stay at home all weekend, filling in his time watching the Live Aid concert, and re-reading a James Herbert novel.

Pete had been able to disguise from his mother most of the minor injuries he had sustained as a result of his fight with Carter, and subsequent tumble down the stairs at Lucy's house. The jarring pain in his ribs and his bruised left foot were suffered in silence. The black and blue lump on the side of his forehead, the size of an egg, together with a fast maturing black eye, had proven more problematic. Deciding that the time for playing games and being secretive with people had to come to an end, Pete gave his mother an uncensored account of his run-in with Carter. Apart from being given a brief lecture about the need to avoid turning out like his father, Pete escaped with only a light reprimand.

Helen and Charlotte were full of concern for Pete's welfare once they heard about the previous Friday's events, and witnessed his physical appearance. Together with Jake, they sauntered up to the local high street with Pete at lunchtime to try and raise his spirits. At the chip shop, Pete treated himself to battered fish and potato covered in lashings of salt and malt vinegar, a combination he always turned to whenever he was in need of comfort food. Walking to the nearby park, Pete sat on the swings with Helen to eat his food and chat, while Jake and Charlotte larked about on the roundabout.

By 2 p.m., the athletics events were well under way, with the quartet nicely ensconced on a grass verge overlooking the javelin and shot putt competitors. When Helen and Charlotte disappeared in search of refreshments, Jake felt it was an appropriate moment to raise something with his friend.

"I overheard something interesting on Friday night before it all kicked off," began Jake.

"What's that?"

"That slimeball Sam cleared up the missing advert mystery from February. He's a school magazine volunteer, and was bragging about how he made sure only David's verse was included in the Valentine's issue, throwing all of the others, including yours, into the bin."

"Really?"

"Yeah. Can you believe that? All that trouble he caused between us two."

"I suppose in the long run he was doing me a favour," said Pete.

"Aren't you mad?" asked Jake.

"Only for the temporary rift he caused between us two. Not about Frances."

Pete and Jake sat in silence for several minutes, broken by Jake when he realised someone was approaching them from the main running track, situated at the far end of the school grounds.

"I think someone's coming over to talk to you, mate. I'll … er … just go and see how Morgan got on in the one hundred metres," he said, making his excuses and leaving.

"Hello, Pete. Mind if I sit down for a minute?" enquired Frances, sheepishly brushing a strand of hair away from her eyes as she anxiously awaited Pete's response.

"Be my guest," said Pete impassively.

Frances sat down next to him on the grass, and opened with a series of icebreaker questions, attempting to gauge Pete's mood.

"How are you?"

"Fine."

"Did you watch Live Aid?"

"Yes."

"Have you had a good day?"

"Okay."

"Why aren't you taking part?"

Pete shrugged his shoulders with an "I can't be bothered" gesture.

"Am I only going to get one-word answers out of you?" she asked nervously, in case her gentle sarcasm backfired.

Before the previous weekend, Pete would have been ecstatic to be receiving such singular attention from Frances, but the combination of her confession and the subsequent fight with Carter, had left him so mentally and physically drained that he was incapable of projecting a false positive front, even for her benefit.

"I hope you are still talking to me?" persisted Frances.

"I'll never not want to talk to you," answered Pete, speaking with a newfound conviction and gravity that had always been absent in previous conversations with her.

Another difficult silence followed, broken only by the sound of a starter's pistol from the running track, and the ensuing wave of cheers and applause that greeted the victor.

"I'm sorry if my news caught you off guard on Friday. I wasn't intending to say anything to anyone. It just kind of slipped out. Hearing Morgan was with you kind of panicked me. You must think I'm a right slag."

"I don't," said Pete, shaking his head.

"Have you told anyone else?"

"Of course not, and I don't intend to."

"Thank you. I just came over to let you know that I saw what you did on Friday. The way you confronted that thug. I told Lucy, too, once we got rid of him. I'm sorry that your evening was ruined when you left so suddenly, but Lucy said it was for your own safety. If everything had kicked off again and the police were called, then the whole thing would have gotten completely out of control. I did come looking for you, but you were nowhere to be found. David and I…"

"David?" interrupted Pete abruptly.

"Yes, David. When he found out, he was concerned about you, in case you were badly hurt or that idiot went after you. Lucy is a very good friend of his." Frances paused, smiled sadly and continued. "Please, Pete. I just wanted to say thank you. I know you are a decent person. You're not like most of the lads who are only after one thing. You care about people. I've noticed that about you."

Frances placed her hand gently on his arm. Pete turned to face her for the first time, and at that moment it took all of his resolve to resist collapsing into her arms and holding onto her forever.

"It was you, Pete, wasn't it?" she whispered. "You've been sending me the tapes. That's what you were going to tell me."

Pete looked away again, his cheeks reddening.

Frances smiled. "Please, don't be ashamed. There's nothing to feel sorry for. I'm flattered. The songs you chose really do speak for themselves. But I have David at the moment, and I'm guessing your opinion of me has been sullied somewhat."

With no response forthcoming, Frances continued. "After the holidays, regardless of my situation with David, I would really like us still to be friends."

"You're not just saying this because you feel sorry for me, are you?" asked Pete, once he had digested what Frances had said. "I can't stand people pitying me."

"I mean it, Pete. Please, give it some thought, and then we'll see how things stand in September when the dust has settled a little. I'm going away on holiday on Wednesday, so probably won't get much of an opportunity to speak to you after today."

Having said what she had come to say, Frances stood up and wiped the grass from her skirt. Leaving Pete with a smile and a slight farewell wave, she wandered back to the running track to where her friends were gathered.

Pete lay back and closed his eyes. The chat with Frances had subdued some of the burning angst that had been raging inside of him. He felt as if a huge weight had been removed from his shoulders now that she knew the identity of her anonymous admirer, and by her understanding reaction to his admission. All that was left in its place was a hollow feeling of extreme fatigue. Wanting nothing more than to curl up and go to sleep in order to escape the burden of his nonstop thoughts, overworked emotions, and battered body, Pete stood up and wandered away from the sporting activities, walking down the footpath that took him past the deserted Science and English buildings, and then out beyond the boundaries of the school.

"Pete. Pete. Telephone."

The sound of his mother shouting up the stairs jolted Pete out of his much-needed slumber. Momentarily disorientated, he reached out for the portable clock on his bedside cabinet, holding it up in front of his eyes. It had only just gone 7 p.m.

"Pete," persisted his mother from the foot of the stairs. "There's someone on the telephone who says they need to speak to you. Urgently."

"Coming," he croaked, as he lethargically shuffled downstairs.

"Hello," he said, expecting it to be his father.

"Is that you, Pete?"

"Yes. Who is this, please?" he politely enquired.

"Gwen. Barney's wife. I really need to speak to you, Pete. Are you free tomorrow evening at 6 p.m.?"

"Yes," he replied.

"That's good. Can we meet at the usual seat on Palace Green?"

Pete was puzzled. Why would Gwen be calling him unexpectedly? The only time either Barney or his wife had ever rung was to arrange his attendance at the carol service the previous Christmas.

"I'll have to check with my Mum."

"Please try and make it, son. It is important."

"I'll do my best," he said, hanging up.

When Mrs Barnett appeared alone from Dun Cow Lane and walked over to meet him, Pete stood up to greet her.

"Hello, Pete," she said meekly, with a brief, tired smile. There was no trace of her usually abrasive, humorous personality. "How are you today?"

"Fine, thank you, Gwen."

Once he had replaced the telephone receiver the previous evening, Pete had assumed that the purpose of the pre-arranged meeting was to unveil a fit and healthy Barney, freshly returned from his period of rest and recuperation. After such a dismal weekend, the phone call from Gwen had raised Pete's spirits. He had missed his kind and good-natured friend. Now Pete was confused by Barney's absence. His buoyant, expectant mood was replaced by rising panic.

"Ah, that's good. That's good," she repeated, sitting down and making herself comfortable. "You look like you've been in the wars, though," she remarked, noting Pete's minor facial injuries.

"It looks worse than it is. It's nothing really."

Gwen gazed at the group of youths on the green throwing a rugby ball amongst themselves.

"I've got some bad news for you, Pete. Not the kind to say over the telephone. I'm afraid to tell you that Barney's gone."

"Gone," said Pete. "Gone where?"

Mrs Barnett turned to face him, lines of deep sorrow etched into her usually happy face.

"A better place, one hopes, somewhere he can find peace

at last. He'd been poorly for a couple of years. Cancer. We knew it was inoperable, but he tried to go on living as normal a life as possible. He never stopped praying for a miracle, right up to the very end in the hospice."

Pete felt numb, unable to fully absorb or believe the magnitude of what he had just heard. He shut his eyes and bowed his head to try and make the reality of the moment go away.

"But what made him so happy, in his final months, was getting to know you," continued Gwen, placing a comforting hand on his back and rubbing it gently. "It made Barney really happy to see you come out of your shell a little. He always used to say to me, 'Gwen, there's something bothering that lad, but I'm damned if I can get it out of him.' He saw a lot of our son, Richard, in you, when Richard was your age. You probably aren't aware that we lost Richard when he was only sixteen years old. Knocked over and killed by a drunk driver. We've spent every day since then living with the what-ifs and regrets, and the thought we never got to say goodbye. We've never gotten over the loss. Even then, Barney was always thinking of others, channelling his grief into something positive, like running the youth club. It gave him so much pleasure to see youngsters like yourself getting involved, helping keep them off the street."

Pete raised his head and looked all around him. It felt strange to be sitting in the same spot where he had first met Barney the previous year, as if he had come full circle to complete a journey he never even knew he had embarked upon.

"I expect Barney told you this was his favourite place to sit whenever he wanted time to spend alone?" said Mrs Barnett.

"Yes," replied Pete, his voice cracking.

"This is where I'll come in future whenever I want to spend time with him. His ashes were scattered here two weeks ago. I expect he's here now, wanting to tell us off for being so miserable," she chuckled. "This place was the closest thing to heaven on earth for him."

"The first time I met him, he told me how much Palace Green meant to him," agreed Pete.

Gwen nodded her head thoughtfully. "Before I forget, Pete, there's something Barney would want you to have." She opened up her handbag and removed a small brown envelope, before handing it to Pete. "It was meant to be for Richard, when the appropriate time arose, but I can't think of any better home for it than with you. It will only sit in a drawer gathering dust otherwise."

Pete opened up the package and pulled out the contents. It was Barney's silver chain and cross. "Thank you," he said shakily, putting the jewellery back into the envelope and resealing it. The gesture from Gwen, and seeing Barney's personal effects away from their owner, filled him with a surge of emotion that he struggled to contain.

Gwen instinctively read Pete's distress, and wrapped a comforting arm around him. The pair stayed that way, saying nothing, oblivious to time and the world passing them by.

Lightning Source UK Ltd.
Milton Keynes UK
UKOW051803240112

186001UK00001B/8/P